Date Due

MAY 16 2006			
JUN 13 2006			
APR 17 2007			

LAST STOP SUNNYSIDE

LAST STOP SUNNYSIDE

A DANA LEONI MYSTERY

PAT CAPPONI

HarperCollins*PublishersLtd*

Last Stop Sunnyside

Published by HarperCollins Publishers Ltd

First edition

HarperCollins Publishers Ltd
2 Bloor Street East, 20th floor
Toronto, Ontario, Canada
M4W 1A8

www.harpercollins.ca

Library and Archives Canada Cataloguing in Publication

Capponi, Pat, 1949–
Last stop Sunnyside / Pat Capponi.

ISBN-13: 978-0-00-639412-9
ISBN-10: 0-00-639412-4

I. Title.
PS8605.A65L37 2005 C813'.54 C2005-905498-0

HC 9 8 7 6 5 4 3 2 1

This work is dedicated to two grand Canadians:
June Callwood and Reva Gernstein

LAST STOP SUNNYSIDE

Chapter One

The knock is surprisingly gentle. I've heard the stomping of numerous feet up the three flights of stairs for some minutes now, accompanied by enough wheezing, coughing and complaining to wake the most medicated of deep sleepers. I put down my book and move to flick open the token lock, a hook and eye arrangement such as used to be found on old screen doors at summer cottages. Multiple sets of shoulders crowd and shove their way in.

Gerry collapses on my bed, shuddering the metal frame; he's red-faced and breathing hard. Resembling a sumo wrestler gone to seed, he's not built for mountain climbing; his two companions, Michael and Diamond, manage to remain on their feet.

"So what's up?" They have the air of a delegation, but not the confidence. No one is speaking.

Gerry holds up his hand, pantomiming the need for a little more time to catch his breath. Clearly, he is the designated spokesman. His once white T-shirt is grey and speckled with ash, and his only pair of jeans are desperately in need of laundering. As is his hair and scraggly beard.

His words finally come out in a rush: "Someone stole Maryanne."

"Stole Maryanne?"

"Yeah, they just came and took her, and all her stuff. Wouldn't let us talk to her, ask her where she was going, nothing."

This is serious. Maryanne is their cribbage partner, and the owner of the board.

"Tell me what they looked like, these people." I already know she has no family to speak of, so it's either the hospital (unlikely since she's no crazier than usual) or another blatant attempt at poaching. Though everyone in here is a societal cast-off, many are on provincial disability pensions, making them more attractive and lucrative tenants than the welfare folks whose maximum allotments are hardly worth collecting. Landlords have been known to lure away people from other homes with offers of one-time partial rent rebates, even cash bonuses if they bring a friend along with them. These promises typically become "misunderstandings" once the shift in addresses is accomplished.

Maryanne wasn't naive, she knew the score. And she liked it here at Delta Court.

"One guy was bald and fat; he had some kind of accent when he told us to mind our own business." This from the gaunt young man with the faraway eyes whom Maryanne had taken under her maternal wing; she called him Diamond, so we did too.

"Dana, I told them they shoulda just got me or you right away," adds Michael, hitching up his jeans aggressively while staring accusingly at his friends. "What the hell are we supposed to do about it now she's gone? Nobody thinks around here."

Michael's never been accused of oversensitivity. He's angry, and when he's angry, he lashes out. It's how he's managed to survive on the streets since he ran away from home at thirteen. Gentling him has been a long-term project of mine. It beats taking up knitting.

"Maybe there was nothing to be done, Michael. She didn't ask for help? Didn't scream or struggle or anything?"

"No, but jeez ..." He runs out of words, and tugs at his hair instead. "I'm sorry, didn't mean to pop off at you guys. It's just, it's just not right, you know?"

His voice cracks, the muscles in his face tighten, and we all look at the floor, or the walls, as he struggles for control. No one speaks, no one moves.

Gerry ducks his head deep down into his chest. I know he's crying. For him, Maryanne's leaving is another loss stacked on a lifetime of losses. I sit beside him on the bed, put an arm around his shoulder. I can feel him trembling.

"Look, I can try to find out where she's gone, it shouldn't be too hard; maybe she'll even come back on her own. No matter how good they made the new place sound, she's going to miss everyone here."

I'm not lying, there's a strong possibility she'll get herself evicted in record time. Maryanne sober is a very different woman from Maryanne drunk. It's mid-month, wine's been in short supply since the cheque money ran out, and what may have looked to the poachers like a sweet-tempered, easily managed, middle-aged matron will morph into a foul-mouthed, aggressive nightmare.

Diamond shuffles his feet, uncomfortable with the sadness flooding him.

"Maybe she was mad at us. For something. When you find her, you could tell her we're sorry."

The other two nod, eagerly, hopefully.

"If I can track her down, I'll tell her."

It's not much, but it's something for them to hang on to, and they mumble thanks as they retreat out the door.

Left alone, I plug in the kettle for coffee. My place is small, but by rooming house standards, it's a penthouse. It has a private bathroom with a shower stall, a sink where a kitchen might be if anyone had thought to put one in and the luxury of only one bed.

There are two other rooms on my floor. In the one directly across from me four men have been shoehorned into beds that take up all the floor space. It's sadly fortunate that none of them have much in the way of personal possessions, as there are no bureaus or closets, just bare walls with cracks like lightning bolts working their way down from the ceiling.

Miss Semple occupies the room in between, her roommate another elderly woman, though not nearly as capable or competent, who mumbles constantly just below her breath, either prayers or complaints, no one can be sure. Just once she has spoken to me, enunciating each word. I was coming up the stairs and she was on the landing, looking lost. I smiled at her, and she said, "I'm not crazy, you know. I spent a few years on the streets, and maybe I was yelling, but I was never crazy. I was just confused, wondering where everyone had gone, my family, my friends."

"I know," I said, though I didn't.

The floor below us has five rooms, one of which belonged to Maryanne. Another is shared by Michael and Diamond, and the last three are packed to bursting with men and women either stepping up from the street or about to step down, transients who rarely stay more than a month or two.

Gerry has the first-floor bedroom, a little more furnished than most, in keeping with his status as longest-serving tenant. Two old men, silent and cowed, take up the other beds in the room. Whenever I'm in there, their faces are turned to the walls, thin blankets drawn up to their necks. A small office, kept locked, a bathroom and the common room fill out the rest of the floor.

The walls of my room are a garish yellowy orange, the landlord probably bought the paint at a serious discount, and they bulge in places where plaster repairs were never sanded flat, but I like the odd shape of the room. It has the feel of an attic space, with a sloped ceiling and two windows, each with four tiny, cracked and milky squares of glass, staring out onto King Street West. It took a while to get them to open, they were jammed shut with old paint and crud, but with Gerry's help I'd managed to prop them up. I love being able to hear all the street sounds, the whoosh of cars throughout the night, the snatches of conversation from passersby, even the rumble of the King streetcar making its way across the city. Less pleasant are the fights that often erupt when the bars across the street close, and drunks stumble and curse their way home. Still, it's all evidence of life, and movement, and possibilities, like living by train tracks, knowing one day you too could get aboard and be whisked away to some other place.

A Parkdale address once held a certain cachet, due to its proximity to Lake Ontario and the hugely popular Sunnyside Amusement Park, which had been a major draw for thousands of Toronto families every summer. The area's more vocal and politically active ratepayers and business associations complain that Parkdale has been turned into a dumping ground for alcoholics, drug addicts, ex-cons and de-institutionalized mental patients. But none of these groups was responsible for Parkdale's decline. It was the exodus of the wealthy that started the rush to the bottom, after the closure of the park and the building of the Gardiner Expressway, which cut off easy access to the lake in the fifties.

Now, instead of the glitterati, it attracts scruffy community legal workers, tenants' rights workers, NDP organizers, lefties of all shades and stripes eager to do battle with evil landlords, the Liberals and the business associations, while the latter mutter ominously about communists and outside agitators. In spite of all the hyperbole and invective, which tends to reach a raucous crescendo at public meetings, the streets are mostly safe, except perhaps for the wee hours before dawn.

Parkdale is my home, once through necessity, now by choice.

I've humanized my room with books and plants I grew from clippings that my friend Charlene cut from her garden. I dug up an old knotted rug from the basement along with a dresser with two working drawers, and scrounged a kettle and a hot plate.

It's enough for me.

I've lived here for two years now, in this falling-down mess of a building, with its dim lighting and quirky heating system, its occasional outbreaks of pests large and small, and its strange and fascinating collection of tenants.

It's not a charitable or missionary impulse that keeps me here. These men and women see something in me that I haven't seen in myself for some years now, and I am grateful to them for that and for the privileged position they've given me in the house. I'm sure it helps that I'm the only woman in here under fifty, which creates a constant jostling rivalry for my attention.

Coffee in hand, I prop myself against the pillows on the bed that has miraculously survived Gerry's collapsing on it, though I think I can detect a new sinkhole in the aging mattress, and realize that I can't hear a single sound from any of the twenty-five people, twenty-four now, who live here. It's eerie, unsettling.

It is very odd, out of character for Maryanne to just pack up and leave without a word. We are, in all the ways that count, her family. She'd brought fun and laughter into the place, weaving a community of sorts out of very disparate threads. Gerry, whose experience of life had been limited to the grey walls of a series of mental institutions; Michael, a young tough desperate for affection; and Diamond, who seemed as fragile and other-worldly as a dream. I feel their distress like a gnawing ulcer, deep inside, and whatever plans I'd had for a quiet day of reading are out the window. I have to move on this.

I can get another cribbage board, scrounge it from one of the drop-ins in the area, and ask some questions at the same time. At least it will get me out in the sunlight. Sometimes, like others here, I need external impetus to physically leave the building, brave the crowded sidewalks and the resultant overload of stimuli. Sometimes whole days go by without my venturing farther than the sprawling porch. I know it's unhealthy and often remind myself, with mixed success, to get out more.

The house, with all its drawbacks, has a womb-like pull about it, as though the dank, narrow corridors and closed doors don't actually confine us, but protect us from all that is harmful in the real world.

In my tiny bathroom, I wipe steam from the mirror hanging crookedly from a single nail protruding from the wall, and despair. Though I'm blessed by an olive complexion, allowing me to get by with a freshly scrubbed look, makeup being an unnecessary expense, I'm cursed by hair that curls wildly, no matter how short I cut it or how much conditioner I pour on it. I'm told I have an attractive face, elfin-shaped, atop a slender five-foot-six frame, but none of us ever see ourselves as others do. I attack the mess of curls with a comb, losing a few more of its teeth in the thicket, snarling all the while.

That bright burst of colours and sounds, so different from the darkening gloom of the rooming house, surprises me every time I step out the door. I always pause here, on the porch, taking it all in, mentally adjusting before heading down the stairs. Passengers disgorged from streetcars at the intersection of King and Dufferin create a constant stream of pedestrian traffic westward that peters out in a few blocks; they tend to keep their heads down, preoccupied with their troubles or their thoughts or their children. There's wariness, too, a careful distancing from some of the rougher characters loitering on the corners, hands thrust out, palms open.

There are streets I can see from my own vantage point on the porch, some called avenues, though they are narrow and almost treeless, that would grace any proud neighbourhood. They create long stretches of quiet, of everyday, middle-class normality between the more anarchic Queen and King Street arteries.

These peaceful streets aren't barricaded, exactly, but the down and out tend to avoid them, even as shortcuts, perhaps feeling too visible and out of place. On other "mixed use" streets, tensions are higher, conflicts more likely, as anxious parents watch the comings and goings of disreputable characters into falling-down buildings, and worry about their children and their escalating insurance costs.

Homeowners don't seem to shop or stroll locally. They're not spotted in the doughnut shops or bars. The very reputation that made their houses affordable for them seems to keep them from enjoying the neighbourhood.

As I walk up to Queen Street, I recognize that there are indeed times when the neighbourhood feels like one big institution, an all-purpose holding facility for the mad, the criminal, the simply poor. Judging by media coverage of the area, bodies should be a foot deep in the streets, but on a sunny day like this, even the dealers crowding the corners, jostling each other in their loud, competitive hawking to passersby, seem inordinately cheerful, the tension that ages and scars their faces gone for the moment.

There's a tolerance here for difference, eccentricity, the less-than-legal that can't be found in other parts of the city: police don't harass the panhandlers, and no one we know worries too much about property values falling, since almost everyone rents or rooms or boards, looking only to keep their footing, not to fall any further than this.

You can't get a latte or a double cappuccino, but every bleak, hole-in-the-wall restaurant has a liquor licence, or at least a notice taped to their grime-smeared windows declaring that they've applied for one. Dollar stores, cut-rate bruised and bashed food emporiums, cheque-cashing outlets, missions and bars complete our business and entertainment district. I pass a squat, red-brick building garnished with graffiti that houses our sole culture allotment—the local library, at the corner of Cowan Avenue, which also doubles as a senior citizens drop-in for those escaping from the grandiose sounding "retirement villas" that pock the area.

"Dana!"

I look around, startled out of my musings. It's Joe. He works the area near the strip mall, a sad little venture containing a laundromat and bracketed by a doughnut shop and two empty storefronts. He's hawking a variety of pills (Valium, Percocet) bought cheaply from the psychiatric patients he rooms with and sold for a profit on the street. Once upon a time, he may have been a good-looking guy, but he's been through so many manic episodes that he's aged early and badly. His teeth are jagged and broken and stained with nicotine, his clothes are stiff with sweat and dirt and could stand up by themselves. He used to come to the drop-in, where I do the occasional shift, and I grew quite fond of him. But his dealing inside the building had resulted in his barring.

"Where you been?" he asks me, though I saw him yesterday, and the day before.

"Right here, Joe. How's it going?"

"Slow. Very slow. No one's got any money. You know how it is."

"Yeah. Sorry to hear it. You take care now, okay?"

I keep moving. A block on, there's a guy who looks like he collapsed on the pavement, then crawled up enough to lean against a storefront wall. It's just George. George thinks I'm homeless like he is, and frequently lets me know where I can cadge a meal or find a bed for the night. He's bigger than Gerry, bigger than almost anyone I've ever met. He looks ageless, the fat having smoothed out whatever wrinkles he otherwise might have had. His legs are like slabs of beef, and between them is a used Coffee Time cup for people to drop change in. There are a couple of lonely quarters stuck in the grunge at the bottom. He smiles when he sees me coming, so I pull up a square of sidewalk beside him and sit for a while.

"Hey, George."

"Hey, Dana." He coughs, a brutal, body-shaking, rumbling cough that reminds him to roll a cigarette. He has a collection of butts that he pulls from his shirt pocket, and he picks through them looking for the longest ones. "It'll be lunch soon at the church. You going?" He finds a rolling paper and starts the tedious process of tearing bits of tobacco from the butts and filling the paper. "They have meatloaf today. You like meatloaf?"

"Sure. Who doesn't? Not today, though, no time."

"Well, you could go to the mission; they have sandwiches you can take with you. Bread's usually stale, but they use a lot of margarine."

I can still taste the bacon and eggs I ate across the street this morning, now leavened with a pinch of guilt. The only way to survive, to keep functioning, is to try to ignore it. Like the people who gingerly step over George's feet, trying not to stare.

"And down farther"—he points a sausage of a finger east—

"there's another church that serves hot, but you gotta line up for hours. You okay? Want a smoke?"

"I'm okay, no thanks. Where'd you sleep last night?"

"In the park. More room. Less people than the shelter. Had supper at the mission first. It was good, not enough though. Chicken and rice, all mixed together. Ice cream. And a banana. Where'd you sleep?"

"I was safe, don't worry." I'm wondering how he's going to manage to get up once he's ready to go. "You going to come to the drop-in today?"

"Maybe. You be there?"

"For a while, yeah."

Recycled tobacco has a stench all its own. We sit together in companionable silence, browning in the sun, people-watching. George likes company more than conversation, though it's easier for him with his extra cushioning to endure the hard pavement that's bruising my tailbone. I don't know too much about George, it's hard to break through his food obsession. I do know the important things. He's sweet, even-tempered and still finds it in him to look out for others. He rarely complains about anything, is grateful for the little he's given.

I'm very aware how much better off I am than most people here. I make a living, of sorts, with word portraits of the neighbourhood and its inhabitants that the local alternative weekly publishes when advertising permits. Between that, and the occasional shift at the drop-in for the "socially isolated" where I'm headed, I manage to feed and clothe myself.

There's a crowd outside the door by the time I show up, waiting for opening time, and I'm quickly swallowed up in hugs and "heys" from the usual assortment of street kids, crazies and wannabe toughs that make up the clientele.

Pete rescues me by choosing that moment to unlock the door, and grins at me across the small sea of heads.

"'Bout time you showed up."

"'Bout time you opened up. A person could get sunburnt out here."

We both know I have a key. Pete says he sleeps easier knowing that I have access to his computer for my writing after hours, his phone for emergencies, coffee and whatever food's lying around if I need it. That's the kind of guy he is, and that's why I love him like a brother. In return, I let him drag me to meetings, the seemingly endless talk-fests with city and provincial bureaucrats and professional social workers and housing providers, all looking for "creative" solutions to the continuing neighbourhood decline.

Pete leads me into his office, waving off calls for his attention with a good-tempered "give me a few minutes." *Office* might be a bit of a grandiose term for what is essentially a combination storeroom and paperwork area: baseballs bats and gloves and bases are piled up precariously in one corner, bingo balls and broken pool cues, green garbage bags stuffed to bursting with donated clothing; mouse traps, roach poison and tobacco tins decorate the rest of the room. He sweeps a chair clear of files and perches on his desk. Not your average executive director, he dresses like the rest of us, without pretense or the need to draw lines.

"So how you been?"

We catch up, since it's been a few weeks—my progress with a piece I was trying to write, his kids, gleaming with health and uninhibited laughter in the latest photos. He's my touchstone for life outside this community, for the good out there that we seldom see. Outside the closed door, a swell of voices rises and falls in arguments, laughter, complaints, the discordant symphony of life in the raw.

"Pete, I'm curious whether you've heard of any new places opening up, or new owners taking over? Something a little strange happened with Maryanne. You remember her, don't you?"

"Of course," he says with a little smile.

"She was scooped by another house. Two guys came in and just took her, and we haven't heard a word from her since."

He closes his eyes a minute, grimaces like he's remembering a bad taste.

"We had a guy show up last week, he said he had some openings. He wanted to make an announcement in the middle of the drop-in, and got mouthy when I said no. I had to escort him out while he cursed at me. Bald guy, fat, short, sounded Eastern European. Generally an unpleasant character."

Sometimes landlords see the drop-in as a people bank where they can grab a few tenants without having to advertise or jump through hoops to get referrals. Pete discourages this whenever someone tries it. Otherwise, it might look as though the centre endorses a particular owner, when it doesn't and never has.

"Sounds like the same guy. Did he give a name? An address?"

"Probably, but I can't remember now. Still, it shouldn't be too hard to find out. I'll make some calls, see what I can find out. I hope it's not another Hector." Hector was a notorious bully and thief who'd run his rooming house like a private fiefdom. It took years and a fortuitous hit-and-run accident to get him out of the business.

"Staying for lunch?"

"Sure, but there's just one more thing ..."

Cribbage board and pegs safely stored in my knapsack, I help Pete and another staff member ladle out chicken stew and chunks of crusty bread smothered in margarine. Eighty men and women in various stages of disintegration form an undulating line that weaves through the haphazardly placed collection of tables and chairs.

That done, I take my own plate over to the table where Vera sits alone in regal isolation, and compliment her on the new blond wig she wears like a cap or a crown over her long and thinning grey hair. At one time, she must have been quite beautiful, and probably attracted a lot of male attention. She still dresses well, though her attempts at makeup are less skilful now that her hands shake and her eyes are dimmer; splotches of rouge and slashes of bright red lipstick often mar her face. Pete has had to work very hard to keep Vera housed. She's a hoarder, her tiny room so cluttered with newspapers and boxes, empty bottles and bags of clothing that she's constantly being threatened with eviction. Every few months he goes in to try to help her sort a path through the chaos, and to convince her to part with some of her treasures.

"Where's Janice today?" I ask. Janice and Vera are usually inseparable. Both in their sixties, they happily spend their waning days creating and consuming concoctions, using the European alcohol-based tonic called Stomach Bitters as a base, which—if one's taste buds have declined sufficiently—recall Kahlua, Brown Cows and better days.

Vera leans toward me, looking around first to be sure no one is listening. Her wig tilts forward into her eyes, she impatiently pushes it back, and breathes vapours into my face.

"I don't know, I went to pick her up, we were supposed to go to the variety store to get a few bottles. This was a couple of days ago, and a man said she didn't live there anymore. I'm very worried; I don't know what they've done with her, why they're lying like that. I'm afraid she's dead!"

Big tears catch and puddle on the smears of lipstick she uses to rouge her sunken cheeks.

"She'd never just leave me like that. Never."

I put my hand on top of hers, feel her trembling and speak urgently through my own growing uneasiness.

"Listen, it could be anything, maybe she wasn't feeling well, maybe whoever answered the door was new, didn't know her name, or was too lazy to go check. Don't scare yourself like this; she wouldn't want you making yourself sick. Let me talk to Pete, see what we can find out." I gently squeeze her hand, trying to reassure, trying to reassure myself, even while I'm wondering who else has been spirited away and ominously kept from their friends, their careful routines. No one really keeps track of individuals and people disappear all the time, losing their housing because of non-payment of rent; it's a side-effect of poverty. Sometimes they show up again, after a few months, trying to get off the streets, trying to re-apply for welfare; sometimes they don't.

The simple act of standing up and stepping away from the table allows my head to clear, and I remind myself that this could be just a coincidence. I could be falling into Vera's latest conspiracy theory, although those usually involve the RCMP and unnamed government operatives. She carries a toy gun in her purse, big and plastic and cracked, to defend herself against attack by these shadowy forces. Still, if it is a coincidence, it's strangely timed.

Long days have gone by and there's been no word from Maryanne, or from Pete. Diamond has taken to his bed, depressed and left alone again, as alone as he can be in this crowded house. It's even worse for big Gerry, whose tenure in the building was matched only by hers. Fifteen years together, through a half-dozen landlords and a stream of tenants coming and going, they were a constant for each other. They battled and reconciled and battled and drank and battled and bullshitted, then she's gone. Just like that.

Our common room looks like a shipwreck, as usual. Cigarette butts and pop cans, McDonald's ashtrays overflowing, bits of unidentifiable trash everywhere. The television in the corner has been broken forever; the couch smells of urine and mothballs, and a collection of old, mismatched kitchen chairs surrounds a rickety card table where a desultory card game is in progress. Though the players appreciated the new cribbage board and real pegs I managed to score for them, without Maryanne's gossip and kibitzing there's too much heavy silence weighing them down.

For at least three-quarters of each month, Maryanne was warm and caring, something of a housemother to those who'd never known maternal warmth; she kept a benevolent eye on the tenants, especially the younger ones. She was always ready to share information, if asked, about local food banks, or places that served hot meals, gave out used clothing or legal advice. She even helped clean rooms that had got out of control, those belonging to paper hoarders or bottle collectors who were risking eviction as fire hazards or public health concerns, and she did it cheerfully, respectfully, without expectation of thanks.

Maryanne could make a stage show out of cutting a tenant's hair. Her laughter was infectious, she brought life into the house, and she was loved for it. The few days when alcohol claimed her, and changed her, seemed a small price to pay for keeping her with us.

It was Maryanne, struck by my "library," who had suggested reading nights in the common room. Gerry, Diamond, Michael, Miss Semple—a nice, very retiring and dignified tenant—and of course Maryanne and I made up the core of the "club," with others dropping in and out as the spirit moved them. My job was to read aloud, a chapter at a time, from a book that was selected by majority vote after a brief verbal synopsis of a half-dozen titles. Literacy among the tenants was in short supply, but democracy still thrived.

Mysteries were big, especially writers like Janet Evanovich (her assortment of bizarre and eccentric characters were people we could recognize and identify with) and Stephen King, and as soon as the library got in a copy of the latest Harry Potter we'd tackle that too. These nights, mostly Sundays, took us away from ourselves and our circumstances, broadened our worlds and stimulated imaginations long starved of dreams. Since Maryanne's disappearance, the readings had been put on hold by common consent. It didn't seem right to open a new chapter without her; it would be too final an acknowledgement that she wouldn't be returning.

I wonder what Miss Semple is feeling about all this. I haven't seen her since the last time I read to the group. We were all surprised when she'd joined us; it couldn't have been easy for her to sit with this disreputable group, in this less-than-welcoming room. She doesn't quite belong in the house, doesn't fit somehow. Miss Semple is the only tenant with a regular life, out volunteering five days a week at a downtown mission, always dressed appropriately, smiling shyly and bobbing her head if she passes anyone in the halls, never a complaint or a scowl.

I take a seat on the couch, raising a hand to the card players but maintaining the silence for the moment, wondering once again how to break this mood that hangs like low clouds in the room. Michael's feeling it too. He clears his throat as he throws in his hand, asking, "So what was it tonight, Gerry?"

"Barf in a bowl. Skinned chicken, a lump of potato, carrots. Half a rotten banana."

Since his last bout with illness, caused by the eruption of leg ulcers, he's been getting his meals delivered free from social services. At first he thought he'd struck gold, so did the rest of us, but it turned out to be a source of constant aggravation. He was getting the diabetic versions, tasteless, spiceless and worse, portion-controlled. Never stepping farther than the veranda he usually sent someone out for a Big Mac as a chaser.

"Let's see," Michael drawled, "what did I have? Karen had a special on: Salisbury steak, fries, corn and a big slice of apple pie." He manages a smug, satisfied belch, grinning across the table.

"Yer a bastard, Michael, did I tell you that?"

There's a banging on the front door, strangers for sure, everyone who lives here knows the lock doesn't work. Gerry throws his cards down with some relief and an exhaled curse, pushes his chair back with a screech and trundles off to see who's there. He's the biggest guy in the house, over six feet and way over two hundred pounds: he looks threatening if you don't know him, which makes him the de facto security guard for moments like this. We don't get many callers, and even fewer people we want to see.

Time's suspended for the rest of us as we wait, curiosity pricking through the malaise, ears straining to catch the voices.

Gerry stands at the doorway, pale and anxious: "It's the cops, Dana, they wanna speak to the person in charge."

Chapter Two

Everyone turns to look at me expectantly. Though I have no official status, I read, I write, I've been to university, so it's down to me.

"Bring them in, Gerry."

The room empties out fast. The police are not our friends. By the time two plainclothes officers are led in, no one's left but me. Gerry points a grubby finger in my general direction, and does his own retreat as I rise to greet them.

"Can I help you, gentlemen?"

It's as though their presence increases the wattage in the room, the usual grunginess and mess stand out in high relief. I'm conscious of the state of my clothes, the tired jeans, rumpled sweatshirt, well-worn running shoes in sharp contrast to their tailored suits and highly polished footwear, aware too of the smell of the outside that they carry with them like an exotic perfume doing losing battle with the mustiness and stale smoke.

"I'm Detective Price, and this is my partner, Detective Jansen," says the shorter and harder-faced of the two, not offering his hand, but reaching into his breast pocket for a notebook and pen. "Are you the super here?"

"No, we don't have one, and the owner's in Europe for a few months. I'm a tenant."

I'm it, is what I mean.

There's a pause as they wonder if it's worth continuing, but Price sighs and clicks his pen to life. I've seen his type before, cracking heads on the street, relishing every moment.

"Your name?"

"Dana Leoni."

I watch his blunt, stumpy fingers carve my name onto the page.

"How long have you lived here?"

I want to cut to the chase, ask them what this is all about, but they are clearly following routine, and expect the same of me. I wave them to the chairs and seat myself. After a long, hesitant moment, either spent wondering if they'll lose an advantage, or pick up a disease, they join me.

"Two years."

"I understand that a Maryanne Wilson used to live here?"

Funny how the temperature can plunge in an instant. I cross my arms in a vain attempt to shield myself.

"Yes, for fifteen years. Has something happened?" Of course something's happened, idiot. Cops don't show up at the door if nothing's happened.

Jansen clears his throat. I study his face as I wait for his answer, he's tanned and his eyes are a deep blue, his aquiline nose has been broken at least once, and his blond hair is cut short over a broad forehead now wrinkled with concern. He leans forward, clasps his hands together on the torn leatherette surface; suddenly I don't want to know.

"I'm sorry to inform you that she's deceased. Her body was found in the lake. It's taken us some time to identify her. We're in charge of the investigation, and we're tracing her movements, looking at her history. Anything you can tell us will be helpful—family, friends, that kind of thing."

I fight an old temptation to mentally leave the moment: there's a loud buzzing fraught with alarm echoing in my head, pieces of consequences flying manically against the walls of my skull, Gerry, Diamond, guilt, loss, pain. This can't be happening.

"She's dead? For sure? You couldn't have made some kind of mistake?"

Price expels an impatient breath, "Of course we're sure. Would you mind just letting us ask the questions? I understand she had a drinking problem."

Not a problem, unless there was nothing to drink. That won't do.

"She enjoyed her wine, yes."

"Did she seem depressed the last time you saw her, and when was that?"

When? It was the night before she left. She'd seemed a bit distracted, but I thought it was the strain of sobriety, understandable really.

"Maryanne didn't get depressed; she was a pretty cheerful person most of the time. It was harder for her after a few days of drinking, but she was used to the cycle and coped well enough." It was the rest of us who had problems coping; she let it all hang out.

"Any history of mental illness that you know about?"

"No."

"Would you know?"

"Yes." He bullies me into continuing with his stare. "There were no pills, no appointments, no symptoms. Others here have been in the hospital, and she would have said, she's the kind of person who would have said, to make others more comfortable, you know?"

He doesn't, but leaves it alone. "And family?"

"I'm afraid I don't know if she has any family left; she never mentioned anyone. About two weeks ago, some people came and collected her. They took everything she owned. I didn't see them, but the other tenants told me. It was a shock, because she'd never said she wanted to leave."

"That's not too surprising, is it? I mean, look around. Christ, she was probably desperate to get out of this dump."

I feel my face flare a brilliant red, the way it does when anger grabs me by the throat. Worse, there are tears in my eyes, and I quickly lower my head, not wanting to give the bastard any satisfaction. I hear Jansen, his voice tight with controlled anger, tell Price, "Why don't you call it a night, Dan." Even I can tell it's more of an order than a request. "You can take the car, I'll finish up here. See you in the morning."

Price is flummoxed. I'm glad, feeling a prick of evil satisfaction at his dismissal. His mouth moves a bit, but nothing comes out. Jansen turns his full attention to me, as though Price has already left the room, leaving him no option but to go. Which he does, taking with him the feeling of claustrophobia his attitude and judgments had created in the room. Jansen is quiet till we hear the front door slam shut, followed by a little tinkle of falling plaster.

"Why don't we start over?" He smiles, a little sadly. I like his smile. "It's still early in the investigation, and the autopsy results aren't in yet, but it looks like a simple drowning. Her body washed up near the beach at Sunnyside. I've very sorry for your loss."

"Thank you." Not just for answering my question, not just for the expression of sympathy, but for getting rid of Price, and for being human.

"She was clearly important to you; you cared about her. That makes you the best person to give me a good sense of her. Take your time; I'd like you to help me to understand who she was."

In an odd way, his gentleness is harder to overcome than Price's staccato interrogation. I'm choked up, unable to get any words out.

"Would you prefer to talk somewhere else?"

I jump at the suggestion. I need to feel the air outside. Need to walk. "There's a McDonald's on the corner, could we ...?"

"Let's go there, then."

Outside, the stars are coming out, joining a sliver of a moon in a cloud-free sky.

I can't believe I'll never see Maryanne again, never hear her voice, her laughter. Never tell her how important she was to everyone in the building. Never get to thank her.

The light inside McDonald's is harsh, too revealing for me. I blink rapidly, taking in the brightly coloured seats, the hunched-up guy near the door with both hands on his large coffee cup like it's the only thing anchoring him to the world.

Jansen gets me seated away from the handful of customers in the place, and goes to the front to order. I'm flooded with memories, jerky scenes replaying in no particular order: Maryanne bullying the little crack addict into clearing out his room; Maryanne with her arm around Diamond's shoulders, sharing an intimate moment; Maryanne going door to door, gathering up clothes and sheets to take over to the laundromat.

Jensen abruptly breaks into these memories, plunking down a tray with a couple of Big Macs, fries and coffees. "Thought you might be hungry."

And I am, oddly. I'm suddenly ravenous. As I bite into the burger, revived by the taste and substance, such as it is, I'm recovering some balance. He pushes over his burger as I finish mine.

"Go ahead; I've already had my dinner."

It's funny, I hate McDonald's food, but I can't stop eating. He's so patient, sipping his coffee, as though he has all the time in the world.

"Thanks." I'm a little embarrassed, but steadier. I take a few stringy fries, liking the salt, the sting of the vinegar.

"Maryanne—"

I realize on saying her name that there's no such person anymore, and trembling sets in. I fight this off, and start again. "Maryanne was, she was like a housemother of sorts. Not to everyone. She was kind of dismissive to those she called Temps, the ones that would stay a month or two then move on. We have a lot of coming and going in the building. When she found people she liked, or people she felt needed help, she'd be knocking on their doors, getting involved with them, trying to help them adjust to the place. Nothing big. Letting them know about card games that go on in the living room, offering to show them the neighbourhood, where to get cheap stuff. And she'd get the other guys to be welcoming, friendly."

A skinny, pimply kid pushing a broom comes too close, and I stop for a minute, gathering my thoughts.

"She had this radar, she always knew when someone was depressed or hungry or scared. At the worst moments, when it seemed like there was nobody and nothing, there'd be this knock at the door. She was a force. She didn't pry though, didn't make people say what was going on, she'd just, just distract you with stories or gossip till you forgot to be miserable."

"She helped you?"

"Oh yes. Me, and others. There's a group of us she knitted together, we couldn't be more different from each other, but there's a chemistry that works with us. A kind of family, I guess." Thinking back to Price's caustic remark about the house, I added, "I know the building's a mess, but it's more than it looks to be. People make the place home. Give it warmth, life. She did that. The drinking, that was confined to the days the cheques came, three or fours days of bingeing. It didn't diminish her in our eyes; it was just something she needed to do. We never talked about it, even to ourselves. And then she'd be back to herself."

I realize it's helping me to talk about her, with this gentle stranger who listens well; there's no judgment lurking behind his eyes, just interest and sympathy.

"She used to troll the discount grocery stores. Buy cans that were dented or had lost their labels. It was like her bank, you know? This huge stash of cans piled almost to the ceiling of her room. If you were broke, she'd choose one, and heat it up on her hot plate. You sometimes didn't know what it was going to be, but that made it fun."

"Did anyone ever come to see her? Family, workers?"

"No. She never said anything about family. Sometimes she'd bring a guy back, when she was drinking, but he'd be gone in the morning. We don't get a lot of outsiders coming in. I know she'd worked a lot of jobs when she was younger, mostly as a waitress, mostly in bars. Her feet still gave her trouble from all the standing she used to do."

"Is there anyone in the house who might know a bit more?"

"People don't spend a lot of time talking about the past, it's generally painful looking back. If it's okay with you, I'll ask around and get back to you. They'll be less threatened if it's just me."

He nods, sits back in the chair. He'd be a terrible card player; I can read the hesitation on his face. He's wanting to say something, ask me something, but he's holding back, unsure.

"Go ahead, Detective."

"Call me Ed."

"Ed, then. I won't fall apart on you, ask your question."

It's his turn to be embarrassed; I have to smile at his reaction. A slight flush, a lowering of the eyes. "It's not related to the investigation, Dana. It's none of my business. It's just that, I've been to a lot of rooming houses in my time, met a lot of the tenants."

As he struggles to phrase his question, Diamond walks past, conspicuously paying absolutely no attention to us. There's no doubt in my mind: he'd been delegated to follow us, to make sure I'm okay. Sure enough, he gets a coffee, and sits where he can see both of us. Ed's still having difficulty, so I pre-empt his question with one of my own.

"You first. What's a nice guy like you doing on a force like this?"

His laugh, loud and sudden, causes a very jittery Diamond to spill hot coffee into his lap, he leaps out of his seat, plucking at his trousers, pain on his face. I grimace in sympathy, as Ed says, "You got me!" There's this admiring look on his face that I could get used to seeing. Suddenly serious, he adds, "Not everyone's like Price, you know. It's a big force, you get all kinds of people, all kinds of attitudes. I love being a cop, most of the time. Love the job. Your turn."

I stare at the clutter on the tray; this is not something I talk about. But I don't want to go home, don't want to think about Maryanne in that cold, cold water.

"I was a graduate student at the U of T. Someone attacked me one night, a few feet from my door. It was pretty vicious. Spent weeks, months, physically recovering, but I wasn't getting any better in my head. Lots of nightmares, lots of fear, especially since they never caught the guy. I ended up here, and decided to stay. Maryanne helped me to stay."

"I'm really sorry."

I shrug, it wasn't his fault. I hadn't liked the cops who'd investigated my case; they'd been brusque and cold.

"But why this neighbourhood? With its reputation, it seems like the last place you'd want to be."

"I was attacked in a wonderful neighbourhood, the Annex,

very middle class, lots of people on the streets. It didn't make any difference to the guy who hurt me. And I do feel safe here. It's hard to explain, but I love the streets, I know the people, I sleep well at night. I'm not afraid."

Ed is making an effort to understand, I can tell. I'm the kind of person who makes snap judgments about people, based on instinct, feelings, intuition. I like him. He points over his shoulder toward Diamond and says, without turning his head, "You have friends watching out for you."

I laugh. "Yes. That's Maryanne's doing. She got us to care for each other. Don't let him know you know, please."

"I won't spoil it." He pulls out his wallet, a battered affair, and finds a card, which he hands over. It's very white and clean and official-looking, embossed with the Toronto Police logo and a couple of numbers connected with the Homicide Squad. He takes a pen from his breast pocket and adds another number. "This is my cell. If I don't answer, just leave a message and I'll get right back to you. Can I get your number?"

"No phone."

"Oh." People are always nonplussed about that. "Okay, I'll just come by, then. To see if you've found out anything from your friends. Are you going to be all right?"

"I'm not looking forward to telling them. Could I ask, how did you find out her name?"

"Prints. It took a while, but they have ways. She had a few D and D's. This was the last address she gave. I'm trying to get ahold of her worker, and when I do, I'll find out where she was transferred to. Get some more information about the night she died. Dana, thank you. I've got a much fuller impression of Maryanne, the whole person. It helps. I'm going to do right by her, don't worry."

"Thank you, Ed." We both stand, he takes the tray away to empty it into the trash bin, watched carefully by Diamond. Together, we head back to the rooming house, and I remember he's carless.

"How will you get home?"

"I'll flag a cab. No problem." We're just looking at each other, it's a bit awkward, then he offers his hand, and I shake it. His hand is warm and firm. "Take care of yourself."

I want to call him back as he walks away. Ask him to stay with me, talk some more, anything rather than go inside, but I turn and walk up the stairs.

That night, when I returned, Gerry was sitting on the edge of his bed, the door open. Michael was with him, pacing in tight little circles. Gerry's roommates, asleep since seven, kept up a steady snoring; nothing short of a bomb going off would wake them up. I went into the room, a barren place, with pill bottles scattered all over the dresser, a stained and ancient thing with broken drawers jutting out. Nailed over the one window was a torn and faded shower curtain that might once have added a cheery note to the room. The walls, pocked with fist-sized holes, hadn't been washed in years, and a grey-brown film from the smoke of countless cigarettes streaked the surface. Diamond came through the door in a rush, his pants still wet from the coffee spill. Any other time he would have been the target of many bad jokes, but nobody said a word. They all looked at me, faces grim and knowing, even before I uttered the words, that the worst had happened.

I hated telling them, hurting them. There were no tears; the pain ran deeper than that. Michael slid down the wall, sat crouched against it, head on his arms. Diamond just stood there, unable to move, while Gerry lay back on his bed, turned his face away, and was still. We stayed like that for a long time, sharing the silent misery. It was a kind of wake, all we could offer Maryanne now. We had no right to the body. If the police couldn't find any next of kin, she'd be buried by the government, and we might never know where. I wondered if they still had paupers' fields, if she'd even be entitled to a headstone.

It was Michael who finally ended our vigil. He mumbled something I couldn't catch, pushed himself up from the floor and, with Diamond trailing behind him, went up to his room. I waited a moment longer, then tucked Gerry's blanket around his shoulders and bent down to kiss his cheek. His eyes stayed shut. I gently closed his door and followed the boys up the staircase.

Days later, Pete hasn't been able to learn anything. He's worried now too about Janice, who still hasn't shown up, and she's been a regular at the drop-in for years. He's been kicking himself for losing the business card the creep left him, but there is so much chaos day to day in the overcrowded, understaffed agency that one tiny piece of cardboard has no hope of surfacing.

It's late morning. I haven't been out yet. I feel exhausted, since I've been having trouble sleeping; a heavy weight of guilt at failing a friend haunts me. I should have moved more quickly to trace her, find her; I should have realized that the abruptness of her leaving was so out of character that it meant something was terribly wrong. I hate to think of what Maryanne must have endured the night she died. Not knowing the truth makes the imagination take over, and it's all bad.

Not surprisingly, I guess, the dreams, nightmares really, have returned, taking me back to the night I was attacked. I find myself once again walking home through gently winding streets, feeling the same pleasure I felt then in the lit-up living rooms, in the lazy drift of smoke up chimneys carrying with it the smell of bone-dry logs burning. I hear and feel the hard-packed snow crunching under my boots, see the full moon luscious and brilliant in the darkening sky. There's no foreboding, no urge to shout out a warning.

I'm on my way home to a late dinner and a glass of wine, smiling the same smile in anticipation of waving to my cat, Joseph, always faithfully waiting for me in the front window, and between one footstep and another, my head explodes all over again, my vision shorts out in a fury of sparks, and down I go.

That's where the nightmare stops. I always wake up at that point, breathing in great gasps, unable to turn off the rest of the story, having to go through, touch each stage, in sequence. I'm in Emergency; I remember a lot of yelling, running and machines beeping frenetically. Questions are hollered at me that I can't answer. I have no words. No use for words.

I remember too the list of injuries they rattle off, when things have calmed down a little, and they've moved me into a room, to a screened-off bed. Concussion and a skull fracture, internal bleeding caused by being violated with something other than a penis. I tune them out, go off on a wave of merciful morphine.

I was still in hospital when the two detectives told me they had no leads, no witnesses, no DNA. A month had gone by, and nothing. He was still out there; he might always be out there. Their faces grew angry when I railed at them. They stopped coming.

The physical recovery was long and often excruciating. What

was worse was the fear I felt every waking moment. I couldn't shake it. I went home to my parents, stayed in my old bedroom and refused to come out. They didn't have any idea what to do with me; I cut them off when they suggested going back to school, or even going for a walk. I knew I was a target out there.

Eventually, on the advice of our old family physician, they committed me to the psychiatric ward of the hospital. When I left there, I left everything and everyone behind; I found my way to this house, this security, a security that is threatened now by guilt and fear.

I close my eyes on the memories and the grief, needing to give in to the fatigue that weighs me down. Maybe I'll be able to sleep undisturbed, thoughts drowned out by the traffic on the street.

The knock that wakes me up and starts fibrillating my heart is a strong knuckle rapping, in short, machine-gun bursts. I sit up quickly, and the book I was reading before the heat and humidity carried me off last night falls to the floor. Confused and a bit scared, I stay on the bed, trying to clear my fuddled brain.

Another racket follows, this from the stairway, voices raised in alarm.

"You never tell anyone where she is, idiot." That's Gerry.

"But he said he knew her." Our resident drug addict, Tommy. He uses everything from Aqua Velva to rot-gut wine to pills when he has the money. His room is on the second floor.

"I don't give a damn what he said, no one goes upstairs. Jesus Christ, where's your brain?" And Michael. Hail, hail the gang's all here.

"I'm sorry."

"Your whole life is sorry."

"Hold on," I call out, forestalling another assault on the door. I go to the door and open it on Ed, the cop, who looks relieved.

"Hi, Dana, I think I need you to let me in before ..."

The quarrelling threesome have made it to the landing. Gerry has old Mr. Jenkin's cane, I'm not sure how he got it away from him, and he's holding it like a baseball bat. Michael's fists are knotted impressively, while Tommy peers nervously out from behind them.

"Who the hell are you?" Michael snarls, moving forward slowly.

Ed puts up one hand, palm out in a classic *stop* motion. And he wins my eternal affection by taking them all very seriously.

"Easy, gentlemen, please. I'm going to reach into my back pocket for my police ID." He looks at Gerry and adds, "I met you the last time I was here, remember?"

Gerry growls, "I never saw you before in my life." Ed is dressed in jeans and a sports shirt, instead of his suit, that's enough to throw Gerry off remembering. Gerry holds the cane higher and keeps his eyes on Ed's hand as he slowly pulls out his badge case and flips it open for the three intrepid defenders.

"Well, okay then, why didn't you just say so," grumbled Michael, while Tommy pales and starts slowly creeping backward down the stairs. "Dana, you want to see this guy?"

Everyone looks at me expectantly, including Ed, so I sigh, and open my door wider.

"Thanks, guys, I appreciate your help. It'll be fine."

They mumble their "sures" and "anytimes" and "just call us if you need us" and retreat, while Ed steps inside my small space, manfully holding back a smile.

"Quite a posse you have there."

"They're a little jumpy 'cause of Maryanne."

He's looking around my room, dismay and disbelief battling for supremacy on his face. The paint job has that effect on people; it had that effect on me when I first moved in, but now I suppose I've got used to it. Still, for just a moment, I'm seeing the place through the eyes of an outsider. The miserable, miserly windows open but admitting no discernible air, the narrow, metal-framed bed with its lumpy mattress, the single-ringed hot plate and the solitary cup and spoon beside it. But what has him riveted is the "lock" on the door.

"What the hell is that?"

"I know, I know."

"Your landlord should be shot." I think of the redoubtable Mr. Mansur, now travelling through the Middle East, blissfully unaware of this fatwa on his life.

"Look, I'll bring a drill next time I come, and I'll install a proper lock. This is ridiculous. A crime waiting to happen."

He moves through the room, stopping at the plants and books piled up against the wall. This is also where I keep clippings of the articles I've written. He picks up one copy, and starts reading. I don't know what to make of this, but my ego is such that I want to see which one he's got even more than I want to snippily inquire if he has a search warrant.

"This is very good," he says, turning to me with those blue eyes of his.

"Thank you?" I put a question mark on the end of that, like what are you doing here, going through my stuff, threatening my landlord.

"I wanted to talk to you some more. But it's sweltering in here. Can we go get some coffee?"

"Sure."

"Think they'll let you leave with me?"

"Yeah. By the way, thanks for, well, thanks for ..."

"Not shooting them?"

He has some mischief about him, this one. I smile back at him. We descend the three flights without incident, and as we pass Gerry's room, I pop my head in. He's back in bed, the cover pulled up over his head, his usual sleeping position.

"Just going out for coffee. I'll be back soon."

His voice comes back, strained through the pillow, "Ya going with him?"

"Yes. It's all right. See you."

He harrumphs skeptically. Outside, there's a bit of a breeze, taking some of the edge off the heat. We stand for a moment on the veranda, and suddenly I don't want to be inside again, not even for coffee.

"Ed, do you think we could go up to Sunnyside? Could you show me where Maryanne was found? It probably sounds a little weird, but I think it would help. You know, one minute she's here and as permanent as anyone else, the next you guys are at the door saying she's gone. We can't see her or touch her. I just feel I ought to know."

"Sure, if you want. It'll look like any other section of the waterfront by now, there are no markers or anything. But, anyway, it should be cooler by the lake. I'm parked just down the road a bit." We walk the short distance in silence. When we reach his car, he opens the passenger door first, and I duck inside, impressed by the dark leather seats and his hi-tech dashboard, which wouldn't look out of place in the cockpit of a small plane. He joins me, pushing a button to lower all the windows at once.

"You're making it difficult for your shadow to keep up with us." He turns and grins at me, and I have to smile back. "The air conditioner will kick in in a few minutes."

This is much more luxury than I've enjoyed for some time. I relax back in my seat. For a cop, he doesn't seem bothered about the rules of the road, executing a nice U-turn in the busy traffic to point us in the right direction.

Pete and I occasionally take the members of the drop-in to the public swimming pool, at least those who own or can scrounge up a bathing suit. Since I never learned to swim, I stay out of the water, but it's always nice to lie in the sun and listen to the children splashing away. At night, the atmosphere changes dramatically, all the regular people go back to their homes, sated by their day in the sun, leaving the long stretch of waterfront to the homeless who gather together in small groups or singly to bed down. Sometimes there's a lot of drinking, and occasionally a fight, but the police tend to be scarce, and people cope more or less by themselves.

Ed parks the car and kills the engine. We sit there enjoying the last moments of chilled air. The water stretches out in front of us, ice blue and still. Seagulls pirouette just above, nattering away at each other, and even the grass looks lush and inviting. It's an odd contrast that I've never come to terms with. So many people are locked into tiny, dark, stifling rooms in the area, there's so little natural greenery even in the parks, yet here, only blocks away, so much openness and space and beauty.

We start walking, slowly, enjoying the breeze from the lake, and the fresh smells.

Here and there, families are spotted about the grass, under trees or out in the open, suntanning. We're passing a young man pedalling a bike full of ice cream bars, and Ed reaches into his back pocket for his wallet, and looks at me expectantly. We move on, the taste of ice cream and chocolate melting on our tongues.

We pass the park where children giggle on swings pushed by

their parents, or chase each other in endless circles. I feel the stress drop away. Ed picks up on this.

"If you like this, you'd love the view from my place."

"Where's that?"

"I have a condo down at Harbourfront. I'm one of those rare cops who live where I work. From my windows, you can see a big chunk of the lake, watch the ferries going back and forth to the island. Sail boats drifting along. Even in winter, there's a different kind of allure, with the ice thickening and the snow falling. It reminds me that there's something more to life than murder and misery."

I'm abruptly brought back to why we're here. It feels like a punch in the stomach. He's remarkably sensitive for a cop, picking up on what I'm feeling immediately.

"Sorry. I didn't mean to ..."

"I know. It's okay. I just forgot for a minute."

It's an ordinary stretch, as Ed had warned me, nothing cordoned off, nothing to show a body had washed up here, nothing to interfere with people's sense of well-being.

"She was found by some of the homeless just after dark. One of them flagged down a police car."

He stands quietly with me while I close my eyes and say a silent prayer. It's been a long time since I've prayed, and I couldn't even tell you who I was praying too. Not to the God of my childhood, not to the martyred saints whose pictures were plastered on every wall in my home, not to the Jesus writhing on the cross. Something bigger, something that can't be captured by our imagination, or portrayed by religious artists. Something that encompasses the lake and the land, the families and the lost, the sky and the sun and the clouds. And even me.

A furry ball brushes past my legs, barking joyously and diving straight in after a stick thrown by its owner, head forward as its body slices through the water in single-minded pursuit. It feels like a moment of grace. And it's good to laugh, to be alive to laugh. As the dog returns, it showers us with spray from its fur, but that's all right too.

I pick up a small stone from the beach, smooth and dark, and pocket it.

Ed leads me to a bench under a spreading tree, and we sit together for a moment in silence. He muses softly, "You know what I find even harder? People whose deaths don't disturb anyone. When we can't find a single person to mourn or remember or even identify a deceased. It makes me wonder about life, the kind of life that doesn't touch even one individual. You cared, your friends cared about her. That says a lot about her, and about you."

I'm on the verge of tears, fighting to hold them back, so I just nod and hope he doesn't notice.

"Dana, I'm afraid we're closing the case. It's going down as a suicide. We have no options here. I've spoken to the operator of the last home she was in. He came to the station to see us. He was pretty shaken up, blaming himself for her death. She'd only been there about a week, and that night she'd come back to the house falling down drunk, she'd cut her face, probably on the sidewalk. The landlord said he wanted to call an ambulance, just in case, but she got abusive, screamed at him to mind his own business, and said she wouldn't be staying 'in this dump' any longer. He got fed up then, it's happened to him a few times, people staying days or weeks then taking off, stiffing him for the rent. He yelled back at her as she stormed out that she had twenty-four hours to get her stuff, he'd leave everything at the side of the house, and spent the rest of the evening packing her things into green garbage bags. They were gone the next night, so he thought she'd collected them. In that neighbourhood, they were probably stolen."

"What's his name, the landlord, and where's the house? We've been trying to find out where she 'moved' to."

He digs in his pocket for his notebook, riffles the pages.

"A Stephan Mallick, at 180 Fortune Street. He bought the house a couple of months ago, says he didn't really understand what he was getting into. Talked about being fed up, selling and getting the hell out of the business.

"Anyway, the autopsy results are consistent with drowning, she had water in her lungs. The bruising on her face and body, in light of what he told us ... and there are big rocks near the shore where she was found; it makes sense there'd be some damage to the body. And the coroner confirms she had high levels of alcohol in her system. There's nowhere else to go with this, Dana."

"Could I ask, did you run a check on Mallick?"

"No, why would we? There are no suspects here. It's not a murder."

He's watching me, so I give him a weak smile.

"You're a good guy, Detective."

"Ed."

"You're a good guy, Ed. You didn't have to do this, bring me out here, be so gentle. I want you to know I appreciate it."

"But you're not buying it. That it's a suicide."

"Give me some time. This has all been something of a shock. I believe you did your best, and I thank you for that."

I can't hide the depression that settles over me, or the distance that's now come between us. The drive home is quiet, broken only by the hum of the air conditioner. As he pulls up in front of the building, he undoes his seat belt and turns to me.

"Listen, I'll go over the file again, see if I've missed anything, if there's anything I can use to keep it open. I promise."

"Thank you. You take care of yourself."

He doesn't pull away till I'm inside. I go straight up to my room, and with some relief close the door to my refuge. I'm troubled by this verdict on Maryanne, the violence that was used against her. The fact that whoever did it might never be brought to justice resonates deep within me. It's been years, but the emotions roiling in my stomach and my mind are still raw.

I'm feeling better the next day; it's Saturday and I've slept till almost noon. I'm going over what Ed told me, while drinking my third cup of coffee.

There are many in our community who believe all cops and all landlords are the enemy. I try to stay open, though it's a challenge sometimes. We have more than our fair share of bottom-feeders housing the vulnerable, the aged and abandoned; men and women who make a nice living squeezing blood from stones. I like Ed, but he's wrong.

Maryanne had been through too much, hung on too tenaciously, to just give up.

And she was a mean drunk, more likely to strike out at others than to hurt herself.

Something isn't right. Not that suicide as a way out is unthinkable for any of us; it's never had the same taboo here as it does out in the real world. It occurs more frequently, and is received with more understanding, even empathy, by those left behind. But Maryanne—I can't see it. And neither will the others. I'm feeling a bit claustrophobic in my room, but if I go downstairs, I'll have to tell them what I know, and I don't feel ready yet.

"Dana!"

Michael's outside the door. I let him in, surprised at the big smile he's wearing.

"Everybody's ready for you, look!" He thrusts a book in my hand; it's new, very new. And hardcover. The latest Evanovich. I know better than to ask him how he got it.

"Michael ..."

"Please, just come read, I can't stand it anymore, everyone being so miserable. This will help, I know it."

He has a good, if larcenous, heart. I can't refuse.

Our club has indeed assembled in the common room, including Miss Semple, perched in a chair nearest the door. I join Gerry and Diamond at the card table, while Michael sprawls on the couch.

Any hope I have of postponing the news is dashed when Gerry asks, "So what did the cop want?"

"He said that all the evidence points to suicide. That they're closing the case."

"The bastards! What do they care?"

"Look, I know it's harsh, and I don't know if I believe it, but there's not much we can do except remember her, and keep doing what she enjoyed so much, these nights we spend together reading. I think it's great Michael got us a new book, it's a way to celebrate her, keep her with us."

Not knowing what else to do or say, I open the novel and start into the first chapter. They do listen, Miss Semple with her eyes closed, the better to see the pictures the words evoke, Gerry with his head down, resting on his folded arms, Diamond leaning forward, Michael still smiling at his little coup. We get through the first fifty pages, then I fold the page, close the text and look around.

"Man, it would almost be worth going to jail if she was coming to collect you!" Michael declares, referring to Stephanie Plum's often physically challenging attempts at bounty hunting. "Though I'd want her to wrestle with me first."

"In your dreams," scoffs Gerry. "I like the pictures she makes with her words. That black hooker, I can almost see her!"

"Well, she's sure the right size for you. In fact, she could be your body double. Me, I like Ranger best. I don't know why she just doesn't drop the cop and stick with him. What about you, Diamond?" Michael turns to him, genuinely curious.

"I, I like the scenes with the grandmother."

"Yeah, they're pretty funny, her waving that gun and all. See, Miss Semple, just 'cause someone's old doesn't mean they can't be armed and dangerous."

"I'll keep that in mind, Michael. Dana, that was lovely, thank you. It's made me think. I know it's just a novel, not real life, but it seems to me that a great injustice has been done to our friend, and sometimes, just like in the book, ordinary people have to set things right. Maryanne would not kill herself, we all know that. Someone hurt her very badly and it seems that person will never be punished unless we do something."

Wherever Evanovich had taken us, we're right back in the common room now, staring at each other in shocked silence. Miss Semple, having dropped this bomb on us, demurely folds her hands on her lap, and waits.

"Goddamn," Michael breathes, "we really could. We really, really could!"

An enthusiastic chorus of agreement bursts from the others.

Oh Lord, I ask myself, looking at each of their faces in turn, all alight with rare purpose, what to do with this? Introduce some realism.

"This wouldn't be a game; it could be very serious, even dangerous. You understand that?" Heads nod in unison. No hesitation. What the hell.

"Okay, everyone around the table." I wait, thinking hard while chairs are dragged into position. People have never moved so fast around here. "Rule number one. No one goes off on their own, we decide collectively what needs doing, and who's to do it. Rule number two. We tell nobody what we're doing. We don't know what's going on here, and till we find out, we don't know who to trust. Agreed?"

More heads nodding. There's so much life in the room now, the transformation almost takes my breath away. Miss Semple has colour in her cheeks, years have dropped away from her face, and that carefully maintained physical distance has been forgotten as she is crowded in on either side by Michael and Diamond.

"Here's what I've learned so far." I tell them exactly what Ed told me, including the bruising on the body and the address of the house, as well as the news Ed didn't know, that another woman, Janice, might have been taken. "It seems to me the first thing we have to do is scope out the house, see who comes and goes, try to get a sense of the layout of the place."

"Diamond and I can do that," Michael offers, "we'll take shifts. I'm better at getting up in the morning so I'll get there at, what d'ya think, 8:30, or so?"

"Sounds good. If we can cover the house till after five every day, it should be enough to start. Diamond, are you in?" His eyes are more focused on the here and now, he's more present than I've ever seen him.

"For sure. Absolutely. For Maryanne."

"For Maryanne," we echo, as Michael slaps one hand on the table, which is quickly covered by Gerry's meaty paw, and Diamond's, then Miss Semple without hesitation rests hers daintily on his, and finally my hand caps them all. "For Maryanne."

Chapter Three

It's a long night. It takes a while to convince a disappointed Michael that we don't need the taser device that Evanovich's character carries in her purse with such disastrous results, although he assures us he can "easily lay his hands on one."

Our resources are scant at best. We have two watches, mine and Miss Semple's. One goes to Gerry, who is declared "shift boss"; his job is to ensure both Michael and Diamond are on time for their surveillance work. Gerry's up every morning at 5:30, not by choice but because by then he's wrung every possible ounce of sleep out of his system; between his frequent daily naps and his early curfew, he spends more time in his bed than on his feet. The other watch will be worn by whoever is keeping an eye on the house.

We don't have rain gear, so we're limited to sunny days, and we don't have cell phones for easy communication in emergencies. Michael, who is functionally illiterate, won't be keeping notes at the scene—we'll have to depend on his memory. But he's observant, a survival trait he's perfected during his years on the street, and resourceful. I'm less sure about Diamond, he's so ethereal, but he gets a few pages torn from a notebook I keep and a functioning pen.

We all know Fortune Street. It's crowded with rooming houses, and in the summer it's not unusual to see men and women hanging out on porches and stairs, smoking and engaging in desultory conversation. Michael's natural garrulousness will serve us well, giving him an excuse to pick up on any gossip or information that might be offered about our target. And there's a scruffy parkette, with a couple of pigeon-poop-encrusted benches, better suited for Diamond if it gives him a clear view. He'll carry our new book with him, but says he'll only pretend to read it. "I won't get ahead of where we are."

I describe Janice to them. "She's about my height, in her sixties, she's pretty skinny, her hair is braided, and a dull grey. If you see her, follow her, see where she goes. If it looks like she's going to be anywhere for a while, come get me, okay?"

Miss Semple continues to surprise us. "Perhaps I could be of some use," she suggests. "I'll write up minutes of our meetings. And there's something else. When a house is bought or sold, there are records kept at City Hall. I know a little about title searches, I've done one or two in my time. Would that be helpful? I could take a few days off from my volunteer work with the seniors at the mission, if you think I should?"

I'm aware we're all staring at her in shock, so I slap the table enthusiastically to get three pairs of eyes off her before she notices. "Terrific. I'll dig up some bus tickets, and some paper."

"No need, thank you, Dana. They give me a bus pass. And it will be easy for me to get a notebook. You people have enough to do without worrying about me."

"Wonderful. Now there's another question that's been bothering me. How did they find Maryanne, where did they run into her? They must have had some time with her to convince her to move in with them. Think back to the last few days she was here. Did she go anywhere? Anywhere at all?"

This time it's Diamond who surprises. "The day before, she came to my room and asked me if I wanted to get my jeans washed, she was going across to the laundromat. I remember 'cause I had to stay in bed till she brought them back."

There's a large, well-used bulletin board in our grungy laundromat, with layers of messages and ads dating back months, maybe even years. It's too late tonight, but I tell them I'll check first thing in the morning. We might be fooling ourselves, but it feels like we have a plan, and a possible clue.

"Okay, that's enough for tonight. I'll talk to Pete at the drop-in, maybe I can get him to walk over to the house with me, see if we can get in. So if either of you guys see us tomorrow, ignore us; you don't want to call attention to yourselves."

We all retire to our rooms, though I don't think anyone but Gerry actually gets to sleep. I'm wired, very awake, my mind going faster than my pulse. This feeling of doing, of fighting back, is so powerful. I can't help but wonder how my life might have taken a very different turn if I'd been less passive in the face of police inaction in my own case, if I'd taken a hand and pushed harder for a resolution. All those months straitjacketed by terror. All the hiding, all the nightmares.

I hated being afraid. It made me feel small, pathetic and hugely vulnerable. When I finally won release from the psych ward, when they referred me to this rooming house after I refused to return to my parents, I thought I'd die of fear the moment I walked in the front door. It didn't help that Gerry was the first tenant I encountered. He looked like an angry bear shambling down the hall. I remember how I squeezed myself against the wall as he passed, how I stopped breathing, and tried to merge with the plaster, tried to disappear. Even so, it didn't take that long to understand that this was the best place in the world for me; if I wasn't to stay barricaded in a room the rest of my life, I had to find my courage, re-take my life.

Gerry. Big, bad Gerry was so lovely, a few days later, when he found me on the veranda, as he clumsily reassured me in his gruff, phlegm-filled voice that there was no need to be scared. That he and "the others" would look out for me. I remember how I laughed at that, almost hysterically, tears running down my face, and how he leaned forward, took hold of my hand, promised me he meant what he'd said.

A few nights later, Maryanne tapped on my door. She was mostly recovered from what I now know was an episode of binge drinking. Her hair was wrapped up in a loudly patterned scarf, the sleeves of her blouse rolled up above the elbow, and she was carrying a bucket, with cleanser and a couple of sponges tossed inside it.

"Nobody ever cleans these rooms for new tenants," she said by way of introduction. "And the last guy in here was such a pig. I thought I'd give you a hand making it liveable."

She did just that. We spent the evening scrubbing, Maryanne tackling the very grungy bathroom, and me the rest. It was fun, and reassuringly normal, reminding me of weekends at home, polishing furniture and cleaning floors with my mom. Maryanne gave me her Who's Who sketches of the rest of the tenants of Delta Court, making me laugh all the while. When the place, if not exactly sparkling, was at least free of suspicious stains and dirt, we shared a cup of tea side by side on my bed, and I felt at last that I might make it here.

When I emerge to start my morning, I find Miss Semple sitting with Gerry in the common room. Gerry managed to send Michael off to the early shift, and, shortly after I join them, he excuses himself to take a catnap, leaving us alone.

Miss Semple hands me a few loose-leaf pages covered in neat, clear writing. It's all there, our meeting last night, who's to do what and when, our rules, our makeshift plan.

"You've been busy."

"I find I don't need as much sleep as I did when I was younger. It's nice to have something worthwhile to do to fill the time."

Miss Semple positively bustles off, and it's time for me to move too. It's another sun-drenched day. I pause for a moment on the veranda, just enjoying the brightness and warmth, then jaywalk across the street to the laundromat. There are no customers in the dingy establishment.

Someone has pretended to clean all the surfaces and the floor over night, succeeding only in moving the dirt around in grimy, psychedelic circles and swirls, but I'm not here to inspect for cleanliness. I walk over to the bulletin board, which is tilting crazily under the weight of all the pinned-up notices: beds and televisions for sale, babysitting services, flea market flyers, missing pets and lost watches. I look for rooms to rent, there's a lot of those, and I copy down phone numbers to call from the drop-in.

The big question we're still facing is how these new landlords made contact with Maryanne in the first place. They couldn't have just walked in off the street and grabbed her without any prior conversation; how did they know where she lived? Compared to most of the people in the house, Maryanne was a social gadfly. She was a regular at the food bank, and enjoyed local flea markets, but she wasn't attached to an agency or drop-in, and didn't have a worker that I knew about. When she was sober, which was most of the time, she was sweeping and tidying and dusting in the common room and the hallways, happily gossiping with the tenants, playing cards, drinking coffee and having fun. She liked the local bars, but limited herself to a drink or two, preferring to buy her own bottles and cut out the expensive middleman.

Janice would have been much easier to get to, to convince. She was constantly on the lookout for a better deal, she never liked the rooms she found herself in, and she always had trouble with the other residents wherever she landed, accusing them of theft or nosiness or other miscellaneous mischief.

There were commonalities, of course. Both were in their early sixties, and both were committed drinkers. As well, each of them were on full provincial disability pensions, and neither of them had, if memory served, any family members still playing an active part in their lives.

I tuck the phone numbers in the pocket of my jeans and decide to go for breakfast next door, my head still buzzing with questions. I love breakfast, which is good, because it's very cheap at Karen's. I love toast and bacon and eggs, sunny side up, with the little pile of home fries on the side, everything washed down with slightly metallic-tasting orange juice. The place isn't actually called Karen's, and it's more of a bar than a restaurant, but Karen has staying power and the owners don't. It's always either up for sale or sold. The beer smells of last night haven't diminished at all, and only the front tables are wiped clean, and more or less organized with cutlery and napkins. Karen comes over, and plunks down in the chair opposite me, her large breasts bouncing with the shock. Though it's early, there's already sweat stains spreading under her armpits. She groans and drops her head on her arms, mumbling through a mass of hair: "Too much partying last night. I swear to God, I meant to go to bed early, but these friends came by, they had some primo weed, and the next thing I knew it was three in the morning. Do you have any Aspirin?"

"Sorry, no, I don't. Why don't you run to the corner? Nobody's here but me."

"Nah, too much like work. Hey, Michael was in. I was sorry to hear about Maryanne." She lifts her head up just a bit, then lets it fall again. "I liked her. I mean, even after we had to bar her, she was pretty cool. I'd run into her on the street, and she'd be all glad to see me. She wasn't a lady to hold a grudge, was she? Not like some folks I could mention." She more or less straightens up, yawns widely. "So what'll it be, the usual?"

"Yeah, please."

"Coffee's almost ready." Placing both palms flat on the table she eases herself up. "Shit, it's gonna be a long, bloody day."

I watch her walk back into the bar. She's hefty, not fat, but that uniform and its pukey orange colour don't flatter her. Her lifestyle is more for people in their twenties, and she's got to be edging close to forty. It seems like there's always a party at her place, and she's always recovering from the side-effects. What's convenient is, you can get more than beer and a meal here, her boyfriend deals pot, and she sells to regulars like me, when I have the money for the little extras of life.

Diamond comes in, walks toward my table. I smile at him. "Still tailing me?"

He looks at me, appalled. "No, I mean, yes. I mean ..."

"It's okay," I said, regretting the joke. "Pull up a chair. Can I buy you breakfast?"

He's conflicted about that too. "That's not why. I wanted."

"Diamond, relax. You're making me nervous. I'm glad for the company."

I haven't seen him in here before, have rarely seen him leave the house, though I'm sure he must. He sits opposite me, takes a deep breath.

"I'm glad we're doing this. I wanted to thank you."

Whole sentences. We're making progress.

"I'm glad too. It would be awful just to accept the official version, when we know it's wrong."

"She helped me a lot. When I first got here, I was so depressed, I could hardly talk."

I try to stop myself from smiling at that. It's not like he talks anyone's ear off even now. "She helped me too, through those first weeks. The whole area came as a bit of a shock to me." He nods at that, confirming my suspicions that he had known better places, better days.

Karen's back with a half-pot of coffee. "Hi there. This your boyfriend, Dana? He's cute." I thought he'd die of embarrassment as she poured him a cup, topping mine off at the same time, and dumped a few creamers on the table.

"Not yet he isn't. What would you like?" He's still a bright shade of red.

"Toast. Please."

I sip my coffee as he shakily tries to pry the lid from the cream. "Maryanne. She kept me together." He's staring into his cup, mesmerized by the changing colour as the cream hits the black coffee. "She knew. She knew when things were bad. She was there for me. I let her leave with those men. I didn't do anything."

"We didn't know what to do. I've got guilt too, but it doesn't help. The best thing is to put our energy into finding the bastards who killed her."

He nods, slowly, still miserable. His lips move, as though he's testing out words and sentences, rejecting them before they can escape. He is so tightly contained, so locked into his brain. I wait, knowing enough to keep quiet.

He shudders, sits straighter, but still keeps his eyes down. "Maryanne always told me to talk to you. That we had stuff in common. But I was, I guess I was ashamed. About what happened to me. How I screwed up so badly." He looked across at me, eyes a little watery. "Maryanne would say to me, 'Welcome to the club, Diamond, you think you're the only person in the world who ever messed up? My whole life has been one mistake after another: men, booze, you name it!'" It was quintessential Maryanne; he had her down pat. We both smiled, lost in the memory.

"She told me her parents drank and fought like animals and lived off welfare all through her childhood. When she grew up, she didn't know any other way to be. She wanted something different, but she was caught, she said. Every way she turned, everything she tried, led right back to the bottle. 'And here I am, Diamond, in this dump. If I'm very lucky, I'll get to stay here till I die, but you, you don't belong here, and I'm going to make sure you get out.'"

He gulps down his coffee, draining the cup.

"I told her how I was always so perfect. Perfect son, perfect student. I had to be. It was expected. But by the end of my third year at university, I just couldn't cut it anymore. It was like something broke inside of me. I couldn't study. Couldn't go to class. Couldn't even open my door. I ran. Didn't tell anyone, not even my parents. I spent some time on the streets, just wandering around lost, then a few months ago I found this place."

I'm just listening, keeping very still, hoping Karen will stay away.

"I was so ashamed. I just wanted to die. She knew. Wouldn't leave me alone. I almost hated her at first for that. But then, she helped. Just her being there helped. Then you. And the guys. And the reading. I felt, I felt better. Part of something." His hand shakes as he brings the coffee cup to his mouth. He must be exhausted. All these words, this tentative trust.

"University of Toronto?" He nods. "I was there too. English Lit."

"Medicine."

"Wow. That can be brutal."

"Parents. Both doctors. Expected me to be one too. There's no excuse for failure. I heard that all my life."

"High expectations can be as bad as no expectations. I was supposed to marry and have a lot of babies. School was for boys. I ran from that."

He likes that, I can tell by his grateful smile. That I would share something of myself. His toast and my breakfast arrive with Karen's idea of a flourish. She plunks the plates down on the table and pats Diamond's shoulder reassuringly. "Let me know when you want refills." He's quiet till she leaves.

"I've made such a mess of things. I never even told them I left. I didn't know how."

I dunk a piece of toast into a runny egg and make a suggestion. "Sometimes a letter can suffice."

A light comes on in his dark eyes; it hadn't occurred to him. "A letter. Yes. They wouldn't worry so much. And I wouldn't have to see them looking at me. Like I failed them."

We spend the rest of our time together eating and drinking more coffee, drafting his letter and then leaving words alone for a while, just being together in comfortable silence, feeling the connection between us grow. Then he says, "I like being called Diamond. Maryanne called me that. But I want you to know my real name. It's Steven, Steven James."

I take this gift the way it's offered, solemnly, seriously. "Thank you, Steven." And I reach across the table and shake his hand.

When Diamond leaves, I stay behind, drinking more coffee, staring at yesterday's paper, but not really seeing the words. Karen is being kept busy by the "morning rush," five or six demanding regulars, all men in their sixties and seventies who flirt with her as they order, feeling their oats along with the greasy eggs she throws down in front of them. Diamond's got me remembering Maryanne, her determined interference in my own life.

She encouraged me to grow comfortable with the house and its peculiar rhythms. I'd be pulled out of the relative safety of my room, to sit with Gerry out on the veranda, or to join the guys in the common room as they patiently taught me their favourite card games that whiled away hours at a time. With Maryanne nudging me along, I became the house scribe, filling in application forms for people seeking to replace their identification, reading the occasional official communication from pension or welfare offices, helping craft job applications. After a couple of months, I'd lost a lot of the fear I'd come in with.

Stepping into the streets of this strange community was a whole other matter. Maryanne relentlessly nagged me to "stop hanging around here all day," bugged me enough that, though I balked at first, I found myself out on the sidewalk, feeling naked and vulnerable in the glare of the sun. My first few excursions sent me scurrying back to the comparative safety of the house. It seemed that everything that had ever given my parents nightmares was here in spades: drunks, hookers and dealers everywhere, along with zoned-out characters who screamed at the sky and shook their fists in people's faces without provocation.

I'd come rushing back, on the verge of an anxiety attack, only to be met by a sarcastic Maryanne, looking pointedly at her watch. "Ten whole minutes. My, my. Were you worried about sunstroke?"

Essentially driven from the building, I kept trying. Some of the side streets were almost bearable, streets like Cowan Avenue, Melbourne, Gwynne and Elmgrove, where the houses weren't carved up into dark, forbidding rabbit warrens, and where parents who didn't look haunted played with well-nourished children. It was something of a marvel to me that regular life, the way it was supposed to be, could be found just steps away from the rooming house.

When I had mapped out some of the area, and grown a little in confidence, I tried Queen again, a few blocks at a time, walking west to Cowan, down Cowan to King and back to my place. I learned that the drunks who hung out on the benches in front of the library, often fighting with one another, throwing wild punches that would go astray as often as they connected, weren't any threat to me. I even found some sympathy for them, once my fear level dropped; their faces were battle-scarred and broken, they were often missing legs or arms, not to mention teeth.

I learned to deal with the panhandlers without panicking. At first, I would come close to cardiac arrest when someone in tattered, evil-smelling clothes would get in my face, spittle flying, bellowing as though their ears were filled with wax: "DO YOU HAVE A QUARTER? I NEED A QUARTER!" Or the more sophisticated sort, like the men who would sidle up to me and ask with wheedling insistence, "Would you have any change? I'm on welfare, and I really need something to eat, it's been days." And if I looked in my pockets and found nothing, they would add, as though making a generous concession, "I suppose a bill would do, too, if you have one." The ones who said nothing, who simply sat on the pavement with one hand out, or with a saucer or cup in front of them, were harder to ignore. They were the most broken and, on a closer look, the most medicated.

I learned not to stare at the haunted men and women who would rummage through public garbage receptacles that had already been picked through half a dozen times before, in search of food or some discarded treasure. And I wouldn't stand open-mouthed, staring at those who, like pigeons swooping down on crumbs of bread, grabbed up cigarette butts from gutters and sidewalks, straightening up long ones and immediately lighting them, the shorter ones going into torn pockets for later.

There were days when I simply went back to my room and cried, overwhelmed by the misery I had witnessed. Vivid replays over and over again of a large, distressed woman on the corner of Brock and Queen slowly pulling her sweater over her head, naked underneath, as store owners and passersby gawked and snickered. A tall, terribly skinny man trying to make off with a banana from a fruit stand in front of a tumble-down grocery store, chased by the raging proprietor, and held for the cops. Two hard-faced women with a tribe of hollow-cheeked, squabbling children in their wake paying more attention to the case of twenty-four they're dragging in a shopping cart than to their kids. Teenage hookers, still plump with baby fat, teetering on heels, stuffed into short skirts and unbuttoned blouses, making their way to their corners.

I would hide out for a day or two, shaken and miserable, determined never to venture out of these walls again. I had a deep, physical longing for the shady streets I had known in the Annex: the carefully tended gardens, the clean restaurants and bookstores, and the many parks where bodies didn't huddle on and under benches. Closing my eyes, I would take myself back to that time, not so long ago, when I could, without a thought, turn the key in the lock, enter my apartment and close the door behind me. I would savour that moment, as I lay on my metal bed with its lumpy, stained mattress, linger over it, that simple, unthinking act, that ability to be safe. I re-lived each footstep down the narrow hallway, into the living room with its comfortable couch and armchair, where no strangers coughed and fought and threw down cards, felt my arm stretch out to turn on the stereo, felt the pleasure in the music that poured from the speakers. I would turn to the kitchen, calling once again for the cat, as I grasped the handle of the fridge, so tall and white and clean, pulling it open, and revealing shelves filled with milk, juice, fruit, yogurt and meat. I might pour myself a pop, or glass of juice, or peel an orange, or make a sandwich. The possibilities were endless. I lingered over that too, almost feeling the delicious chill as I stood there, blithely gazing in. I let myself turn to my cupboards, as I had done so often, in search of the cat's dinner, every shelf a pirate's treasure of tins and packaged goods, salmon and tuna and chickpeas and soups, nothing dented, nothing missing labels. Bending down, I would pick up the mewing bundle of fur, fussing over it, then set it down to eat its gourmet dinner while I turned on the stove and started to cook my own dinner, in my own kitchen, in my own apartment. I remembered how I would pour a glass of wine, set my place at the neat little wooden table, choose a book for pleasure and read while I ate. Sometimes I would watch television after the dishes were washed and put away, or work on papers that were due. Then, when it was time, I would go into the bedroom, and soon I would be under the duvet, my head resting on the plump pillows that hadn't supported a dozen other heads, my eyes closing, no screams or furniture crashing against walls, no screech of tires or rattle of streetcars shattering the night. No monster lurking to steal it all away.

Sometimes it would all be so real, my imagining so vivid, that when I opened my eyes I would be shocked and disoriented to find myself in this room. I realized, after a while, that it did me no service to keep going back to what had been. I was here now, that other world was lost to me, and I should let it go. If I was to survive.

I might never have ventured beyond Cowan, except for Maryanne. She'd shown up at my door one afternoon, in her black elastic-waist pants and flowered blouse, carrying her purse.

"Dana, I need your help. There's a drop-in that got a whole shipment of scarves and hats and gloves from one of the churches around here. I saw the notice while I was at the food bank, and it said they were handing them out today."

I groaned, not wanting to stand in long lines with my hands out. It was too close to begging. "Isn't Michael around?"

"Nope, he ran out of here before I could ask him. C'mon, Dana, you could use a good walk, and it's lovely out. I want to bring back enough for the whole house. It'll take the two of us to convince them, though; they're too used to me squeezing them for more. You wouldn't want people going without in the cold, would you?"

"Ooh, that's low, Maryanne. Where is it?"

"Up near Roncesvalles. If we leave now, we'll get there before the crowds."

Out on the street, in the late fall weather, with a slight breeze playing with the bits of newspaper and discarded Styrofoam cups, it was a beautiful day. Even though I cringed at the idea of asking for anything from anyone, maybe it wouldn't be so bad knowing that the folks in the building would benefit.

As we passed Cowan, I confessed, "I've never been farther west than this."

"Really? Why on earth not?"

I turned it into a joke, not wanting to admit that the people I'd encountered freaked me out. "I was afraid I'd never find my way back home. The pigeons would eat all the breadcrumbs, and there I'd be, stranded in the Parkdale wilderness."

"Right. It's not like you could ask directions of one of the fifty to a hundred people walking around. Dana, believe me, compared to some neighbourhoods I've lived in, like Scarborough, this is really safe. I know some of the people look a little strange, but they're just like Gerry, they come out of the same place. They're on a lot of pills, and they're not used to being outside in the world. They wouldn't hurt anybody any more than Gerry would."

It wasn't fear of them so much anymore as fear of the emotions they stirred up inside me, I thought to myself—though, if I were absolutely honest, sometimes it was simply fear.

"I've spent a lot of years here now. Between Lansdowne and Roncesvalles there's so many places, boarding homes, rooming houses, mostly run by mean bastards who will take anyone with a cheque. They never care much about the other tenants' safety. I think I must have lived in most of them before I found our house. Compared to some of the landlords I've known, our guy is a real prize. He's careful who he lets in, and if we tell him someone is really bad, he listens."

I'd only seen him a few times, before he set out on his travels, but he had seemed a decent sort, practical, interested.

"We don't have roaches or lice, or rats. Mice yes, but he has the exterminator in once a month. Believe me, we're very lucky compared to most. Look over there"—she pointed up the street.

"That's the BiWay. Cheapest jeans and sweaters, underwear and socks in the neighbourhood. They have sales all the time. I love going in there."

The sidewalks had begun to thicken with people, all poorly dressed. Some of them looked pretty tough, in leather-looking vests, with knife cases on their belts, a lot of tattoos, and with chains dangling from their belts to the long flat wallets sticking out from their back pockets. Everyone was either very skinny or very fat; there seemed to be no in-between.

My heart sank as I realized we were all heading in the same direction. Sure enough, Maryanne proclaimed, "Here we are." She checked her watch. "We shouldn't have to wait too long."

"What is this place?" I asked her, making an effort to keep my voice steady.

"It's a drop-in for mental patients and poor people. They play cards and watch movies, sometimes there are hot meals. The man who runs it is an all-right guy, not too full of himself."

Oh great, I thought. If I'd worried about them on my walks, I'd sure as hell worry when trapped in a crowd of them. I checked out the faces around me, as casually as I could, faces that were either chalk white or badly sunburnt, some caved in from missing teeth.

There must have been over a hundred people gathered in front of the door. I noticed, at the edges of the mob, middle-aged to elderly women who stood a little apart, not talking to anyone, some wearing coats or layered up with sweaters even in that heat. Scattered here and there were their male counterparts, shirts grey with grime and dirt and perforated with cigarette burns; they mumbled to themselves, leaned against the mailbox and street light as if all their energy had deserted them. These men and women were clearly from Gerry's neck of the woods, the mental institution down the street. Some were rigid in their spare movements; others shook like they had high fever, while everyone, the toughs and the crazies, coughed up a storm. I had to stifle a strong impulse to run screaming back to the relative safety of my room. I was furious with Maryanne for exposing me to this. What had she been thinking? Or maybe this was all normal to her, I realized in a moment of clarity. She'd stopped seeing this as something appalling. It was just another part of her world and, by extension, mine too.

The door opened, and a bearded man stood in the entrance, effectively blocking it, as he called out, "Okay, now, those of you who are just here for the drop-in, go right in. For anyone who's here to pick up scarves and hats my name is Pete, and I need you to line up for me in front of the long table." He was tall and strong enough not to be buffeted by the rush inside, which impressed me, and he traded jokes and insults with some of the guys who pushed past him.

Maryanne grabbed me by the arm and stepped into the melee. My heart was going a mile a minute, but we made it inside unmolested. I was glad the table was close to the front door, since I had no desire to venture any deeper into that cavernous space. Someone had turned on a television set, and the sound of an old sitcom competed with the roar of voices from the back. Maryanne and I stood in line, not a long line, I was happy to see, and shuffled forward without too much delay. Pete had to turn his chair to search in the boxes piled behind him for requested colours and pairs of mittens; it was all quite efficient, considering. Before I knew it, Maryanne was introducing me as if I were a prize catch.

"Pete, this is Dana. She's a *university graduate*. She's practically running our rooming house for us. She's sensible, good in emergencies, she likes people, and people like her. I heard you're looking for part-time staff, so I thought I'd bring her along to meet you. She doesn't have enough to do, and she could sure use the money. And we need a bunch of gloves and scarves and whatever else you're giving out, for the residents at our place, if you have enough."

My mouth was hanging open. I stared at her in shock, totally sandbagged.

Pete had taken it all in stride. "Tell you what, Maryanne, you sit here and I'll have a chat with Dana in the office."

He got up and she pushed me around the table, while I tried to get out some words of protest and denial. Before I knew it, I was in a very cramped space, perched on the edge of a chair, still poleaxed.

"Tell me about yourself," Pete said, as he leaned back in his roller chair, looking very comfortable.

"Ah, listen, I didn't know, that is, Maryanne never said ..."

"That's okay. You're here now. So tell me, what did you study?"

"English Lit. At U of T. But ..."

"Good. And what are some of the emergencies you've dealt with at your rooming house?"

I took a deep breath and tried to collect my scattered thoughts. "I helped out a few times. People asked me to. There was a man who kind of lost it; he was banging on everyone's door in the place, hollering stuff that wasn't making any sense, scaring people. I talked to him for about an hour, calmed him down a bit, he thought there was poison gas leaking in the house. I found him a bus ticket to go down to the hospital, get himself checked out. And there was an incident with an intruder, our front door doesn't really lock, he was sleeping in the common room, and I got him to leave first thing in the morning. And I stopped some fights, nothing big."

"Good. Sounds like you have some experience. Tell you what, Dana, Maryanne's right, I do need part-time staff. Not everyone can handle this kind of place, so we don't get a lot of applicants. I'll introduce you around, and you decide if it's something you'd like to do."

I clamped my lips together to stop from saying, "Are you out of your mind!" And kept them clamped when he mentioned the hourly wage, which beat the hell out of welfare. It hit me hard that I was deeply tired of trying to subsist on next to nothing.

We left the office, and I overheard Maryanne asking about colour preferences as I turned toward the back of the drop-in. Every table was full, every inch of space taken up by someone. I felt very small and physically vulnerable; anyone here could have taken me apart piece by quaking piece. Pete was right behind me, asking if I played cards. Who would have thought, when Gerry and Michael made me play euchre and cribbage, that they'd been teaching me a marketable job skill? "Good," he said, "follow me." As we snaked through the tables, Pete introduced me to a dizzying array of faces, and found a couple chairs near the coffee bar at the back.

I almost collapsed into mine. Pete smiled at me sympathetically. "It's a bit much the first time, eh? But you'll get used to it, and I'll be here to help. The goal is to create a place where socially isolated adults feel some sense of ownership and safety. We try to anticipate problems before they blow up, which means keeping your eyes and your ears open. We also spend a lot of time on the phones, calling the provincial benefit office or welfare workers, if someone's cheque is late, or if people get cut off, and we call around looking for shelter space if someone's homeless. Or a detox bed if needed. There are hot meals twice a week; we have volunteers from the membership who do the cooking and cleaning up."

Faces were indistinct, everything and everyone blurred into one another as I tried to take it all in. Then a voice called out for Pete, and I saw a very tall women threading her way toward us, a very tall woman with a five o'clock shadow and tattooed arms.

"What a nightmare," she said, pulling up a chair. I thought for a moment that she was sympathizing with me, but she went on, "It's getting really hard for a lady to make a buck these days. Bloody cops are everywhere, scaring away the johns, stirring up trouble. Like there's not enough real crime around to keep them busy."

Pete grinned across at her. I tried not to stare. She was wearing very thick makeup, but her Adam's apple was unmistakably there.

"I only made about sixty dollars, spent more time on my feet than on my back. Anyway, Pete, here's the ten I borrowed. I'm off to bed. If Charlie comes in will you tell him to get his ass home?"

"Sure. Cindy, this is Dana, she's going to be helping out around here."

For the first time since she'd sat down, she looked at me full on. "Hey."

"Hey," I said back, a little faintly to my ears.

"Relax, honey, it ain't Kansas, but it ain't so bad, either. Okay, see you guys."

She left while I was still blinking, trying to reset my vision. I was ready to tell Pete to forget it, ready to leave, to run. He attracted people like a human magnet: in less than half an hour, I was introduced to more drop-in members than I could possibly remember. Some were timid, which I could relate to, others boisterous, loudly welcoming me to their "club." In spite of everything, I felt myself getting hooked, as my mind raced to take it all in. No one was blatantly hostile or challenging; everyone seemed remarkably good-humoured considering what their lives must be like. They also didn't seem to need a lot of direction or intervention. It was their place, and they were obviously comfortable there.

"Gotcha, don't I?" Pete asked, startling me.

I grinned back at him. "Yes, I think you do. But I also think I've got a whole lot to learn."

He nodded, serious for a moment. "It'll take time, no question. And you'll make some mistakes, just like I did when I started. But these guys have been through enough in their lives that most of them don't bruise too easily. They'll survive your apprenticeship, and so will you."

There was a constant demand for bus tickets, and Pete excused himself to get some from his office, leaving me to play out his cribbage hand with a guy who talked mostly to himself. Pete came right back out, looking frustrated and annoyed. I watched as he waded into the middle of the drop-in and hollered for attention.

"Listen, I've managed to jam up the lock on my cabinet. Can anyone break it open for me?"

At least a dozen hands shot up, provoking some laughter. Pete held up both hands, palms out, adding, "Can anyone break it open without wrecking it?"

A guy who looked like an old biker stood up to hoots of "Go Derek," and scattered applause. "I'm your man!" he said. In less than a minute, Pete was distributing TTC tickets while Derek returned to his seat.

Maryanne picked that moment to wander back, cradling a bag stuffed with loot, looking like she owned the place. As Pete returned, she plunked the bag down and pulled out a chair, a smug smile on her face.

"See, I told you she'd be perfect for you. Everything's gone,

Pete, it didn't take long, and nobody went without. So when does she start?"

That was Maryanne. Pushy, outrageous at times, arranging lives and distributing charity without apology or advance notice. Everything I have going for me these days stemmed from her intervention.

Brought back to the present by Karen asking me if I want more coffee, I shake my head, close up the newspaper I haven't really read and ask for a bill. I'm still steeped in the past as I head west on Queen, hearing echoes of Maryanne's laughter.

Chapter Four

Pete and I don't have much of a plan. We're just going to knock on the front door and hope someone answers. I'm conflicted about how honest to be with Pete. I trust him absolutely, but his funding comes from the province, and I don't want anything our group is doing to jeopardize that.

I'd called all the numbers from the ads posted in the laundromat across from our building before we left the centre, trying to age my voice, adding a soupçon of vulnerability, but those who answered weren't from the address we're interested in. A dead end, as was my effort to find Mallick in the phone book.

Though Fortune Street is less than a ten-minute walk from the drop-in, it takes Pete and I more than half an hour to negotiate our way. The area is filled with rooming and boarding homes, and we're stopped every few feet by men and women wanting to share news, or ask questions, or bum bus tickets. Pete is patient and accommodating. I've learned a lot from watching him with the folks who use the drop-in. He expects the best from people, and they tend to respond with just that. Other places I've been place huge emphasis on rules and compliance, whereas Pete values the relationships he builds, not the power.

Fortune Street is notorious in the neighbourhood, the last stop before homelessness or jail. The houses are old, and falling-down tired. People sprawl on peeling stairs, bottles of beer in hand, laughing or arguing or grimly silent. Police are frequently called here, to break up fights or to bust fugitives. There are no trees, not even in the scrub parkette, no green lawns and hardly any cars. You have to be tough to live here, even tougher to survive the experience.

Looking around, I'm positive there's no way either Maryanne or Janice would have voluntarily moved here; it makes no sense. Pete agrees.

"I can't see it either. Here's the place." We stop in front of a big, rambling house at the end of the street, while I swivel my head around as unobtrusively as possible looking for Michael or Diamond. I can't see either of them, which is good. The house is three storeys, and all the visible windows are closed and curtained. Odd, in this heat: I know from experience no rooming house has air-conditioning. The front door, as we approach up a cracked and weed-clogged cement path, is solid wood, with an ominous warning sign taped to it. Orange lettering on a black background declares that a guard dog is on the premises.

There's no bell or knocker, so Pete raps his knuckles on the door. He tries this three times, then uses his fist to pound a little louder. I keep my eyes on the curtains but can detect no movement, however slight. Other eyes are watching, though; we're the only action on the street.

"Let's try the back." Pete leads, I follow, worrying about the dog, though we haven't heard any barking.

"Christ, it's like Fort Knox." He's right. Even the small glass pane in the back door is covered with cloth. The back yard is as unkempt as the rest of the house, clearly not used. Pete bangs for a while on the door, with the same negative results.

"This is weird, Pete. It's like nobody lives here."

"But the cops must have been inside, right? You said they talked to the owner?"

"Yeah. Ed didn't actually say he'd been inside the building, but I suppose he must have. I wonder if he'd tell me, if I asked him." I find I like the prospect of talking to him again.

"On a first-name basis, eh?" Pete teases me. I punch his shoulder.

"He's not a bad guy, for a cop. Are you game to check Janice's old place with me?"

"Sure. Who knows, maybe she left a forwarding address, and we can both relax."

He doesn't believe it any more than I do, but it's a cheering thought, that this gnawing fear I've been experiencing could be for nothing, that Janice has just decamped on her own, set up housekeeping on another street. Thinking back to the last time I saw her, I have to laugh. She was gloriously drunk, with Vera as always by her side, also the worse for wear. Belching fumes from the bitters, she resisted going home, cursing her house-mates and me as I tried to walk her out. She got as far as the sidewalk in front of the door, when, exasperated and filled with righteous denial that she'd even touched a drink, she pulled out her false teeth and flung them at my feet in the ultimate grand gesture.

Her old place is a few blocks over. As we walk back down Fortune, I can't shake the feeling of being in an old western movie, at high noon. There's dead silence and many pairs of eyes follow us.

"Dana! Pete! What the hell, there goes the neighbourhood."

A laughing figure detaches itself from a group of men hanging out on the porch of a particularly decrepit establishment. It's Derek, I see with some relief, the lovely old biker whose breaking and entering skills had come in so handy for Pete on my first visit to the centre. He's a man with a serious drug habit and a poet's soul. We all hug each other, somewhat gingerly, since Derek has one arm in a sling.

"I haven't seen you in months," Pete tells him. "I was starting to worry."

"Can't kill an old dog. They had me locked up for a while, that's all. How you guys been? How's everything at the drop-in?"

"What did you do to your arm?" I ask. It is swollen about three times its normal size.

"Just a bad shot. Happened before, no big deal. Looks worse than it is." Sometimes when he injects himself, with heroin or whatever else he can find, he's already too stoned to do it right.

The tension on the street has lifted; we've been validated by Derek's acceptance of us.

"Have you seen Janice on this street, maybe coming from that house?" I ask him, pointing back at the building.

"Janice wouldn't be caught dead here, you guys know that. I think that building's empty, I never see anyone coming out. But I'm not watching all the time, you know."

We chat a bit more, Pete telling him to come by the drop-in for a hot meal, maybe a change of clothes, and we continue on our way as Derek returns to his friends. As gentle and sweet as Derek can be, I've seen the other side, the street fighter who still retains lightning-swift reflexes, killer instincts that have kept him alive over the years. I had been working an evening shift at the centre, and had just come out of the office when I heard angry raised voices. Derek was arguing with a taller, stronger man who I hadn't seen before. Suddenly, like a rattler striking, two rigid fingers went right for the stranger's eyes, intending to maim, or disable. My shout froze them both just in time.

He'd never hurt me, or Pete, but it was a lesson for me, a reminder that just below the surface all the harsh lessons of the street ruled both the mind and the body of those who lived long enough to learn them.

The street where Janice used to live feels a lot less dangerous. There's a mix of housing here, apartment buildings, single-family himes, even a few trees. The front door to her house is wide open, as are the windows, in a vain attempt to get the air flowing. A man is walking out onto the porch as we climb the stairs. He's tall, toothless, shirtless and needs to wash his hair. Pete asks the questions.

"Hi, we're looking for Janice. We understand she may have moved."

"Yeah, thank Christ. What a bitch that woman is. Trouble from the day she moved in, nagging and bitching all the time."

"Did someone come get her?"

"Yeah, two guys. Hope they locked her up."

"Can you remember what they looked like?"

"Nah. But one of them was maybe German. Talked like Colonel Klink, you know?"

"Did she say where she was going?"

"Who the hell cares? Long as she was leaving."

"Is there a super in the building?"

"You're looking at him."

We thank him, and retreat back to the street.

Pete and I stop for beer and wings at a local bar. There are huddles of serious drinkers in here, little laughter, lots of cursing. We've both been quiet, thinking our own thoughts. Pete sighs, puts down his glass.

"You know, I offered a number of times to try to get her into a seniors' residence, but she was smart enough to know it would mean she'd have to give up drinking, and—how did she put it? 'It's pretty late in life to be forced into sobriety, isn't it? Don't worry about me, I live by my wits and it keeps me sharp. People who go into those homes have their brains turned to porridge.' And she was right."

"Poor Vera, she's really lost without Janice. Too bad they couldn't have shared a place."

"I think they both recognized that would have ended their friendship pretty quickly. One of the reasons they've managed to stay friends so long is because they can both retreat to separate corners when they're tired of each other."

"And the other reason, aside from the drinking, is that neither of them has anyone else. You'd think, Pete, that with so little, they'd be left alone to finish out their lives in whatever peace they could find."

He nodded his head slowly.

"I've checked with the Information and Referral Centre. That house on Fortune hasn't been on their recommended list for years. The hospital doesn't use it either, according to the case managers I talked to."

There's a provincial psychiatric hospital that borders the neighbourhood, it feeds patients into substandard buildings all the time. There's not a lot of choice for those branded mentally ill.

"I could try to get a building inspector to check it out, for illegal use," Pete continues. "And I will. If they ever had a licence to run a rooming house, it must have expired by now. But you know how reluctant they are to move on anything. They still use the same old excuse: where will people go if we close them down? And I can't see reporting this to the cops. After all, what do we have? One dead body that they've labelled a suicide, and one woman with a history of impulsively jumping from one place to another whose friends are worried about her. No evidence of foul play. No force used that anyone noticed. But something is going on, I feel it."

"Me, too. Pete, how do we know that there aren't others who've been scooped up? Disappeared? Damn, we need to get into that house."

"Don't go doing anything on your own. That guy who came to the centre was bad news. When I told him to go, he looked like he was going to try to hit me, and I'm a lot bigger than you."

I just nod, feeling guilty and miserable.

"You talk to your cop, see what he thinks. Maybe he'll have some ideas."

I borrow his cell phone and call Ed at the station. He's not there but his voice mail is active. I leave a message, asking him to drop by the house when he gets a chance, that I have some questions and concerns he might be able to help with.

The bar is dark and cool, a relief from the heat outside.

I'm remembering all the sad, tawdry tales we've heard from the members about their landlords. "What was the name of the guy who gave Jocelyn twenty bucks for sex, then took it out of her welfare cheque?"

Pete chokes on his beer. "God, I'd forgotten about him. Harrison, wasn't it?"

"Yeah. And that lady who had Rose sign over her inheritance to her? So she wouldn't waste it on booze? Mrs. Klemper, on Beatty. Rose never saw a dime."

"Vince!" Pete adds, "remember that jerk? The one with the broom handle he used to 'keep order.'"

"They really come out of the woodwork, these bastards. I hate feeling so powerless, Pete. It drives me crazy."

"We'll figure something out. I promise."

We stay for an hour, talking about more pleasant things, then Pete leaves, and I head home. The sun is starting to set, hordes of people are out on the street, escaping airless apartments and rooms. Young hookers are staking out their territory, and the johns are cruising slowly by, checking out what's on offer. The dealers are out in significant numbers as well, hawking dimes of hash and pot, and small homemade envelopes of powdered cocaine. Business as usual.

Unholy screams and shouts break through whatever dream I may have been enjoying. I leap out of bed, pulling on jeans and a T-shirt. I waste seconds trying and failing to find my watch to see what time it is, then, remembering I lent it out, tie my shoes and stumble out the door and down one level imagining lurid scenes of murder and mayhem.

There's a huddle at the bottom of the staircase, as people (the Temps, as Maryanne used to call them) clutch at one another and point to the far corner of the hallway. "There! It's there! Can't you see it? There it goes again, watch it!"

Someone steps on my foot, trying to back up the stairs. "What's going on?"

"It's a rat!"

"Stomp it!"

Though part of me wants to slink back to my room, the word *rat* having sent shivers down my spine, I can't stand all the yelling and I want it to stop.

"Quiet! Everyone shut up for a minute." I nudge past the

huddle, taking baby steps down the hallway toward the small, dark shape they're all freaked about.

"It's not a rat." Tommy, the resident problem child, speaks through a crack in his door. "It's my pet."

"Your pet what?" I ask, not taking my eyes off the thing.

"My pet squirrel, I found him. A car squished his tail, so I brought him home. He's mine."

"Jesus, Tommy, there's got to be twenty million cats in the neighbourhood, and you've got to have a squirrel?" I haven't had my coffee yet. "Squirrels aren't pets. Do you hear me? Not. Pets."

I take a deep breath, then, "Were you feeding him?"

"Of course, peanuts, lots of them."

"Give me a handful."

He disappears into his room for a moment, then pops his head and a hand out. I take the peanuts from him, lean over the rail and yell for Gerry. He's there, laughing and choking on his cigarette, but pulls himself together to do what I ask, and props the front door open.

"Okay, everybody stay still."

The Pet has obviously chewed his way out of the room; little piles of sawdust near a low hole in George's door, and little sawdust paw prints along the threadbare carpet attest to that. I toss a peanut over the rail to the stairs below, then another, and another, and slowly, with many stops and starts, the furry little escape artist rises to his feet and, like a slow-motion slinky, starts his descent.

A triumphant whoop from Gerry as he slams the door signals success. I almost break into a chorus of "Born Free," but I want to sleep more.

After an abortive effort to sleep, I give it up and go downstairs to check in with the group. Michael, Gerry and Diamond are sitting at the card table with Miss Semple, who is taking notes. It's easy, for the moment, to see the woman she must have been during her working life, efficient, competent. I pull up a chair, and our second official meeting begins.

"If I could start off," Miss Semple begins, "in the last few days, the boys have noticed that one man, in his early thirties, blond, about six-foot-two, arrives around ten in the morning. He has no car, we think he takes public transportation. Shortly after, another man, the same one who took Maryanne, leaves the house and gets into a BMW, metallic grey, with four doors. We have the licence number. Michael hung around one evening and caught the BMW arriving, just shortly after dinnertime. The driver let himself in with a key, and the blond man left a few minutes after. It's almost like a change of shifts. No one else has come or gone, at least not while they were watching."

We mull that over in silence, then I tell the group of my visit to the house, and to Janice's last address, with Pete.

"So they took that lady too," Michael says, disturbed.

"I'm afraid so. I think we may want to wander by that place at night, see what lights are on, if any. And look for that car."

Heads nod.

"It's weird about all the windows being closed like that, and covered up. Half the rooms here don't have anything like curtains, and most rooming houses I've been in, that's the last thing the owners worry about," Michael says.

"I know, Michael, it struck me as odd too."

Miss Semple stops her note-taking for a moment and makes her own report.

"I'm afraid I failed miserably at City Hall. Things have changed a lot since I was last there. Everything's computerized and complicated and, worst of all, expensive. They charge fifty dollars for the information we want about the ownership."

"Fifty dollars!" snorts Gerry. "That's, like, almost a carton of cigarettes."

"Or twenty-five Big Macs!" the perpetually hungry Michael adds.

"Or five brand-new mysteries," Diamond pitches in, surprising us.

"Whatever, it's beyond our resources. Thanks for looking into it, though; it was a good thought. I've got a call in to that cop. Haven't heard back yet, but if I do, I'm going to try to convince him to check on the tenants. Don't know if he will. In the meantime, Diamond, why don't you go for a walk up Fortune tonight?"

"We should follow that car when it goes," Michael adds. "I could maybe borrow one long enough to find out where that bastard lives."

"We can't help anyone if we're all in jail. No car 'borrowing.' But it's true, it would be good to 'tail him back to his lair.' Maybe I can work on that. I know someone who might lend me hers. I do still have my licence." I've renewed it faithfully every year, since I have no desire to do my driving test again. It had taken me three tries before I'd passed, in spite of driving school. The mechanics of parallel parking baffled me. One of my best friends, Charlene, a woman of many talents, drives an old clunker she's offered me before.

"Now we're cooking," Michael says. "In the meantime, we'll keep up our surveillance, me and Diamond, just in case someone does come out that door."

Tommy appears at the entrance of the common room, desperately trying to hold on to three mangy cats, all of them spitting and yowling and biting. His face and arms are sliced with scratches and blobs of blood, but he's glowing with purpose.

"Which one do you think is best?"

"Best for what," Gerry asks. "Cat stew?"

I kick him under the table, then try to differentiate between the squall of animals, finally just pointing to a little orange tail flicking furiously.

"How about that one?" He looks, nods his head up and down like one of those bobble heads people put on their dashboards, and backs away.

"That's all we need," mutters Gerry, sulking because of the kick. "Fleas and fur balls and cat piss."

Miss Semple interjects, "It might be nice, having a cat in the house. They make good company; I used to have two. And they are very clean animals, Gerry."

He snorts at that. "Then maybe it'll teach Tommy a thing or two."

"Quirky," she'd said. "Temperamental." I have other words, not nearly as kind The plan had been simple, deceptively straightforward. I would wait for Stephan Mallick to leave, and follow his car when he turned onto Queen, but now I'm unsure that the car will respond when I need it to. I know I'm not a great driver, neither is Charlene, judging from the tickets lying on the dashboard and scattered on the floor, but I know that when you turn the key in the ignition, something is supposed to happen, a nice growling sound, or even a not-so-nice grinding. I get nothing, like the car's on strike. Or dead.

Charlene had made a deal with me. In return for working her

Saturday night drop-in shift, she'd pick me up at the rooming house and show me some of the "eccentricities" of her car, an aging, rusting Honda Civic, and leave it with me for the day.

My first try, I'd kept watch, feeling almost professional, and an hour or so later looked on helplessly as the BMW drove away, leaving me in its dust as Charlene's car refused to turn over.

Charlene was apologetic, to the car. "Poor baby," she cooed, as I looked on incredulously, "you don't know Dana, do you?" The next day we tried again. She'd taken me through all the steps and incantations to bring the wreck to life, patted the steering wheel fondly and left for work. I'm very fond of Charlene, but I really hate this car. Sitting here in the heat is no fun either. I get thirsty, or I have to pee, or my stomach sends urgent Feed Me signals. I didn't even bring a book, fearful that I would lose concentration. The sun is baking the interior, and there's not a cloud in the sky. I try winding down the windows, but that only brings in the exhaust from cars that do what they're supposed to—drive—leaving me headachy and even more miserable. To escape, I think about Charlene, how I got drawn into her world.

Her family is better than television. I love the stories, conflicts and histrionics that she relates with some relish over cups of tea in the home she shares with her famous uncle Jeremy, the only one of her relatives she can stand. They are two sides of the same coin, eccentric, verging on downright odd, writ large for the stage they both know so well. Her mother's older brother is tall, whip thin and has a voice that can rumble like gathering thunder, rocking the gallery he always plays to, if only in his mind.

It was Jeremy I met first. One very cold winter evening I was heading back home from the drop-in. It was a terrible night, the driving snow feeling like ice pellets striking my face. I was walking along Queen Street when I spotted an old fellow apparently collapsed against the wall of a deserted apartment building. Residents become accustomed to assorted drunks and druggies sleeping it off in public areas; it's as much a part of the scenery as the few trees and bushes, panhandlers and hookers. As long as there isn't a great spill of blood, we tend to walk on by.

Still, ever since Pete told me the story of locking up one night, and on the way to his car seeing old Charlie with his back against a brick wall, frozen and unable to move, while tons of snow continued to fall, I'd kept an eye out for similar tragedies in waiting. Pete had been able to get Charlie back to the drop-in, warm him up and then drive him to his rooming house. Charlie had told him his legs had given out, and that he'd called out to people for help, but no one responded. Charlie always looked pretty rough, more skeleton than flesh on his face and body, and passersby probably thought he was trying to hit them up for change, which ordinarily he would have done.

I could see this fellow was different. His clothes were clean, his shoes shiny and expensive and totally impractical for the season, his hair styled with some care. I stopped, and crouched down beside him. He was conscious, barely, and trembling from the cold. I offered to call him an ambulance, but he shook his head, and croaked at me to please help him up. It turned out he'd slipped on a patch of ice and went down hard, knocked himself out for some minutes and was too dazed to stand. I enlisted a few passersby—people do respond if someone who looks like them asks them to—collectively we got him into a cab, and I rode with him to his house in High Park.

I'd been worried about the cab fare, having no money at the time, but thankfully Charlene answered the doorbell, immediately bursting into tears at what could have happened. She embraced her uncle, then ran out to pay the driver. Their house was typical of the area, three floors, beautiful staircases, bay windows, solid furniture, everything highly polished and gleaming. We eased him out of his coat and bundled him upstairs, where Charlene managed to take off his wet pants and shirt while I averted my eyes.

Charlene left to make some soup while I stayed with him, staring in awe at the pictures covering every inch of his walls. Black and white photos of scenes from stage plays, *Hamlet, Macbeth, Othello*, autographed colour portraits of actors I recognized but couldn't name, masks and costume bits hanging here and there. He even had a mirrored and lighted dressing table, like an old Hollywood star.

He was very pale, but even so he had such a strong face, all angles with a great beak of a nose. He waved me closer, and I leaned toward him, taking his hand.

"How are you doing?"

"Much better, child, thank you. I wasn't sure that I'd see this room again. It would have been dreadful to die like that, on the bloody pavement. I don't understand people anymore. No one stopped to help, even when I called out. They were all suddenly blind and deaf, or I was invisible."

"It happens to people in the city. Self-protection, I guess. None of us wants to see what's happening around us. It's too scary. Too much. We shut down. A cop once told me that they always know when tourist season starts, 'cause they get all these 911 calls from out-of-towners about 'man collapsed.'"

He snorted derisively, just as Charlene reappeared with a lap tray holding a steaming bowl of soup.

We sat together, the three of us, as he shakily lifted spoonfuls to his mouth and the colour began to return to his face.

"What makes you different?"

"Experience," I replied, telling him about my part-time work, and about Pete and Charlie. I wanted him to speak again, his accent was lovely, upper-class English; I could have been sitting in the drawing room of a lord. He was exhausted though, and as soon as he had finished his soup, his eyes started to close. Charlene and I made to leave him to sleep, but his eyes popped open briefly and he said to her: "Don't let her get away, Charlene. I like her."

The three of us have been fast friends ever since.

(A BMW pulls around the corner, startling me; my hand is reaching for the key in the ignition before I realize that Mallick's car is still parked in front of the house. I'm surprised there's more than one BMW in Parkdale. I let myself drift back to Jeremy.)

In subsequent visits, I learned he had spent years doing small parts in Canadian theatre, a workman on the boards. Never given the big roles, the great roles, he nonetheless developed a following among the faithful audiences that trekked out to Stratford or the Shaw Festival to lose themselves in the magic. Women adored him, he was often photographed squiring the wealthy and the glamorous to parties and theatrical openings, but aside from these very public appearances, little was known about his private life.

"Not that I was hiding, you understand, but I am a man of my generation, and, I suppose, of my class. Even if I had been inclined to bed the fairer sex, I wouldn't have wanted it splashed about in the tabloids." He gave a genteel shudder as he considered that possibility, over a cup of tea in the kitchen.

He'd been approached to do a television drama, the first of his career, a supporting role as an aging mentor, and the production had almost wrapped up when things blew up in his face. A young third assistant to the director, a skinny, charmless fellow in his early twenties, filed a sexual harassment suit against him. Jeremy was known to be very wealthy, insiders within the theatrical community knew he was gay, and the combination of those two factors left him wide open to sharks. Since he was very private, the fellow must have assumed that Jeremy would settle the claim quickly, in order to keep it out of the press. He didn't know Jeremy.

Jeremy was outraged. He'd never been alone with the accuser, never mind touched him. And the charge that he was some sort of chicken hawk offended him deeply; he was not a man to chase after "spotty boys." As much as he dreaded being "outed" in the press, he knew that if he paid off this man, he would always feel violated.

He'd filed a counter-suit, for defamation of character and blackmail, and hired a private detective to investigate the accuser's background. The tabloids loved it, and the dignified, courtly actor was splashed across their pages, portrayed in the very terms he'd feared. It was a difficult time, and Jeremy retreated from the spotlight, suffering from depression and treating it by increasing his drinking.

The investigator proved a good investment, showing the young man had three previous claims against male actors that had been settled out of court. Jeremy won his suit, and if the fellow ever worked again, his salary would go to pay off the hundreds of thousands Jeremy had been awarded. Still, he felt, in the public mind, he had been diminished, tainted, an inglorious end to his career. He locked himself away in his house, refusing all visitors, all calls, beginning and ending his days with tumblers of Scotch.

Charlene's mother wrote to her in Vancouver, where she was busy establishing herself as part of a small, struggling company putting on interesting and innovative plays, that it "was time to put Jeremy in a place where he can be cared for."

Charlene flew home immediately, determined to rescue him from her mother's scheming. Travelling straight from the airport to her uncle's retreat, she banged on the door till he answered, falling into his arms and holding on for dear life.

She'd loved Jeremy from the first moment she laid eyes on him, his twinkling eyes looming over her crib, his dazzling smile so captivating, and he too had lost himself to the charming, bright infant she had been. In spite of her mother's acid disapproval, or perhaps because of it, they became everything to each other. Charlene's mother was an unhappy woman, undemonstrative, unyielding, cold and haughty. Their home on the Bridle Path was cold too, a cavernous space of pillars and plinths laid out like a museum. She had plans for her only daughter, plans that involved a straitlaced academic education, marriage and children—in other words, "upper-class normality." In this she had an ally in her husband, equally reserved as befitted a successful banker, but they were constantly frustrated in their efforts by Charlene's irrepressible personality, expressed in rebellion and the occasional tattoo. She ran away from boarding school, to her uncle, ran away so often that Jeremy gave her a key and her own room.

Her mother blamed Jeremy, accused him of stealing her daughter, of alienating her affection, of ruining her life. It was not in the least surprising that she would use his time of distress to get even with the "wastrel" brother, to impose her will on him, to lock him away. Charlene frustrated her once again by moving in with her uncle, ensuring he ate and slept, removing bottles of liquor from the house, and simply swaddling him with love and affection.

It took some months, but between the two of them they came up with a plan to redeem Jeremy's reputation. Jeremy would form an incorporated foundation that would fund a community theatre group, dedicated to exploring social issues and sparking social change. Charlene would run the company, gather the players and write up grant applications to supplement the dollars available.

Charlene has a great hunger for experience, for life without a net, all grist for the mill of her creativity. She really believes that emotions of any depth have atrophied in the upper reaches of society, due to class in-breeding and constant stifling. Her own upbringing had been, except for Jeremy, so sterile, bloodless and buttoned-down that when she came to the drop-in to visit me, she immediately fell in love with the chaos and characters. Pete liked her, and so did the members, and it wasn't long before she started doing shifts, less for the money than for the experiences and stories.

Loud honking hurtles me back to the present. An unwary pedestrian has narrowly escaped serious injury, as he attempted to jaywalk through the traffic. I sigh, and crane my neck to be sure Mallick hasn't disappeared on me. He's still parked there.

No wonder Charlene uses TTC most of the time. She could afford a much better car, I bitch to myself; she has her own trust fund from her grandparents. I'm certain a large part of her affection for it is the pained look her mother gets when Charlene pulls into the circular driveway on the Bridle Path, and parks beside the BMW and the Mercedes, her exhaust sputtering black clouds and the faulty muffler disturbing the bucolic setting.

There was barely room for me in this poor excuse for a vehicle. I'd shoved aside mouldy Styrofoam cups and hamburger coffins, files, notebooks and ratty paperbacks, dumped the contents of the ashtray and cracked open the driver's side window. It didn't help. Stephanie Plum had Ranger to hand her a new car every time one failed or blew up. I feel an irrational bite of jealousy.

This time I'm going to do it, I think to myself, follow that man wherever he goes. I've been waiting two hours, I'm bored out of my mind, and suddenly there's a loud knock on the passenger side window. Two of the guys I know from the drop-in, Richard and Gord, grin widely as I lean over and roll it down.

"Hey, Dana, you bought yourself a car? Didn't even know you could drive. How long you had it?" Half of Richard's body is in the car with me, no mean feat given his size.

I explain that it isn't mine, but trailing the men are their girlfriends, Lorraine and Suzie, and soon the car's surrounded. It's like one of those sixties "happenings" I've read about. Gord pops the hood, becomes mesmerized by the engine, and that attracts other passersby; they kick the tires, ask questions about mileage that I can't answer, recommend other models, and still people keep coming. Lorraine, in a feathered cowboy hat and faux leather jacket, begs for a ride, "just around the corner, c'mon Dana, it'll be fun!" and is half into the back seat with Suzie right behind her before she sees how messy it is. "Ooh, yuck", she says, and starts cleaning the garbage off the floor and the seats, carting it over to a city garbage container, telling me I'll feel better driving without "all that crap" getting in the way. Suzie piles in, all two hundred pounds of her, causing the car to rock on its wheels. Lorraine is next, loudly arguing with the boys who tell them to shove over, make room for them. I have no idea when Mallick drove away, but when I look through a gap in the crowd I see his car is no longer there.

Frustrated and tense, I order everyone out, and they exit, grumbling and insulted; I pretend not to hear Lorraine's gripe: "Some thanks I get for all the work I did cleaning it out!" I pack it in, and use the phone at the drop-in to leave a message for Charlene begging one more day, and walk home.

Today, I'm parked farther down the road, I'm wearing a baseball cap and shades, and I'm practising being invisible. Having had some experience at this sitting and waiting, I have a can of pop in the car. I made sure I had something to eat and that I went to the washroom before I left home. Lucky for me, there's some cloud cover, enough that I get occasional breaks from the heat. I know from Michael and Diamond that Mallick always headed east on Queen when he leaves that house, so I'm well positioned to follow him when he shows. If the damn car starts.

When his BMW soars past, I'm so excited I have to deep breathe to remember all the steps Charlene took me through, but after a few throaty coughs the engine catches and I'm off. I can't believe it. This is so cool; here I am, in disguise, trailing the bad guy.

Michael would love this. I love this.

I have to put on the brakes at the intersection of Ossington and Queen because a psychiatric patient from the mental hospital is doing a little jig in the middle of the street. He's not wearing anything but a sheet, which flaps in the breeze, making it more cape than cover. Mallick's ahead of me, but I'm not too worried, he's stalled behind a streetcar that's come loose from its overhead moorings. There's no danger of him speeding away. I manoeuvre carefully around the escapee, who tries to open my driver's side door, but I get it locked in time, lower my window a bit, and ask "What's up?"

He stares at me for a moment, then, delighted, says, "Hey, Dana, it's me, Oran, from the drop-in, how you doing?"

Oran. Of course, I remember now. Usually a quiet guy, keeps to himself.

I roll the window right down, and, with one eye on Mallick's car, and the other on Oran, say, "Hi, I'm doing fine, how about you?"

He sticks his head inside. "Oh, not too bad, you know how it is. I'm back on the ward now. Whatcha up to?"

Cars are blaring their horns at us, I'm right in the middle of the intersection, talking to a nude escapee, but I manage to continue our conversation.

"Well, Oran, it's like this, I'm tailing a bad guy, and I'm in a bit of a rush."

"No shit?" He's clearly impressed. "You go straight ahead, then, I'll catch you later." He moves a little away from me, and he's almost struck by a car that swerves violently around us, while the driver shouts obscenities punctuated by a thrusting finger, before being stalled again two cars behind Mallick. I lean out the window, calling to him.

"I'd like to, Oran, but to tell you the truth, I wouldn't be very comfortable thinking of you back here. These drivers get a bit impatient. There might be an accident."

"You think?"

The streetcar has started to move, and so has Mallick.

"Yeah, I do. I wonder if you'd mind going over to the sidewalk?"

"Sure. Which one?" Oran's head is back in my car now.

"Whichever one you want."

"Okay. Will you come visit, maybe bring Pete too?" I nod quickly, and wait till he's on the sidewalk before I pull away, spurred on by the cacophony of horns.

It doesn't take me long to catch sight of Mallick. Remembering snatches of television cop shows and movies, I keep a few cars between us, so he doesn't "make" me. I haven't driven for a long time; it requires all my attention not to bump into other vehicles or hit squeegee kids while trying to keep him in sight. He's making it easy, though, obeying all the rules, including the speed limit, further evidence of his guilt in my mind. If you're committing big crimes, you don't risk being stopped by cops for running stop signs.

Before I know it we're over on the Danforth, and traffic is so thick I could park and follow him on foot. I watch his turn signal flicker on, and do the same with mine, as he turns into a small side street and then into the driveway of a nondescript detached home. I drive farther up the street, craning my neck back in time to see him put a key in the door. I spend the next twenty minutes trying to parallel park, finally squeezing in between two bigger cars without scratching or denting anything. I lock up, and affect a casual stroll back down the street, getting the house number, and a glimpse of open windows. There's nowhere inconspicuous to hang out, to keep an eye on the building. But I know where he goes when he leaves Parkdale, and that's a start.

Chapter Five

It cost me thirty-five dollars to fill Charlene's tank. I hadn't wanted to risk running out of gas and losing Mallick. I hadn't been thrilled with her request to work her evening shift, but now I realize, as I make my way to the drop-in, that I could use the money.

Though poverty and boredom make every day pretty much the same as every other day, there are still vestiges of Saturday Night Fever in the community, a sense that it's a time to party, to cut loose. It can make for unsettling behaviour, as expectations collide with empty pockets. There's still days to go before the cheques are out, and hunger and nicotine cravings are at their height. As I prepare the coffee and straighten tables and chairs for the onslaught of members, I grin in anticipation of their reaction to my choice of videos.

There's a crowd already gathered on the sidewalk. People start showing up a half-hour to forty minutes before the door opens; they mill around, break into conversation groups, argue or joke while others stand alone, encased in silent misery or talking to unseen companions. A third-year psychology student from the University of Toronto, William—not Bill I remember being told—is supposed to be working with me. Pete has asked me to evaluate him, unsure as to his suitability or comfort level in the wide-open setting. I see him now, hanging back from the crowd, looking lost.

As soon as I open the door, it's like a gold rush as people head inside, some taking up seats in the television area just to the left, others heading into the back for the card tables and the coffee bar. I grab William and ask him to organize the popcorn brigade, volunteers who've mastered the art of stove-top popping in our blackened, battered pots. He looks somewhat offended, as though it's too menial an activity for him to engage in, but he gathers the folks who eagerly start the oil smoking and sputtering.

I announce that coffee, usually costing a quarter, will be free tonight, a strategy worked out with Pete for times that are fraught with tension. In the wake of muted cheers, I carry the video to the VCR, refusing to answer questions about what they're going to see. I manage to push all the right buttons, and as the WWE logo comes up, I am queen for the evening. William can't believe it; I think he was expecting a foreign film with subtitles. The men, and some women, crowd around the television set, finding chairs or spaces on the floor, exchanging mini-bios of the wrestlers, choosing favourites and booing villains.

If William is still around on Halloween, he'll lose all respect for me, if he still has any to lose. I tend to rent horror films, one step above slasher flicks, for that particular evening. Not my cup of tea, but fun is fun, and I love to see people enjoying themselves.

But work calls. There are now about a hundred men and women crammed inside the drop-in, half that number around the television area and the rest at the card tables.

The front door is propped open to allow some of the cigarette smoke to escape, and guys keep coming. I take a seat with a couple older gentlemen, perennial euchre players, positioning myself so that I can keep a covert eye on the place. People are coming up to me, congratulating me on "my" car. News travels fast when nothing much is happening. I settle into a mantra: thank you, it's not mine, I just borrowed it from Charlene. I'm left feeling I've disappointed them.

Paul, sitting opposite me, has to keep his hand tucked close to his chest, held there by his withered arm. Years ago, he'd leapt in front of an oncoming subway car, looking for an instant death but managing only to destroy the left side of his body. It doesn't interfere with his ability to win, though; he loves to beat me. His partner, Jimmy, messily slurps coffee and smokes his hand-rolled Exports; he keeps jumping up and rushing over to the television when the hooting and handclapping breaks out, not wanting to miss anything. It makes for a long game, but Paul is used to distractions, using it to his advantage to pull ahead.

I've learned to listen to the rhythm and quality of sound on nights like this, not to jump at every expletive, not to assume trouble's broken out when voices are raised. I see that William still hasn't mastered this. He's hiding behind the coffee urn, and his eyes are very wide. I call him over, ask him to play my hand for a while; they'll be gentle with him.

I wander around, like a hostess at a party checking in with the guests, stopping here and there to chat for a moment, to laugh at a bad joke, or to answer a question. I catch sight of Vera, slumped in one of the few chairs near the front door. Bedraggled and miserable, she hasn't bothered with either wig or makeup, her clothes look slept in, and her long hair is matted and greasy. It hurts my heart to look at her. I drag a chair over to her, and sit down as she turns to face me, her eyes blood red with dark half-moons below. Pete has tried to reassure her that we are doing everything we can to find Janice, but, as each day passes with no news, the emotional toll on her increases exponentially. I take her hand; it's cold and limp.

"Vera, you look terrible. You're not sleeping at all, are you?"

"How can I?" Her voice trembles, and tears are falling down her pale cheeks. "I keep hearing her calling me; she's so frightened and alone. Someone's hurting her, I know it, and I can't make it stop." Her left hand balls into a fist and she strikes her thigh once, twice, three times. "I try to talk to her, tell her we'll find her, but I know, I know that we don't matter, her and I, we're old and we're drunks and nobody cares."

"That's not so, Vera, you're not alone in this. We're searching for her, and I believe we'll find her." I can't tell her more than this, she'd be at Mallick's door in an instant, then we might lose her too. "Tell me about her, Vera, anything you can, it might help us."

She looks at me, confused. "What do you want to know?"

"Tell me where you two met."

She rubs her eyes and face on the long sleeve of her dress, it's thin with age and the original colour has faded to a uniform grey.

"It was a long time ago. Years ago. We wound up in the same rooming house, just for a few weeks. I'd hear her yelling at the landlord, at the other tenants. She was glorious. She could curse better than anyone I ever met. So much fight in her, so much life. They kicked her out, of course, threw her stuff out on the street. I helped her put it all in garbage bags, snuck some of it up to my room to keep it safe. Till she found another place."

"Did she ever talk about her family? Her past?"

A little shrug of her bony, bowed shoulders. "No more than me. All that's done with, long buried. No sense picking at scabs." Our heads are close together, so I can hear her over the raucous shouts and catcalls from the crowd around the television. I want to keep her talking, pull her out of her misery.

"She was married, lost her kids to Children's Aid. Too much fighting and too much drinking. Same as me. No one to blame but ourselves. Nobody left who knows us. We didn't have to rake over the wreckage we'd made of our lives, we knew without saying. After being so alone for so long, we had each other. She could make me laugh, think of that! To be able to laugh in our circumstances!"

She turns again to me, with a half-sob catching at her voice.

"What I really wanted was to learn to scream like her, to curse and shriek and fight, to be so alive."

Derek has come in, he's standing nearby watching the second wrestling video, laughing at the antics on the screen. His injured arm is out of the sling. He looks over his shoulder at us, once Vera has stopped speaking.

"Hey, Dana, nothing like a little culture on a Saturday night."

"Beats opera or ballet. Good to see you, man. How's your arm?"

"Healing." He walks over, crouches in front of us. "Any word about Janice?"

I shake my head, while signalling him with one finger not to say anymore. Vera narrows her eyes in suspicion, glaring at him.

"I asked Derek to keep an eye out for her."

She starts to cry again, softly. "I need to go home now, Dana." Looking at both of us, she pleads, "If you find out anything, you'll tell me right away? Please." I assure her we will, and watch her slowly gather herself up and make her way out the door.

Derek is looking very intense, clearly moved by Vera's grief.

"Sorry, I shouldn't have butted in like that."

"It's okay. She's pretty shattered, it's a nightmare for her. Not knowing where her friend is."

"I like Janice. I mean, she's a pain in the ass, but she's got spirit, you know? You think she's in that house you and Pete were looking at?"

"I don't know, Derek. There's no movement there, no one comes or goes but the owner. I have a bad feeling."

He thinks for a minute, makes a decision. "If you want to get inside, look around, maybe I can arrange it. Some skills you never lose, even if you're not, ah, practising anymore. I just want to tell you, if you want some help, I'm here. And I have some friends who'll help too. Shit, we all had mothers, you know?"

I stare into his face, till he says "What?"

"Hard to see you in nappies, that's all."

I tell him about Maryanne.

"That's very fucked up. I'll keep an eye on the place for you, and when you're ready to go in, you tell me, we'll figure a way. You should have told me earlier."

"It's complicated, Derek. I don't want anyone else hurt. Give me a few days, I've got some ideas I want to check out. And don't say anything to Pete yet. He'd kill me if he knew."

"You got it. But be careful. There's some real slime out there."

I find I feel better knowing Derek is onside. He's been through stuff I can't even imagine in his five-plus decades of life, and just the fact that he's still on his feet says a lot. He's ridden with some of the heaviest outlaws there are, tried every drug going, and most of the jails around, yet still managed to retain a strong core of humanity.

A half-dozen card games and a few interventions between testy individuals later, I notice Charlene's arrived to pick up her car. Although she's looking a little deflated tonight, she's still her usual stunning self. She favours East Indian clothes (at least in this incarnation), long cotton skirts and paper-thin blouses, accented by silver bangles that travel up both her arms. Her raven-black hair, framing a tanned and attractive face, drops below her shoulders, and is shot through with streaks of white.

Usually loose, it's gathered tonight into a tight roll, her perm apparently suffering from an attack of the frizzies. She's trying to move toward me, but keeps getting stopped by little knots of men and women happy to see her.

After her first few incursions at the drop-in—to her credit she kept coming back, though for weeks she'd confessed to me that she'd cried herself to sleep each night—she'd decided to offer her skills in theatre to a small group of members, who, initially skeptical, soon couldn't wait for the sessions. She was very different from the harried workers that were often their only contact with the rest of the world. She laughed a lot, once she got her bearings, an infectious, deep-throated laugh that brought out smiles from those around her.

Her comfort level now is remarkable, though she stuck very close to me for weeks. I was her "mentor," the way Pete had been for me. I stopped her from falling into the same traps that had caused me to stumble from time to time, gave her thumbnail bios of individual members, as well as timely warnings about the few predators that stalked the place in search of victims. Dealers, scroungers, small-time hoods, a bully or two, and people I thought of as succubuses, who'd leach all your time and attention if they could. Charlene got an exaggerated notion that I was an excellent reader of people, with special insight and skills. But I wasn't really.

Pete was very impressed with her commitment. Most people tended to start out well as volunteers, then leave beaten by the members' apathy or the grim surroundings.

I was proud of her too. If she could come into my world, I would immerse myself in hers, however weird it was. She placed me on her board, a board that was a necessary requirement for outside funding. They were a hand-picked, very compliant group of people gleaned from her and Jeremy's acquaintances. She said I could represent the community. It wasn't an onerous role, and gave legitimacy to my frequent excursions. I couldn't afford movies and didn't have a television, but I did have live theatre whenever I wanted.

It takes me a while, but I manage to get to the office ten minutes after her.

"Hey, Charlene, got your keys; you're baby's safe and sound."

She looks up from the desk where she's sitting, staring blankly at the wall. She flashes a grin at me, but it's gone almost as quickly as it appears.

"I knew she'd take good care of you."

I harrumphed; it would be ungracious at best to let my real feelings be known.

"What's up?" I knew Charlene pretty well by now, well enough not to be immediately concerned. Her theatrical qualities didn't begin and end on the stage. It could be anything from a bad hair day to an actor not living up to her expectations.

"I don't know for sure. There's some funny—funny peculiar—stuff going on, and I can't put my finger on it. It's as though there's a gremlin in the theatre. Things are breaking that shouldn't, stuff goes missing, then turns up in odd places. I wish you'd come by, look around for me, check out the folks, see if you notice anything that I've missed. You're better than me at reading people."

"You want me to spy on them?"

"Well, yes, I guess. It's really bothering me. We're like a family, you know, and I'd hate to think that one of us is up to no good." She trails off, looking into the distance.

"Don't worry. I'll come by tomorrow, you know I love to hang out there anyway." We step out of the office, back into the controlled chaos of the drop-in.

In the privacy of my mind, I'm thinking Jason. It's because of him that I haven't been to the studio for a while. Not since he'd shown up for auditions and stayed and stayed. He was smooth: from his face, unlined and conventionally handsome in the way of American evangelists; to his manners; to his hair, which he kept swept back in smooth waves. Even his clothes, all earth colours blending into one another, showed no creases. From the first moment I laid eyes on him, I felt a deep antipathy I couldn't explain. It happens sometimes, a good argument that we've all been here before, in previous lives. Jason seduced people by love-bombing them, staring into their eyes as he listened to their concerns and problems, holding their hands, massaging their shoulders and necks. He's helped along in this by the actors believing they deserve to be listened to, coddled and appreciated. In a very short time, he was the one everyone looked to when something needed fixing around the studio, when wires got crossed or scenery fell over, or egos deflated. People came to depend on him, even the electricians and sound people seemed to love him, he was always there, and quickly became the indispensable one. Only Jeremy seemed immune, Jeremy and me. Charlene liked him a lot—how could she not? He took over much of the work she hated, and did it well. He concentrated his attentions on her, whenever she was in the room, playing to her already substantial ego. Underneath it all, I believe that Jason felt he was carrying the whole theatre group.

"I'm sure it's nothing to worry about, just a run of bad luck." We're leaving the office now, standing near the front door, when a young man with a wad of cotton stuck under his nose, sniffing glue or some other inhalant, passes by us and upsets a table he was trying to lean on. The table collapses along with several cups of coffee and at least one ashtray. This coincides with some wrestling move on the video that gets the crowd in the stadium and in the drop-in yelling for blood.

Some wag yells, "Just Say No!"

As I head off to deal with this, Charlene says, "Great. Thanks. Now I'm going to drive my baby home, get into bed and pull the covers over my head. Dana, thanks for taking my shift, I really appreciate it. I just couldn't face it tonight." I stare at her accusingly, feeling just a little betrayed and abandoned, but she kisses my cheek and whispers, "It's almost closing time. You'll cope just fine."

And I do of course. I get the young fellow to his feet and out the door, while some of the members mop up the spillage. Then I move on to deal with one dramatic epileptic seizure, two arguments that threaten to come to blows, a fellow trying to shoot up behind the coffee bar, another who can't remember where he lives, all topped off by a stirring rendition of "O Canada" emanating from the women's washroom, courtesy of a large and quirky homeless woman. I realize I haven't seen William for an hour or so; looking around, I see he's flat against the wall near the office, he's pale and trembling.

"What's up, William?"

"Look, I don't think I can do this. It's not what I want. The smells, the aggression—Christ, the noise! I want to help people, counsel them, but not in this kind of place. I'll finish tonight, then I'm gone. Will you tell Pete for me?"

I could argue with him, I suppose, convince him to come back, try again, but I'm tired, and I don't like him or his attitude. If I open my mouth, I'm liable to attack rather than reason, so I just nod abruptly and turn away, back to the people I care about.

Thankfully, the night is winding down, and I'm tired, ready to pack it in. It takes another thirty minutes to get everyone out, dole out TTC to those who need it, call shelters for those without a place to sleep, but then I'm done. I turn out the lights, and lock the door behind me.

It feels like I've spent the night digging ditches. I'm still tired when the sun wakes me up. I make a strong cup of coffee and retreat to the bed with it, listening to the morning music of car motors, pigeons and seagulls, the drumming of feet on pavement, the shuddering of walls and windows at the passing of the King streetcars. Sundays are down days. I remember getting dressed up for church as a child, in princess dresses (or so I thought) and shiny shoes, holding tightly to a plastic purse with gaudy cartoon characters cavorting over its surface. After a special breakfast of pancakes and bacon, my mother and I would walk hand in hand up the street, joining the parade of parishioners, mostly women and children, heading for salvation.

I wonder if any of the bright, lively children who made up the Sunday school class still attend. Perhaps they have their own children to dress up now, before draping themselves in dark funereal dresses and scarves, leaving their exhausted husbands snoring in bed. I shiver, as though recalling a narrow escape. I haven't been back to church in years. Haven't been to confession. I feel sometimes that both God and I broke out of this unnatural confinement together, leaving bricks and mortar and stained glass for the wider horizons of real life.

Our group is going to meet this evening, in Michael's room. I plan to propose that Miss Semple accompany me on a ruse that might gain us entry to Mallick's east end "retreat." If she can create an official-looking survey form at the mission, on behalf of a fake advertising or marketing firm, as well as a little pile of extra documents that we can fill in so that it looks like we've approached other houses on the street, we may be able to pull it off. No one could be suspicious of her.

I play with samples of questions, wondering what we can get away with. Occupation, level of income and education, citizenship, number of individuals in the home (or kept captive in other places), any subscriptions to magazines, favourite painkillers and cleansers, type of car, Internet provider, investments, criminal record. Okay, maybe I need to edit a bit. I make another cup of coffee, and start turning my notes into a questionnaire. It's a pleasant morning by the time I go across the street for breakfast, ordering a nostalgic plate of pancakes, and I've honed the "survey" to twenty questions.

Coming back from Karen's, I see that Gerry's seated on the veranda, and there's someone with him. It's Ed.

They look, the pair of them, like old friends. Both have their feet on the rail, and as I cross the street, Ed is offering Gerry a cigarette, which he takes and lights. I don't remember Ed smoking.

"Hi, Dana, got your call. Gerry said you'd be back about now."

Gerry's looking a little guilty, which makes me wonder what they've been talking about. By Ed's chair is an oddly shaped box and a Canadian Tire bag. He sees me looking. "I brought you that lock for your door. I can install it now, if that's okay?"

"Yeah," says Gerry, "it'll make me feel better if you have a decent lock. 'Specially these days."

It would look churlish to protest. "Sure, thanks, come on up."

Three flights of stairs later, I'm opening my door and letting Ed in. He makes himself at home, opening the box and pulling out a drill, then tearing the plastic and cardboard wrapping off the lock, which looks more substantial than either the door or the frame. I don't know what to do with myself, though I'm glad I made my bed and tidied up the papers I was working on.

He looks a little smug to me.

"Next time you want to talk to me, call my cell. I gave you that number, right?" I nod. I'd been more comfortable using his office number. "I've been off a few days, just picked up your message this morning."

The whine of the drill and the mechanics of installing the lock keep him busy and quiet while I consider how to ask him about Mallick. "Proactive policing, that's what this is. Crime prevention at its best." He's clearly satisfied with himself. He tests the two keys that came with the lock, then hands them to me. The lock is massive, and the cleanest, shiniest thing in the room. "I know you've eaten, but maybe you'll let me take you for a drive? We can talk in the car."

I'm happy with that. This room is way too small for two people. He watches me lock the door, proudly pointing out the deadbolt "system," then we're down the stairs and out the door. Gerry's disappeared.

"I didn't know you smoked."

"I don't. But I've started to carry a pack with me. It's a real ice breaker with some people."

"Hmm."

"Thought I'd drive you down to Harbourfront. We could walk around down there. Do you get there much?"

"No. It's a bit out of the way for me. You and Gerry seemed to have hit it off."

"Yeah, he's quite a character. And a good friend to you. I wanted to reassure him my intentions were honorable."

I laugh, and start to relax.

"He tells me you don't date at all."

So much for relaxing. Where did this come from?

"I haven't heard that term for a while. Dating. It sounds so, I don't know, adolescent. But no, I don't, I haven't."

"Any reason?"

I haven't been in a relationship since the attack, haven't even felt that pleasant stirring under the skin that I used to enjoy during the man-meets-woman preliminaries. I've grown comfortable within my celibacy, though I guess I've known it wouldn't last forever. I didn't want to awaken memories that might have been etched on my psyche.

When I was "active," I had always tended to go with the "opposites attract" option. Something about men leading the conventional life, with their short haircuts and dark suits, riveted me. If there was also a sense of humour, active intelligence and openness, I was, historically, lost, at least for a while. But there are opposites and there are opposites. A homicide detective in his late forties, early fifties was bound to have attitudes and beliefs that, piled together, would create insurmountable barriers.

"Not really," I lie. "Just how it is. What's your sound system like?"

He punches a button and classical music floods the car. I close my eyes a moment, just revelling in the orchestral majesty of Bach. It's like being at Roy Thomson Hall, only much more comfortable. Too soon he pulls into a parking space, next to what looks like a shopping mall, and the concert ends abruptly.

I'm glad for the wide-open spaces. He doesn't let up, though.

As we walk, manoeuvring through crowds of tourists from a multitude of nationalities snapping pictures and lining up for pop and ice cream, he continues his personal questions.

"Are you from Toronto?"

"Yes. I was raised around here." This is more comfortable territory. If I keep talking, maybe he'll forget about the "D" word. I have to confess, though, it does feel good to have this man strolling by my side, tall and strong and self-assured. "My parents emigrated from Italy. I'm not sure why they ever left, they never adjusted to life in Toronto, they wouldn't even make serious efforts to learn enough English to follow the news. It seemed like the city was too large, too open for them to ever get comfortable. Everything new was threatening, especially blacks and East Indians and women's rights and gay people. Not to mention drugs and clubs and hookers. They watched me like hawks when I went through puberty. It was stifling. My father worked construction and my mother occasionally cleaned people's homes; they scrimped and scraped by. It taught me to hate closed communities, and closed minds. And lives that were constricted by fear. I had to run away to go to the University of Toronto. Don't laugh."

I catch him in mid-grin, which he quickly straightens out into a tight line.

"Sorry. It just sounded funny. They didn't want you to go?"

"No. Too far from our street."

Now he does smile. "What did you study?"

"English." I grinned back at him. "Literature and philosophy and the humanities, all terribly impractical. It was wonderful, mind-blowing stuff. And I was an honour student. The years I spent there were the best in my life."

"Do you think you'd ever go back to university?"

"I don't think so. It was great, but since I've lived in Parkdale, I've come to prefer real life. There's something oddly insulated about academia, it's a separate world in its own way. Professors are preoccupied with interdepartmental wars, and student politics are more about ideologies clashing than really making a difference. As much as I loved it and needed it, it's a closed chapter for me."

"That's a shame. You can't find much intellectual stimulation where you're living now."

"You'd be surprised. I know it's not forever, but for now it's where I belong. What about you?" We're on a boardwalk now, which runs parallel to the water. Ferries and party boats are docked alongside, some with their gangplanks down.

"Born and raised in Gravenhurst. Great place for a kid to grow up. My parents took in foster kids, so though I was an only child I was never lonely. And it taught me that not everyone had it as good as I did. I worked with disadvantaged kids at camp every summer, then after high school I thought I'd either teach or find a job at some agency or other dealing with teenagers. I kind of fell into policing. A friend of my parents worked for the OPP, he talked me into it. By then, though, I was itching to be in the big city, so I signed up with the Toronto force. I liked the uniform, at least at first, then after a few years on the beat I couldn't wait to make detective so I could wear my own clothes."

"You wear them well," I said, remembering the suit he had on that first time he'd come to the house. "Do you have kids of your own?"

"I was married for a while, but it didn't work out. No kids, and under the circumstances that was a good thing." He points up to a towering condo building. "See up there, about thirty floors up? Just above those window washers?" There's a couple of guys balanced on a board that's held up by what I hope are really strong ropes; they're using squeegees and not looking down. It makes me feel a bit dizzy, watching them.

"That's where I live. And this," he sweeps his arm around to encompass the lake and the land, "is the view from my window."

"Nice." I don't want to talk about his place. Don't want him inviting me up. My chest feels constricted. Change the subject. "The reason I called you, Ed, is I've been checking out Mallick's place. It's closed up tight; no one except him ever comes in or out."

"And how would you know that?"

"One thing at a time. Another woman, a lady from the drop-in where I work part-time, was also removed from her house by Mallick. Her best friend hasn't seen her since." I think for a moment. "Did you check out the building?"

"Of course. Her bedroom was on the first floor, off the kitchen. Everything was very clean; it looked like a decent place."

"Did you get a look at the other rooms, other floors?"

"There was no need. What are you getting at?"

"There's something wrong, I'm sure of it. Maryanne's leaving like she did was odd enough, and now Janice—she and her friend are so tight, so dependent on each other's company, it makes no sense that she'd just cut her out of her life. I wondered if you could do a check on Mallick, see if he has a criminal record?" I can see the impatience gathering on his face, so I push on quickly, before he can interrupt.

"And I wondered if you could talk to him again, ask about Janice, try to see her, make sure she's all right?"

"Dana, I did ask if we could keep Maryanne's case open. But there have been three bona fide murders since her death. I've been told to close the file. I have no right, no reason, to harass the man. Listen, I know her death was a blow to you, but there is nothing evil going on, no kidnappings and no murder. It was a tragedy, no doubt, but that's all it was. The sooner you and your friends accept that, the better." He takes a few seconds to gentle his tone, which was showing some frustration with me. "I know what it's like to search for answers, Dana, to try to make sense of something so terrible, so final, as death. There are no answers, no one to blame, you'll just drive yourself crazy till you accept that."

We walk silently on. Sailboats are out on the water, patches of white on the deep blue of the lake, and several of the large tour boat operators are hawking tickets. It's the same lake as Sunnyside, but here there is a greater sense of space, and it's certainly more commercialized. Even so, there's so much to look at, so much more going on. And the air feels cleaner, maybe scrubbed for the tourists. We take up a park bench and stare out at the boats and the gulls soaring over them. I'm glad to be here, even though there's a tension between us now, a different kind of tension from the boy-girl stuff. At least he won't be suggesting I go up and check the view from his place. I'm relieved, and a little saddened.

"I'm sorry, Dana."

"No, that's okay. I understand."

"Now's probably not the time to ask, but I like you, Dana, and I'd like for us to do this again, when you stop being mad at me."

Unsure how I feel about this invitation, I ignore it, while trying to reassure him.

"I'm not mad, Ed, I know you've done your best."

In heavy tones, he finishes my thought. "You just can't let it go."

"I can for now. You know, I came here once before, I think it was for some Italian festival day. I remember wanting to play with the birds, grab at the dogs people kept on leashes. I must have been four or five. I couldn't get my parents to let go of my hands, I was so frustrated, I started to cry and they thought I was tired."

Thinking back, it foreshadowed my life as a teenager, as a young adult. "To be surrounded by all this, and not to be allowed to experience it, to be held so tight, it seemed ridiculous and punitive."

He nods, understanding. "It was never like that for me. My parents were great believers in self-reliance. They taught me to swim, taught me how to use the canoe, and I could spend the whole day exploring. I'd teach my foster brothers what my parents taught me, these city kids who'd never even seen a boat, never mind caught a fish or listened to the call of the loons. I think that's why I live here. I need the water, need the expanse. Come on, I'll buy you lunch; you must be hungry by now, with your appetite. There's a great spot right on the water."

A couple of McDonald's hamburgers at a weak moment and he thinks I'm always starving! We head back to the shopping area and, after a brief wait, take our seats on a patio overlooking the lake. Ed orders wine and I try to get comfortable in this very different setting, where the waitress doesn't pull up a chair and plunk herself down. And where the cloth napkins are starched and as white as the tablecloths, and, instead of the occasional mouse, sparrows hop from crumb to crumb. We talk about other things than murder and dating, staying on safer topics that slowly reveal ourselves to one another.

It's late in the day by the time we pull up to the house; I'm out of the car before he can make any move toward me, knowing I'm not ready for that particular complication. I lean in the open window, glad of the bulk of metal between us, and thank him for the afternoon. He shakes his head in slight frustration, but there's a smile on his face as he tells me, in tones that could make it a promise or a threat, that he'll drop by again soon. I watch him pull away, and realize I'm smiling too.

I have my hand on the doorknob when I hear a strangled cry. I whirl around, trying to see what could possibly have made that noise. There, on the sidewalk near the corner, hidden by a city garbage container, there's a hump of something, perhaps a large racoon. Hesitating for just a moment, I creep back down the stairs, heading toward the sound that continues to emanate from the likely wounded animal. I'm equal measures of caution and fear, moving slowly till I make out a human form lying on the sidewalk, trying to crawl toward me. I kneel down, grasping the man's—for it is a man—shoulders. He fights me for a moment, arms flailing, and as I try to calm him, I catch a glimpse of his face, stunned to see it's Michael.

"Oh, man, what's happened to you?" There are tears in my eyes, he looks so broken. "I'll call an ambulance."

He grabs me when I try to rise, croaking out words I have to lean close to hear.

"No ambulance, no cops. Promise me."

"Michael."

"Promise!"

"All right. Let me get some of the guys."

It feels terrible, leaving him there even for a moment, but I run into the house, calling for Gerry and Diamond, who respond immediately, Gerry still mussed from sleep.

The three of us manage to carry him inside, Gerry bearing most of Michael's weight.

"Put him in my room," Gerry puffs. "We'll never manage to get him upstairs."

They hold him while I straighten the sheets, pull back the blankets, then we ease him down.

You can't live in this community for as long as I have and not be aware of the brutal effects of street justice on the human body. Even so, the damage done to Michael's face is beyond anything I've seen. One eye is so terribly swollen and discoloured, I keep expecting it to explode out of its socket, spew itself all over the room where he lies moaning. His wiry body is covered with multi-coloured bruises, and I'm sure his ribs are cracked from the kicks he's endured.

"We gotta call an ambulance," says Gerry. He's crying too.

"He made me promise not to."

"He's probably out of his mind, doesn't know what he's saying."

"No! Don't tell anyone." Michael's eyes roll back in his sockets, and he passes out.

Diamond clears his throat, and looks at the two of us. "I can take care of him. I know what to do, what to look for."

The next few days blurred into one another. Diamond wanted to keep Michael still, which was a challenge. He couldn't talk yet, but thrashed around a lot, moaning. We ran out of the pills Gerry had scavenged from his supply, and Diamond said we needed either stronger painkillers, or powerful sleeping pills. I reluctantly found myself in front of that sad little strip mall talking with Joe, part of me feeling like I should have been swiping at my nose with the back of my hand, or hopping from one foot to another like his usual customers.

"Listen, Joe," I said to him, "I'm in a bind here. A friend of mine, he got himself beaten up pretty badly, but he's afraid to go to hospital."

"Well, yeah, I don't blame him. Once they've got you, they've got you. Then they start shoving needles into you, wiring you up for shock treatments, and it's all over."

I was startled for a minute, until I realized he was assuming I was talking about a psychiatric hospital. A place few are willing to go.

"Okay. So we're trying to keep him in bed, sedated, so that he doesn't hurt himself by moving around. We've run out of pills to do that. Joe, you know I don't agree with you selling on the street. I ..."

"Hey, that's all right. I know you're just looking out for me, and I like that. And now you're looking out for him. Tell you what, I've got some Perks, they'll take care of him. Give him a good sleep; he won't be trying to run around." He slips a little bundle into my hand. "It's on me."

I must have been more tired than I realized, or more stressed, because his simple generosity brought me dangerously close to tears. "Joe, thank you."

"No need, no need. You just keep him away from that place, Dana, they don't do anyone any good. Look at me. Look what they did to me. I shake all the time now, can't keep still. You need more, you come back. I'll be here."

We hugged each other for a long moment. Poor Joe, poor generous Joe. I felt a little like I'd taken advantage of him, but as we parted I could see real pride on his face; he'd been able to help. I headed back to the house with my stash of super painkillers.

The chair I'm in is uncomfortable, deliberately so; I'm afraid I'll fall asleep in this lonely vigil, lulled by the snores from the other two beds. On the windowsill are handmade "get well" cards, a glass jar holding a wilting floral arrangement, a bag of chips, an apple, even a small jar of Nescafé. All gifts of silent encouragement saying, come back to us.

We're still waiting to hear the results of the urine test Diamond has had done. He wanted to be sure there was no internal bleeding, so he took some of Michael's urine with him to a less-than-reputable doctor in the area, complaining of peeing blood. He poured it into the container they gave him, in the privacy of the bathroom, and left it for analysis. They told him to drop by in a couple of days. And Miss Semple donated her top sheet, laundered and smelling of Bounce, for bandages. We cut it into long strips that Diamond wound around Michael's ribs, just in case they were cracked. And that was all we could do, except wait. Keep a close eye on him, and wait.

Diamond has been so gentle with him, lifting his head to help him drink, and to swallow the painkillers. He says that the bland meals Gerry gets delivered have helped; he spoons broth and bits of skinless chicken into his mouth, food that's easily digested. He hasn't left Michael's side for more than minutes at a time, helped by Miss Semple, who empties and cleans the bedpan we've managed to improvise from a scavenged bucket, and who keeps a moist face cloth near the bed to wipe the sweat and grime from his face. For the first couple of nights, Michael wasn't able to speak more than a few words to us, croaking "no" when we suggest again and again that he needs to go to hospital, refusing even more adamantly to report this assault to the police.

I have a bad feeling this is connected to the house we've been watching, though Michael may well have been involved in some other less-than-legal undertaking. We'll have to wait till he's ready to talk.

Diamond has been great. Strong, calm, reassuring to the rest of us who, without his medical background, are terribly fearful that Michael will slip away if we are not constantly with him. He's organized shifts, scrutinized the pills for efficacy and danger, poked and prodded the limp body, and kept careful notes. He looks like he belongs in hospital corridors, not this rooming house. It's an amazing transformation, from a halting, otherworldly young man to this authoritative figure we all defer to, look to, to save our friend. It's been three days since I found Michael collapsed in the street, and if anything the swelling and discolouration seem worse, but this apparently is a normal part of the healing process. And he is healing. He's managed to talk to Diamond, answer questions about what hurts and where.

"Dana." The voice is faint, at first I think I've imagined it, but as I turn I see that Michael's eyes are open and he's watching me.

"Oh man, it's good to hear your voice."

"Water?"

I help him sip from the glass donated by Miss Semple, then ease him back onto the pillow.

"Can you tell me who did this to you?"

"You're going to be mad." My heart sinks, this seems like a confirmation of what I've feared.

"You went to the house that night." I say it like a simple fact, like "it's raining tonight," no blame attached, no accusations.

"We weren't getting anywhere. I thought"—he interrupts himself with a painful coughing, holding his sides with both hands, grimacing. But he won't listen to my efforts to quiet him. "Ouch. I thought I'd scope it out myself in the dark, check what windows might be open. They were all shut tight. I was trying to break the back door lock, I thought I was real quiet." He closes his eyes, pain etched on his face. "They were on me before I even knew what was happening. Called me a thief, beat the living shit outta me. Threw me in the street. Never thought I'd make it back."

"We can call the cops."

"No. They'll just bust me. I've got outstandings, and failures to appear."

He means outstanding warrants for arrest, and failures to appear in court.

"Used to make a living with B and E's. Don't want to go back to jail. Sorry, Dana, didn't mean to fuck things up. You won't kick me out of the club, will you?"

"No, of course not." I'm hiding my own distress, blaming myself for his beating.

A soft knock on the door signals the end of my shift. Diamond's there, a smile breaking out all over his face when he sees Michael awake and communicating, but he needs to examine him, so he ushers me out, and closes the door gently.

Chapter Six

Since that afternoon, I've spent a lot of time second-guessing myself, feeling responsible for Michael's terrible beating. I should have known that he'd take it further than we'd asked him; it was his nature. What had I been thinking, putting everyone at risk like that? Playing at detective like kids playing cops and robbers. Only there were real bad guys and real consequences. Michael could have died. I lay on top of my bed for hours, when I wasn't on duty in his room, just staring at the ceiling, letting guilt eat at me. I couldn't bring myself to keep my promise to Charlene, to go up to the theatre; I couldn't even go down to the common room. What could I say to Miss Semple and Gerry, to Diamond? I felt the burden of failure piled on failure on my shoulders, and it paralyzed me.

Miss Semple materializes at my door. I let her in, and she perches on the edge of my bed, while I sit with my back against the pillows, and listen.

"I know what you're thinking, Dana," she said. "And you'll forgive me if I'm a little plain-spoken. It's not your fault, not your responsibility. We're all part of this, we all decided together. It's disrespectful of you to take all the blame. Perhaps even a little self-indulgent."

Shocked out of my semi-stupor, I can't even protest.

"I've asked myself the same questions. Were we foolish to undertake this? Unprepared? Maybe. But tell me. Are we supposed to abandon those missing women? Forget about what Mallick did to Maryanne? Pretend it never happened? How could we live with ourselves if we did nothing?" She pats my hand. "And how would Michael feel if we gave up because of him? No, we have to go on. We just have to. I've spoken to Diamond and Gerry, and we've decided, with you or without you, we're getting into that house!"

How did so much steel get into such a slight frame?

"We've been keeping up the watch. I've been to the parkette with Gerry, in the evenings. Mallick's car is always there."

"Gerry? Gerry goes out?"

"Yes, dear, while you've been hiding up here," she smiles a little to take the sting out of her words, "Gerry's been finding his courage. It was awfully hard for him, a lot of people do stare, it's his size, I suppose, but he won't let me go alone."

I close my mouth, which had dropped open. She's right, it isn't up to me. We'd made the decision as a group, and they stayed true while I was dithering in my room.

"He's downstairs right now, on the porch. He'd love to see you."

What can I do? I follow her down the stairs, shaking my head a little at this turn of events. When we reach the veranda, Gerry has two chairs waiting on either side of him. I take up one, and Miss Semple takes the other. She's never sat out here before. We watch the cars and people in silence for a bit, people who seem in such a hurry to get where they're going.

"So you're not dead," Gerry mutters at me, by way of welcome, while staring straight ahead and sucking on his cigarette. "Hardly recognize you, you been up there so long."

"No trouble recognizing you, Gerry." I put my feet up on the rail, tilt the chair back and lift my face to the sun. "Though I hear you've been stepping out."

"Couldn't let her go alone. She's as stubborn as you."

I reach over and poke him gently in the side. "You did good. Sorry I wussed out on you guys. I wasn't thinking clearly."

"Shit happens," he shrugs, meaning all is forgiven. In the street, a car horn blares, two, three times, and Gerry yells, "What else did you get for Christmas, ya stupid bugger!"

We watch as one of the new, elongated streetcars disgorges passengers across the street. Miss Semple points to it.

"Do you know, when I was a child, growing up on Elmgrove, there was a free streetcar that would take us down to Sunnyside on weekends. To the amusement park and the roller rink that used to be there."

"You grew up in Parkdale?" I ask, astonished.

"Oh yes, that's why I came back. An attempt to relive those days of my youth, I suppose. My best friend lived right over there on Tyndall; her father was one of the pioneers of cough syrup, of all things, and their house was huge. She had a convertible at sixteen! My family lived more simply, but, my, it was a wonderful place to grow up back then. There wasn't a lot of crime, you never thought to lock your door. Parents didn't worry about their children the way they do now. We played in the streets till it got dark."

We're all listening hard, fascinated.

"During the Depression, there would be all kinds of people coming to the house, looking for a handout, and my mother would always try to feed them. She was from South Africa originally. She came to Canada when she was twenty-two. She'd tell me that when she'd walk on the sidewalks there, blacks would have to step into the street." She shook her head at that. "Of course, it wasn't all that different here. I think there was one black family in the whole area, and the pool at Sunnyside had a 'Gentiles Only' sign. Hard to believe, now, that we'd do something like that. These days, at the mission, I get to meet women from all over the world, Somalia, Ethiopia, Vietnam and Cambodia. It's quite wonderful. " She looks straight ahead, remembering, as another rush of people make their way past the house.

"My, it's like watching a parade, isn't it? I can't think why I haven't sat out here before."

Gerry sighs, throws his cigarette butt down on the much abused front lawn, and says, "I like it. Sitting here. Reminds me that I'm not locked up. At Whitby, there was only grass and water. Hardly anyone but us patients and the geese. And mounds of geese shit everywhere you stepped."

"You were in the Whitby hospital?" asks Miss Semple.

"The mental hospital, yeah. Thought I'd be there forever. There were these buildings, they called them cottages, but they weren't cottages. They were more like little prisons. The guards were called 'staff,' they were there to keep us on the pills and needles, keep us in line. I forgot, after a while, that there was anyplace else. Got there too young. Kept there too long." He sighs, and starts rolling himself another cigarette, bits of tobacco flying here and there. This is a long soliloquy for Gerry, I don't remember him ever talking about his institutionalization. Not so subtle changes are happening with our little group of detectives.

"First few years I was there, I only wanted to get out. I dreamed every night about going back to my mother, back to my own bedroom. I still don't know why she sent me there. They never said. Then the dreams stopped. I hardly remembered what she looked like. How it was to be out there. I started getting fat. Only thing to do was eat. To pass the time." He lights the cigarette, and the tobacco must have been very stale, because half of it burns away in a little blaze. "Then they told me, after twenty years, I needed to leave. Just like that. And not just me. Shit, this whole neighbourhood is one big institution. Filled with mental patients like me. I see them every day, you can't miss them if you sit out here, and they're panhandling, or just screaming their lungs out, scaring the normals." He coughs, one of those scary, red-faced volcanic coughs.

"Never understood why they locked me up, never understood why they kicked me out. Still, I like it here, not at first, but Maryanne helped, you know? And now you guys, I mean you're not much, but you're better than nothing. And I love the stories. Didn't know about reading, how it could be. Never learned."

Miss Semple sniffs, and I see she's crying quiet tears. Gerry pretends not to notice, though I see one meaty hand reach over to hers, and hold it for a few precious seconds.

"I've been remembering things lately. How it felt when they punished some of the patients, how we couldn't do nothing. Just had to let it happen, or you'd be next. Hated that feeling. I really like that we can do something about those ladies. Fix that bastard Mallick." He turns to face me. "We have to, Dana, and you have to help. That's just how it is."

I nod, knowing he's right. We've all lost a lot of ground in our lives, Miss Semple, Diamond, Michael, Gerry and me. We need to take a stand. We need to fight back. Diamond comes through the door, does a double take when he sees the three of us.

"Here you all are." He sits wearily on the top step. "We can meet in Michael's room—sorry Gerry, your room—tomorrow, if you like. He's much better, but he has to stay in bed a little longer."

"Okay, let's do it in the early evening, say five o'clock." I'm thinking that will give me enough time to work on the plan I'd shelved. In the meantime, I've got to go up to the theatre and see Charlene. None of us move right away, we're taking pleasure in each other's company, taking strength. A loud car horn blares three or four times as another frustrated driver asserts himself. Miss Semple (of all people) and Gerry call out in unison, "What else did you get for Christmas, ya stupid bugger!" and we all collapse in hysterical laughter.

When I first went to Charlene's theatre, almost a year ago now, I was a little nervous just because it was such a new experience for me, and I didn't known what to expect. The auditions for *A Midsummer Night's Dream* had been completed a few days earlier, and I'd been told that this would be the first opportunity for the selected actors to hear and see one another, and for Charlene to get a feel for how they interacted. I took a seat behind the circle to listen and watch as they read through the play.

It was like getting to meet Cinderella before the fairy godmother stepped in with her wand: all the potential was there, but without scenery, direction and costumes, it lacked sparkle and glamour.

I remember how I was startled to realize that, in contrast to the strain and sallowness I was so used to seeing in the denizens of the drop-in and my rooming house, these people had smooth and tanned faces, sometimes creased with smile lines, or crinkles in the forehead from age or concentration, but on the whole they looked well-fed and almost glowingly healthy. Their clothing too, as casual as it was, was clean and fit them. And their shoes weren't falling apart, at the toe or the sole. They were confident. They had enough words in their vocabulary that their conversations weren't littered with profanity. When they took a break, they spoke of vacations and work, children and movies, there wasn't the urgency behind their words that I encountered at the drop-in, that desperation to be heard.

I realized then that I'd almost forgotten there was a whole world of people who lived lives unscarred by want and need. I had to check an impulse to examine my own face to see if I was permanently marked by my time in Parkdale.

And later there were moments of apparent crossover, when the drop-in and the theatre would merge for a nanosecond in my mind, and I'd be struck all over again by what was normal for me. I was watching a rehearsal, sitting in the back of the theatre as usual, and in front of me a man was talking very quietly to himself, making gestures for emphasis. At first, I just assumed he was a crazy—there were many in Parkdale so lonely they needed to create a companion, to have a conversation, maybe just to hear their own voice. It took a minute, but then I realized he was just going over his lines.

I didn't feel anger or resentment, just a kind of wonder. I knew enough about people that I didn't assume their lives were uncomplicated by fears and tragedies, loss and even illness. I didn't make them into the one-dimensional "haves," the flip side of the "have-nots." But that's when I started my long walks in other neighbourhoods, as a constant reminder that there were other ways to live a life, families that were loving and caring, where residents had the energy and the heart to plant gardens where all kinds of flowers and bushes beautified a street, a kind of anodyne to Parkdale.

"God, I thought you'd never come."

Charlene is still not happy. She gives me a strong hug when I appear at the studio, days later than I'd originally planned.

Now that Michael's recovering, I feel okay about leaving the house for the afternoon, but it's clear that things have not got any better here.

"There was a bit of a crisis at the house, I couldn't get away. Has your gremlin been escalating his activities?"

We're in her windowless office on the first floor. It's a chaotic affair, much like the inside of her car before the ladies cleaned it out. She closes the door, which makes the place feel like an elevator stuck between floors, and sinks into the chair behind her desk. I can tell from the dark circles under her eyes that she hasn't been sleeping well, and her hands are a bit shaky. As she talks, she moves piles of scripts and invoices into separate piles, throwing out empty water bottles and chip bags.

"It's so weird, and a bit scary. It's all little things, like props disappearing, things breaking or malfunctioning that always worked before. The lights, they're critical for this play, but they constantly go out, like someone's played with the fuses. Poor Evan, our volunteer electrician, we're calling him every day to fix this and that. And he's been great, but it can't happen when we open. It would be a disaster."

"What else? Be specific."

"Okay, let me think. There are the costumes. When people go to try them on, they literally fall right off them. Someone has carefully, methodically, undone the stitching, so sleeves detach from the gowns and suits. We've had to double-check them every day to make sure they're not messed with, and the seamstress is exhausted; her sewing machine is going all the time. Heels are pried loose from shoes. Tools disappear. None of this is accidental, though I was hoping at first we were just having a run of bad luck. Someone has it in for us, and I don't know who or why."

She's crying now, the kind of crying that happens when stress and strain wear you down.

"I lock up every night. Close every window. I don't know how anyone gets in. If it's done at night. Dana, will you hang around a while and see if you can pick up on anything? I'm at the end of my rope here. If it wasn't for Jason, he's been so supportive, I think I'd just collapse in tears."

I stoically ignore that last bit. "Sure, I'll be here all afternoon. Have you talked to the cast and crew? What about Jeremy?"

"No, not yet. But everyone knows something weird is going on. Except Jeremy. I've kept it from him. You know how he is, he's so proud of what we've built together; it would kill him to think a member of our company would resort to something so foul. " She sighs, wipes her eyes and composes herself. "The worst thing is, I suspect everyone now. I look at them and I wonder which one of them is doing this. It doesn't make for good relations."

"I'll do what I can, of course."

"Thanks, Dana. I know you'll find out who's doing this."

I stay behind when Charlene leaves. I don't share her confidence in me. Though I'm sure Jason is the villain, how do I catch him? And what if, in spite of everything, it isn't him? "Fat chance," I mutter to myself, stepping out of the office into the first-floor open space that does double duty as a meeting place and a lounge for the actors. Though the furniture in here has seen better days, it's all selected for comfort, and the walls remind me of Jeremy's bedroom, festooned with wonderful shots of past productions, old theatre flyers and even bits of costumes and masks.

Jeremy and Charlene were fortunate in their timing. If they had had to apply for the multitude of variances they needed for all the construction from the city's buildings and inspections department these days, they would have met with a lot of opposition. Sometimes it seems like ratepayers do nothing but guard their neighbourhoods from anything other than a single-family dwelling. They organize at the drop of a hat, using pickets, petitions and pressure. "Not In My Back Yard" is their rallying cry.

The once-upon-a-time coach house turned two-car garage and rental flat is unrecognizable now. Jeremy and Charlene hired the best architect they could find, and he created a miracle. There was a lot of depth to their back yard, as is the case with many of the properties here, and much of it is now eaten up by the renovated building.

The theatre upstairs can comfortably seat a hundred people. They had to install bathrooms, cleverly tucked away off the first floor, along with a small reception area, the wardrobe department and the lounge. It worked. And it still left Charlene her garden, which theatregoers could admire as they followed the flagstone path to the studio door.

I've been here so often that I've grown largely invisible. No one pays much attention to me; I'm just another fixture in the place. Like the coffee pot, which I see is working. I pour myself a cup and take a seat on the tatty couch, leafing through a script I've borrowed from Charlene's desk. This afternoon, there's just Becky and her co-star, Barry, in the room, both with their heads deep in their scripts.

I remember being a bit disappointed on my first foray into the studio to learn that it wasn't like a movie set; there weren't a lot of glamorous, recognizable faces, no lights, camera, action. In fact, for a lost soul wandering in, it might have easily been mistaken for a neighbourhood get-together. Everyone, in deference to the summer temperatures, had been casually dressed, which Jeremy tended to bemoan; he made no concessions to the heat. His shirts were always white and crisp, his pants sharply creased. In contrast, the actors waiting to be called for particular scenes were sprawled languidly on the scattered couches and old chairs, in shorts, T-shirts, sandals. The women were without makeup, their hair often tied back with elastics; the men wore a variety of ball caps.

I didn't have much time for drama students when I was in university. Their exaggerated personalities and self-obsessions exhausted me. But in community theatre, it's more collaborative than ego-driven. After all, the success of their endeavour makes them all interdependent, from the advertising people to the lighting and set design, to those who wear the costumes. Everyone brings particular talents, and no one gets paid. There's something very charming, very engaging, about this.

Except for the younger, just out of school types, all the actors have real careers, in all kinds of sectors. Bankers, software designers, teachers, accountants, they spend their evenings, weekends and vacations with their first love, rather than with their families.

Becky, for instance, has three children she's raised, and if there is a cure for narcissism, motherhood has to be right up there.

I was at the studio when Becky had her audition for the current production. Charlene had decided to do *Lady Windermere's Fan*, by Oscar Wilde, and was looking to cast the mother.

Charlene likes to ask her would-be performers about the play, what their thoughts and feelings about it are. "To be sure they have a brain," as she puts it. First off the mark was a middle-aged, rather severe woman who launched into a bitter political diatribe.

"I come at this from a purely feminist perspective, of course. How women were forced by the male hegemony to be these pure vessels, empty vessels, that must be of perfect shape—as decided by men's fantasies—essentially handmaidens to their husbands.

They were burdens to their fathers, displayed in degrading fashion, kept penniless and powerless. And the single great failure was to not be chosen by a man. It was little better than being sold into slavery, for the material benefit of the parents. Not much has changed."

Her reading was more of the same barely restrained fury, the tear-off-the-testicles-and-stomp-them kind of rage, no subtlety, no nuance. I saw Jeremy cross his legs in unconscious self-defense. We were all relieved when she left the room.

Next up was a younger woman, pierced here and there, nose, lip and eyebrow, cracking gum and slumping in the chair.

"Well, I mean, it's so oppressive, isn't it. Not that things have changed much," she said in an eerie echo of her predecessor. "I related absolutely. I've been there, you know? Where people judge you, decide who you are when they know nothing about you. I got my eyebrow pierced a few months ago, and you wouldn't believe the looks I get from total strangers. So, like, I really felt close to this part."

I remember thinking that poor Jeremy must be at the end of his tether. Not a patient man at the best of times, it must have been agonizing for him not to explode at this. And indeed, right at the point where the woman stopped blathering, Jeremy snapped his pencil, startling even himself into a muttered apology.

Next was Becky. Middle-aged, simply dressed in shift and sandals, her hair tied back in an elastic. Self-contained, calm, she thought a moment about the question, while I held my breath in the back.

"My reaction? At first, I was a little ashamed. I thought I knew the play. I suppose I was very young when I first read it. As I went through it, I became quite sad. At what we do to people, men and women, how we construct these social barriers to avoid any semblance of truth, any threat to how things are supposed to be. And I felt unutterably sad for Wilde, proud of him too, for showing people what they didn't want to know. I'm surprised he could even draw a breath in that era. God knows, he was punished enough. As for this particular role, she had no choice. A branded woman, forever marked by one mistake, with no financial resources of her own, at the mercy of those who had none of her depth, her intellect or her drive. Of course, I admire her. She's a survivor, yet still capable of sacrifice."

I almost applauded, her feelings mirrored by my own, but that would have brought me a glare from Jeremy. When she did the assigned reading, she brought all the depth and richness Wilde must have envisioned. I was captivated as soon as she started, and held my breath till the passage ended. I'm glad she's rehearsing today; it will be a treat.

I stay in the lounge for about a quarter of an hour, and in that time at least ten people enter the lounge, looking like they know what they're doing, drifting upstairs or toward the wardrobe room. Some carry tool boxes, or pieces of wood; a few come clumped together, laughing or chatting. No one looks twitchy or any odder than anyone else. I'm thinking this is an impossible mission I'm on; I have no idea who is supposed to be here and who isn't. There's no check-in, no control over the comings and goings.

Becky stands, stretches languidly and throws me a smile as she and Barry collect their things and make their way up to the stage. I have already noticed one difference. Usually, there are piles of personal possessions left here and there in this room. Books, knapsacks, odd bits of shopping people have done on the way here for home, changes of clothes when necessary. Not anymore. That trust within the company is gone.

Other actors start to appear. Among them, I see with a sinking heart, is Jason. They are all listening to him, hanging on his every word. I know I have to speak with him eventually, but I'm not ready for him yet. My frustration over Charlene's blind infatuation with such an unworthy, manipulating bastard peaks at the sight of him, as I knew it would, and I feel myself redden with anger.

His idea of casual dress means whatever shows his body off to maximum benefit. Today, his sport shirt is brilliant white, to highlight his tan, and his shorts are very short, allowing his muscular thighs to take a bow. He is pretty, in a conventional, bland kind of way. He's worked as a model, done a commercial or two, and a few spots on a Canadian series, but nothing of note recently. His teeth are as white as his shirt, and he probably spends longer in front of the mirror working on his hair than most women. It's easy to see he thinks he is much desired. Stage has very different requirements than a catalogue shoot, however: looks are entirely secondary to talent.

I might have been his long-lost best friend, the way he lights up when he sees me sitting there.

"Dana, how lovely to see you. You look great, as usual. Wonderful, in fact. It's been a while." Uninvited, he takes a seat beside me, throwing an arm over my shoulders. "Charlene's been missing you." It's just like him to speak for Charlene; the not-so-hidden inference is that he's closer to her than I am.

"I'm here now. How are you doing, Jason?"

"I'm good, really good." He hesitates, looks around at the others and leans in even closer, lowering his voice to a whisper. "Has Charlene told you about what's been happening? It's pretty sick. Someone really has it in for us." I nod, and he continues on.

"But I wanted to talk to you about something else. You're on the board, aren't you?"

People have strange ideas about the board, and about serving on the board, as though it's some mythic centre of power, elevating those who are a part of it. The reality is, its members are carefully selected by Jeremy and Charlene; the criteria seem to be, for some, a familiarity with theatre, professional or community, or an ability to fundraise among the upper strata of society. Others have PR experience they are willing to share, or accounting skills. Charlene said that it would be good for them to have an "outsider" viewpoint, someone who could bring a wider perspective; I think she just wanted to give me something official to do. Overriding all that is the understanding that we rubber stamp the decisions and directions Jeremy and Charlene come to. And that's fine with me. There is no jockeying for control, no power struggles. It's all very civilized.

"I know Charlene will never say a word. But I can tell how frustrated she is, with Jeremy constantly looking over her shoulder, second-guessing her. He's really past it, but he doesn't have the sense to bow out, you know?"

I actually turn to face him, making no effort to disguise my shock. He's such a weasel, so sure of himself that he doesn't read me properly, he probably thinks I just want to admire his wonderful looks. At least I manage to dislodge his arm.

I've caught him in unguarded moments in the past, seen the daggered looks he's sent Jeremy's way. He seems to have decided that Jeremy was the one who confined him to such a minor part, out of personal rather than professional reasons. Better to blame jealousy of his youth or his looks, or his intimate relationship with Charlene, than his limited talent.

He appeared to take it well, when he was told which part he'd been allotted, quoting the old chestnut about there being no small parts, but I'm sure he was seething underneath; he was used to centre stage wherever he appeared. That, I thought, was when he began his charm offensive to win over cast and crew. I missed his audition, but Jeremy confided that he'd "minced around on the boards like a bad parody of an old queen."

"She's so talented, there's no telling what she could accomplish if she was out of his shadow. Everyone knows she already does most of the work, while he just wanders in when the mood strikes him. And he grabs all the credit, he's the Name, and he'll never let go. I thought, since you're on the board, you might have a word with some of the others. Plant the seed, as it were. I'd do it, if I could have a seat."

He snaps his fingers in a sadly transparent pantomime of a eureka moment.

"That's it. If you could put my name forward, we'd be allies. Between the two of us, we could fix it so that Jeremy is reduced to a figurehead, confined to a PR role."

I want to hit him, first for thinking I'm so gullible, so easy to manipulate. And then hit him again for his attack on Jeremy. He puts his arm back around my shoulder, as though he's promising greater intimacy if I go along.

I'm frozen with rage. He, of course, doesn't notice.

"Please think about it. I know you care about Charlene as much as I do. We'll talk more later; I promised to help with the set. Take good care now."

Yuck. What a jerk. What a conniving, underhanded jerk. He's left me breathless with his audacity. How can Charlene not see what he is? I ask myself. How can I tell her? I can't, of course, I have to catch him red-handed. The bastard. I wait till my fury has abated, then take myself upstairs to the theatre.

Jeremy and Charlene are sitting at a long table, facing the stage. In front of Charlene, fruit, bottled water, scripts, and Mars bars clutter her space. Jeremy, the neat freak, has only one script and his pen.

The set is coming together, a little miracle in itself performed by retired carpenters and set designers in lengthy meetings with Charlene. A labour of love, like most of the work done here. I never tire of this, watching the rehearsals, the slow, careful progression to opening night. Though one might think watching the same scene done over and over again would be stultifying, for me, it only enhances the magic. I love the creativity and bustling industry, the ability to live, even for just a few weeks, other lives.

Becky is being put through her paces. I watch her counting steps on the stage, familiarizing herself with its boundaries. She pulls off her sensible shoes and tube socks, slipping on ankle-length hose and into the high fashion and probably torturous heels she will wear during the production. I see her surreptitiously check that the heels are firmly attached.

The scene is a powerful one, the last confrontation between her character and Lord Windermere. Her co-star, Barry, a tall, balding insurance salesman who's a regular in the company, drifts in and takes his place on stage. Charlene calls a start, and I watch Becky transform herself right in front of my eyes. It's the posture, the way she holds her head, the steel just under the flesh, the long-buried hurt; it's all there, before she says a word.

"You seem rather out of temper this morning, Windermere. Why should you be? Margaret and I get on charmingly together."

"I can't bear to see you with her. Besides, you have not told me the truth, Mrs. Erlynne."

"I have not told her the truth, you mean."

Charlene stops them. "We really need to work on your accents, people. And we don't have a lot of time. Jeremy, could you spend some time with them, and some of the others, help them out?"

"I didn't know we were doing *Pygmalion*," he quips. "But of course. What are your schedules like?" Everything stops while people pull out their books, and wrestle with times. I hear voices just outside; Jason's talking to someone. When he comes in, he walks down the aisle and takes a seat just behind Charlene, reaching over and touching her shoulder proprietarily. She turns her head and smiles at him; it may be my imagination, but I think Jeremy stiffens as he feels Jason's presence. The actors pick up the scene again, Barry doing Windermere.

"I sometimes wish you had. I should have been spared then the misery, the anxiety, the annoyance of the last six months. But rather than my wife should know—that the mother whom she has mourned as dead, is living—a divorced woman, going about under an assumed name, a bad woman preying upon life, as I know you now to be—rather than that, I was ready to supply you with money to pay bill after bill, extravagance after extravagance, to risk what occurred yesterday, the first quarrel I have ever had with my wife. You don't understand what that means to me. How could you? But I tell you that the only bitter words that ever came from those sweet lips of hers were on your account, and I hate to see you next to her. You sully the innocence that is in her. And then I used to think that with all your faults you were frank and honest. You are not."

Charlene interrupts. "Barry, why are you standing as close as you are?"

"I think I'm backing her into a corner, using my superior strength, my maleness, to my advantage."

"You must remember your total revulsion at this woman's behaviour. I suspect you'd want to keep your distance, that it would be difficult for you even to look at her. It's as though you'd catch some dread social disease if you came too close. Think of her as some conniving leper, threatening to destroy all you've built with your wife. Move about four, five feet away—yes, right there—and let's try it again."

And it's better this time.

Step by measured step, Charlene leads them toward her vision, and they follow without a murmur of dissent. Then we come to Mrs. Erlynne's big speech, and I lean forward to catch every nuance.

Barry checks his script, says his lines. "*What do you mean by coming here this morning? What is your object?*"

"*To bid good-bye to my dear daughter, of course. Oh, don't imagine I am going to have a pathetic scene with her, weep on her neck and tell her who I am, and all that kind of thing. I have no ambition to play the part of a mother. Only once in my life have I known a mother's feelings. That was last night. They were terrible—they made me suffer—they made me suffer too much.*"

The hair is standing up on my arms. It doesn't matter that the stage is half-finished, that they are wearing modern clothing, or that a faint hammering can be heard from the back. None of that matters at all.

"*For twenty years, as you say, I have lived childless—I want to live childless still. Besides, my dear Windermere, how on earth could I pose as a mother with a grown-up daughter? Margaret is twenty-one, and I have never admitted that I am more than twenty-nine, or thirty at the most. Twenty-nine when there are pink shades, thirty when there are not. So you see what difficulties it would involve. No, as far as I am concerned, let your wife cherish the memory of this dead, stainless mother. Why should I interfere with her illusions? I find it hard enough to keep my own. I lost one illusion last night. I thought I had no heart. I find I have, and a heart doesn't suit me, Windermere. Somehow it doesn't go with modern dress. It makes one look old. And it spoils one's career at critical moments."*

"*You fill me with horror—with absolute horror.*"

Charlene interrupts again. "Barry, when you're working with Jeremy, pay attention to his posture, how he holds himself. A late twentieth-century slouch is out of place here."

"I'll loan you my girdle," says Becky. "If you slouch it'll cut you in half. Shall I continue?"

At a nod from Charlene, she continues.

"I suppose, Windermere, you would like me to retire into a convent, or become a hospital nurse, or something of that kind, as people do in silly modern novels. That is stupid of you, Arthur; in real life we don't do such things—not so long as we have any good looks left, at any rate. No—what consoles one nowadays is not repentance, but pleasure. Repentance is quite out of date. And besides, if a woman really repents, she has to go to a bad dressmaker, otherwise no one believes in her. And nothing in the world would induce me to do that. No, I am going to pass entirely out of your two lives. My coming into them has been a mistake—I discovered that last night."

"Very nice," says Charlene. "Remember though, her talk about her age and bad dressmakers is a shield, she knows she's coming too close to revealing herself to a man who's not worthy, not even capable of hearing her truth. She keeps coming so close, and then retreats behind this dry humour. We have to show that, almost physically. This need to share herself, barely kept in check."

A discussion ensues about the best way to hold herself during that scene, and I drift away, closing my eyes and thinking of Ed.

As Jeremy and Charlene mutter with their heads together, I look around the theatre. No one is skulking, or looking out of place. I'm thinking this approach is hopeless. And now that I'm a little calmer, I realize that even though Jason is the obvious and, I confess, the desired candidate, I can't blind myself to other possibilities. I sift through the legion of mysteries I've read, Evanovich, Christie, Chandler, George, Doyle. They never just trip over the culprit, there has to be a methodical approach, a winnowing down of suspects.

Jeremy stands up and stretches his back. "Bravo, Ms. Edwards. You do yourself credit. Your interpretation will stand with the best. Now, if you'll pardon me, I must adjourn to my office, and the Everest of papers that awaits me."

He catches sight of me as he heads up the aisle and smiles, waving as he approaches. "Dana, it's been too long since you've graced us with your presence." He bends and kisses my cheek, then takes a seat beside me. "Where have you been, and what have you been up to?"

"Nothing as exciting as this. She really is wonderful, isn't she?"

"Yes, she transports us without the aid of costume or props. I'm quite taken with her. If we had had her playing Lady Macbeth, instead of that poor excuse for womanhood we ended up with, we'd never had closed the production."

"Jeremy, it ran for a month and a half. And it got reviewed." It's rare for community theatre to attract intelligent critics, but Jeremy's productions are the exception.

"Yes, still." He looks tired; there are smudged circles under his eyes. He pats my hand and murmurs, "Perhaps your being here will drive away some of the clouds that have been darkening our little effort." He shakes his head slowly. "I don't recall so many things ever going wrong in so short a time. Has Charlene spoken to you?"

"She has. Try not to worry; I'm sure everything will sort itself out."

"Poor Charlene. She has enough to contend with these days." I see his eyes burning tiny holes in Jason's back. "I must be off. Do come for dinner soon, won't you?"

I can't fail him. In spite of the flutters of panic I'm feeling, I see the edges of a plan, an approach that might work. I hear Charlene call for the actors in the next scene, and no one responds. She sends her assistant, Lillith, who doubles as a stage manager, back to the lounge to corral the players, but Lillith returns alone, and whispers to Charlene, who groans audibly.

"Please try reaching them now. We have so little time. God, it's not like them to just not show."

The bare stage looks ominous, like a prelude to disaster. Jason takes the seat recently vacated by Jeremy (how's that for symbolism, I ask myself) and gives her a one-armed hug. She allows her head to fall against his shoulder for a few heartbeats, then starts gathering up her pile of debris. She comes up the aisle and sits with me for a moment.

"Anything?" she asks.

"No. Listen, no one's going to do anything while I'm watching. And there's no way for me to tell who belongs and who doesn't. This is what I need you to do. First, you have to talk to all the members of your company. Let them know that you're taking steps to deal with this, enlist their help, ask them to be vigilant. It's no good not addressing this."

She groans, but agrees to call a meeting.

"Secondly, do you still have all the headshots and resumés for all the actors? Including the ones you rejected?"

She nods, interested. "Okay, I need to see them, and I need to know who applied for what part. I also need to look at a list of who's working this production, all the volunteers you're using. And you need to set some controls over the door. Maybe a sign-in sheet so we know who is in the building at any given time. Name tags, too. Can you do that?"

"Yes, of course. I'll talk to Lillith. She's certainly not involved in this; she's been away, vacationing in Cuba, and just got back a few days ago. She's very organized. I'll have her pull everything you need, and get someone on the door. Will tomorrow do?"

"Tomorrow will be fine. I'll come by and go through the list, start talking to people." At that moment, Lillith appears, a little pale and almost wringing her hands.

Charlene looks at her, "Oh damn, what now?"

"The phones are down, nothing's working. I had to use my cell. I reached Tim's wife, and she said he got a call after ten last night saying the rehearsal was cancelled, so he went golfing. I've left messages with the others to call us. I had to give your home number out, I hope that's all right. And I've called Bell. Charlene, they said they had a disconnect order from us, called in a week ago! From you, the operator said!"

This is bad. Charlene and Lillith both turn to me, and I quickly rack my brain.

"You'll have to call around. Tell the cast that only you and

Lillith are authorized to contact them. That they should pay no attention to any other calls they may get. And get them all in, Charlene, as soon as you can."

They look grateful for this. I have pangs of anxiety in my stomach and my chest, but I'm all front, projecting confidence where there is only rising fear. It's time for me to exit, stage left, and return to the other mystery in my life.

Chapter Seven

Diamond is keeping his very bored patient in bed. There's only one chair, which we leave to Miss Semple. Diamond and I have brought our pillows to sit on, and Gerry grabs the side of the bed. They listen, rapt, as I tell them of my adventures with Charlene's car, and the ultimately successful tailing of Mallick to his home. I also tell them about my ex-biker pal Derek's offer of assistance, which cheers them, and then I turn to Miss Semple.

"You can say no. It might be dangerous, there's no telling, but I think I've come up with a way to suss him out. We know that he leaves Parkdale during the day, going to the house off the Danforth." I go through the plan, and read out some of the questions I've developed. Miss Semple claps her hands together, very pleased to play a part in this mini-drama.

"I will prepare some forms tomorrow, it shouldn't take me long. I think it's a wonderful idea, bearding the lion in his den!"

To practise, I suggest we role-play; Gerry volunteers to take the part of Mallick. Miss Semple and I leave the room, stand briefly in the hallway, then I knock politely on the door. Gerry opens the door and glares at us.

"What do you want?"

Miss Semple takes the lead. "Good afternoon. I wonder if we

could have a few minutes of your time to complete a survey we're doing in the neighbourhood."

"What's in it for me?"

Gerry's put his finger on a major flaw:, why should he let us in? We toss around ideas, and decide to claim that residents who assist us will be entered in a draw for prizes. Blue Jays tickets, or gift certificates (in case he's not interested in baseball) for local grocery and clothing stores.

Miss Semple and I go back to the hall and start again.

"Yeah, what is it?"

"Good afternoon, could we have a few minutes of your time to complete a survey we're doing in the neighbourhood? You'll be eligible for wonderful free gifts in return for your co-operation."

"I don't know, who you working for, what's it about?"

We're ready for that.

"We're with Advance Marketing, and we're looking at buying trends to help us with product development. Some of the prizes we're offering are quite generous, and it really won't take up a lot of your busy day."

Gerry blows a gust of exasperated air toward the ceiling. "All right, I guess, but I only have a few minutes. C'mon in." We trail him into the room, he sits back down on the bed, and Miss Semple primly arranges herself and her papers from her perch on the chair.

"This is very kind of you; we'll get started right away. Do you own or rent your house?"

"Rent."

"How many adults are in the house? Children?"

"Just me."

"And your occupation?"

"Kidnapper."

Miss Semple nods, and I, the form filler-outer, pretend to tick off an answer.

"Where do you do the majority of your grocery purchasing?"

"Food Bank." This elicits an appreciative guffaw from Michael.

Miss Semple is a straight-faced marvel. "Do you find there is enough selection there?"

"No, the shelves are always empty."

"Do you own an automobile? May I ask the year and make."

"How the hell else did you find me? Sorry, yes, I own a car. Are we almost done here?" He pretends to check his watch, clucks his tongue. "I got misery to spread, people to do in."

"Almost done. You've been very patient. Just a few more, then you can fill out your draw ticket. Did you purchase your car locally?"

"No. I hotwired it."

"Could you tell me the number of televisions in the home, and whether or not you own a computer?"

"Hah! In your dreams. Number of televisions."

"Y'know, Dana, I'm not sure how to put this." Michael, who's been enjoying himself, now looks quite serious. "But you'd get more time with the creep if he thought he had a chance with you." The others nod, including Miss Semple. "If you, well, give him the eye, flirt just a bit, not too much, he'll be falling all over himself."

"Yuck. But you're right, I'll keep it in mind. Miss Semple, I must say, you sound like it's the fiftieth time you've asked the questions, you're perfect. Okay, whenever you've got the forms ready, we'll do it. Who's ready for Evanovich?"

Today, we feel more like Stephanie Plum's peers than a passive audience, thanks to the magic of our plan.

Another beautiful day, the sun high in the cloudless sky has everyone out and about, smiling, cheerful. Walking west on Queen, heading to Charlene's, I decide at the last minute to detour down Fortune Street, lured like the squabbling seagulls, pigeons, feral cats and squirrels by the garbage piled high and carelessly in front of each dilapidated building.

Mallick's car isn't there. I approach as casually as I can, interested in the recycling containers stacked by his driveway, beside several overloaded trash cans. If I'd known in advance, I would have dressed down and grabbed myself a shopping cart, rummaged around like the regular tribe of bottle collectors. I'm walking really slowly, giving myself a slight limp to justify my pace, and there's lots of time to see the dozen or so oversize cans, the kind Pete buys for the meals he prepares at the centre. They're dented and dirty, some with their labels still attached, corn, chicken broth, peas, stewed tomatoes. That's a lot of food for a supposedly empty house. I bend down to tie my shoelace and see a bunch of envelopes. Even squished and stained, they are instantly recognizable as Government of Ontario mail, the kind used to send out disability cheques. There's no time to count them, but there's a dozen. This is getting scary.

As I reach Queen Street, I look back toward the building and mutter to myself "soon," a promise and a threat, maybe even a little prayer thrown in. The next instant, I almost jump out of my shoes as a screech of tires, accompanied by staccato bursts of horn, tears through the fabric of the afternoon. Muscling his way through oncoming traffic, causing other drivers to stand on their brakes and pound their own horns, Ed has broken every traffic law in the book with his abrupt attempt at a U-turn. Price is in the passenger seat, holding on to the dashboard with both hands, and I think I can see little beads of sweat on his forehead. The pedestrians around me have frozen, some in mid-stride; I feel as though I should throw my hands in the air and snarl "You got me, copper."

Ed doesn't park the car so much as abandon it at a skewed angle to the sidewalk, reinforcing the perception of a take-down, till he casually swings himself out of the seat and saunters over. "Hi," he says, as if he hadn't just come perilously close to causing a massive pile-up. "I was just over at the house."

People have started moving again, some no doubt disappointed with the lack of violent follow-through, others relieved. He smiles down at me, but there's an edge to it.

"Gerry's not made to keep secrets. I don't know what it is, but I do know you guys are up to something. Dana, I wouldn't want any of you getting hurt, blundering around, stirring things up. You have to leave these things to the authorities. That's why we're here."

"And when the authorities, as you put it, fail to do their job? What then, Ed?" I shake my head, look down at my feet. "You've decided there's no crime, and if there's no crime, then there's no danger to any of us."

He leans forward, speaking urgently. "I've been back to Mallick's twice since we last talked. On my own time, unofficially. No one answers the door. I'll go again, I promise, but you have to stay out of it. That's where you were heading, isn't it?"

I can be both indignant and self-righteous now. "I'm on my way to the theatre, Ed, not to Mallick's. And I'm late." Deep breath. "I appreciate your concern. I really do. And I like that you almost made Price wet himself." We both turn to look at him. He's still clutching at the dash, staring blankly ahead, as cars ease around the protruding rear end of the vehicle.

"Well," Ed says grudgingly, "it's the least I could do. He looks a little older now, doesn't he? Dana, will you leave it to me?"

"What else can I do?" I'm hoping there's enough ambiguity in that response that it's not an outright lie. Glints of suspicion in his beautiful eyes show me he's wondering the same thing, but he retreats to his car with a shake of his head. I move off without looking back, trying not to dwell on "if only's."

Eloise scares me. She scares everyone, which is ridiculous when you think about it. She's just another volunteer, though I'd never say that to her face. Tall and skinny, with those little glasses perched on the very end of her nose, her eyes peering over them, she's like the librarian from hell. Sometimes I fantasize her into a brown uniform with jackboots. This is her territory, every inch of the small cramped space filled floor to ceiling (okay, not right to the ceiling) with a stunning variety of clothing and shoes and hats and coats of all eras and descriptions. Top hats and frock coats, ball gowns and faux furs, boas and wigs, high-button boots and the most fragile footwear all carefully, even lovingly, preserved. She's the wardrobe lady, keeper of the costumes.

Eloise hates to have actors rummaging through her collection. She especially hates me, or so I feel, as I breach her defenses once again to "shop" for a skirt, blouse and heels to bedazzle Mallick. Because the space is so small, she's fanatical about keeping everything just so; the actors have learned to stand just outside the room and wait while she finds them what they need. I, on the other hand, need to browse, pull this and that out, try it on, put it back more or less where it was, and look some more.

The idea that I very occasionally remove things from the studio really jars her. I take no pleasure in tormenting her; by the time I've found what I need we're both usually hyperventilating, and she's moved that much closer to a coronary. Still, except for her disapproving glares, I love this room. It's my private Holt Renfrew, a far remove from my own limited cache of jeans and T-shirts. The skirt I've chosen is tight, hugging my bottom, the blouse, a light lavender thing, can be unbuttoned just enough to show some cleavage, and the heels, not too high, are the ultimate in suggestive footwear. I pile up my treasure, and Eloise demands once again that I fill out a form that she's created just for me, certain that I'll abscond with her things, or bring them back irretrievably damaged.

As I list the items on the paper, I gather my courage and say in a conversational tone, "Charlene tells me there's been some mischief going on. Have you noticed anyone hanging around that you haven't seen before? Anyone who looks out of place?"

Eloise instantly transforms from Hilda of the SS into a concerned and vulnerable middle-aged woman, and I swear there are tears in her eyes.

"Yes, there have been thefts, from this very room! How long have I been asking for a door to close off my space, a door I could lock? The idea that someone has been in here, after hours, touching everything, taking things." She shakes her head in despair. "There are whole costumes I set aside for this production missing. I've been running around to other theatres, begging and borrowing replacements. It's humiliating, to be so unprepared! I've kept my eyes open, but ..."

I don't think she'd respond well to a hug, so I murmur some sympathetic words and back out of the room with my plunder.

I noticed earlier that Charlene has indeed staffed the front reception area; a man who looked vaguely familiar waved me over to sign in. Jeremy arrived as I was checking the list of names, and introduced me to him.

"Dana, this is one of our stalwarts, one of the unheralded, who put so much of their time behind the scenes, my neighbour, Jim Allan."

He's an undistinguished-looking fellow, slightly balding, short and paunchy. I reached across the counter and shook his hand. "Hey, Jim. So you've managed to get everyone to check in. Thank you, this may help."

"Anything I can do, Dana. Absolutely anything. You just need to ask."

Jeremy beamed at him. "You see how fortunate we are? And his wife, Marlene, what a treasure she's been. Theatre's in her blood, I believe. Do let her know how much we miss her." Jeremy turned to me, "Her mother's very ill, so Marlene has had to leave her family and travel to Quebec to care for her. Jim has stepped into the breach."

Jim's face turned bright red. Perhaps he was unaccustomed to praise.

"You're too kind, Jeremy. I'll be certain to let her know you're thinking of her."

He'd been thorough, Jim had; beside each name was the reason each individual was in today. Jeremy wandered off while I perused the list. The majority were here to work on the set, a few to read through their lines for Charlene. I saw Jason's elaborate flourish of a signature, with "called in to assist the stagehands" tagged on.

When I looked up, I realized that Jim had been watching me intently. He blushed again and lowered his eyes as if he'd been caught out snooping. I smiled at him, one snoop to another, and said, "Good job, Jim."

Jeremy took my arm, murmuring, "Could I have a word with you? Let's step outside for a moment."

The sun was scorching. Jeremy shielded his eyes with one hand, and leaned toward me, saying, "Charlene held that meeting this morning, as you suggested. It was high time. I think everyone feels better that it's out in the open, that something's being done. Thank you for that."

I shrugged, at a loss for words.

"I wondered, Dana." He blew air out forcefully, frustrated with himself. "I wondered if this could have anything to do with that other unpleasantness, that odious young upstart with criminal tendencies. Could he have returned to plague us?"

"I hadn't thought of that, Jeremy, but I think it's unlikely, considering the public thrashing he got the first time. Still, it might be useful to see what he's up to these days."

"Leave it to me," he said, brightening at the prospect of taking action. "I'll call the lawyers I had back then, see what they can find out."

Now Charlene has set me up in her office, which Lillith has made liveable by clearing off the desk. Files are stacked neatly and tagged with yellow stickies. I like Lillith, she's the kind of assistant any executive would kill for. Organized, quietly competent, she doesn't ask questions, just does what she's asked, and does it well.

Today, however, she looks to be on the edge of a nervous breakdown. Her hands tremble, and her voice, usually calm and soothing, sounds a bit strangled. She sinks in the chair opposite the desk.

"I love stage managing, Dana. I've done it so often that I can anticipate almost everything that can go wrong in a production, once the audience is in place and the curtain goes up. But this! The idea of deliberate sabotage! How on earth can I plan for that? I'm having nightmares. You have to catch whoever is doing this, and soon, or I don't know what I'll do! There are so many ways to ruin us, stop the play dead, with everyone in their seats, watching!"

"We'll catch the s.o.b." I can't believe I sound so firm, so confident. Maybe this acting business isn't as difficult as I thought. "And soon. Believe me, I understand the strain you're feeling, the responsibility you're carrying." And I do. Once the play opens, the stage manager is God. It's all down to her. Charlene and Jeremy must keep to their seats, with the rest of the audience; only Lillith can communicate instructions or re-directions to the actors, to meet the challenge of the unexpected, such as an important prop that's not in place when it's needed, or forgotten lines, or missed cues.

"Everyone depends on you. You have to be strong for them. I know you've acted before, I've seen you, and you're pretty good. So act the part now of the confident stage manager who has everything in hand. You can do it."

She straightens her posture, takes a few calming breaths. "You're right, of course. I can't let them see me all nervous and, and, freaked out. That won't help anything. Oh, why would someone do this to us? It's inexplicable. We're all decent people, we're not hurting anyone."

I feel once again the helplessness that is too much with me these days, both here and at home. Lillith continues, "Thank God for Jason. He's spending all his time fixing things the creep keeps breaking. If not for him, things would be even worse. He's promised to stay backstage with me on opening night, when he's not on, just in case. Anyway, I'll leave you to it."

I take my seat and open the first file and lose myself for a few hours, reading and sifting and taking notes, holding off despair at the sheer number of people involved. Whoever is doing this has a serious grudge, and it's unlikely to be the carpenters or the sound and lighting people. Someone's feelings, someone's ego, have been badly bruised, and actors are the easiest to imagine taking umbrage at some slight, perceived or real.

I decide to start with those who auditioned for the major roles, and were rejected. Even that list is long. And the only way to winnow it down is to talk to the actors who made it. They all know one another, since they're often in competition for the same roles, and can give me a sense of the people behind the names.

Becky is back today, hanging out in the lounge, so I approach her and ask for a few moments of her time. When we're both seated in the office, she says, "This is about our gremlin, isn't it? I heard you've been enlisted to track down the creep. If there's any way I can help, I'm game." Never underestimate the rumour mill, I remind myself.

"Thanks. Actually, I could use your help. Anything we talk about in here will be kept confidential. You don't have to worry about it getting back to anyone, including Charlene and Jeremy." Even though she's not on the stage, I'm still a little starstruck. Her real persona is overlaid by the role she plays, and I feel like I'm talking to two people. "I've culled the actors who auditioned for your part." I hand her the headshots. "Can you look through them, tell me a bit about them? I'm interested in character stuff, how they handle disappointment, that kind of thing."

"You really think it's one of us? One of the actors?" I'm afraid I've offended her, but after a moment she says, "God, I hope not, I really hope not. That would be terrible." She sighs, starts shuffling through the pictures. "I may not know all of them, but let's start with this one. Norma." It's the angry ball-buster, the one who caused Jeremy to protect his private parts. "She's angry enough to want to strike back, but she'd be more likely to sue, or file a human rights complaint, than hang around here making mischief. Anyway, she's working, starring in a fringe production put on by an all -women company. I'm sure she's as happy as she'll ever be." She shuffles that photo to the bottom of the pile and concentrates on the next one. "This is Joanne, she's great. I think we're always competing for the same roles, though we never tell each other. Easier to stay friends that way. She's never shown any animosity, and I've known her for years. And this one, oh, what's her name." Her brow furrows in concentration. "Jackie. That's it. Very professional, very good. I'm surprised I beat her out." I'm not, though I didn't see Jackie's audition. We get through the small pile, and there are only two people she doesn't recognize, one of whom is the gum-chewing Lady of the Piercing. I can safely dismiss her as a suspect; she's too visible, too much of an airhead, to pull this off. That leaves just one possibility.

"Can you ask around about this one, Linda Meyer, see if anyone knows her? What she's like?"

"Sure, someone will know her. But do you really think it's a woman who's doing this?"

"No, just trying to cover all the bases. Here's the guys." I hand her the headshots of the men, and we start again.

"Okay. Barry is very sweet, he's a family man, very down to earth, very centred. He wouldn't do anything to hurt the company. And Jimmy, he's doing Lord Darlington, so he has no reason to complain. Oh, this fellow, Jim, I think, he lives right next door. I think he was given an audition just because his wife, Marlene, is such an active volunteer. Though I haven't seen her around much this season. He was terrible, of course, but he's still with us. Quite a trooper in his own way, he doesn't mind the more mundane tasks." I recognize him as the man working reception.

We go through the pictures rapidly; she's familiar with most of the men. I hold my breath till she gets to Jason's picture. She stares at it for a long moment, obviously considering what to say. "He's a piece of work. I'm not sure what he's up to, but he makes me nervous. Everybody's best friend, always volunteering to help, but underneath? And he can't act to save his life. I have no idea why Charlene tolerates him. She usually has better taste." She hesitates, biting her bottom lip. "He seems to have it in for Jeremy. And he certainly could pull off some of the stunts that have happened. He has the time, since he's always here, and the access. But he's ambitious, and I think he's trying a different tactic, ingratiating himself with Charlene, trying to push Jeremy out of the picture—that's more his style. I wouldn't put anything past him, though."

I'm relieved she can see Jason clearly. After Lillith's ringing endorsement of him, I was starting to worry that everyone was enchanted by him.

Only four of the headshots leave her shaking her head, and she writes down their names. "I'll see if I can find out about these guys too. I'll talk to Barry, if it's all right?" I nod as she continues, "This is all so strange. Community theatre isn't as cutthroat as professional theatre. Less histrionics. More opportunity. For instance, I know I'd never get the lead like this at Shaw or Stratford. In my twenty years, I've been allowed to star, to direct, to work on props, set design—almost all aspects of theatre. It's quite wonderful. Tensions do exist, but they're usually kept in check."

"What kind of tensions?"

"Oh, if your star has a bumpy romantic relationship with her co-star, that can spell trouble. Or if an actor is too big-headed to follow directions, that kind of thing. And of course there are resentments, backbiting, gossip. Whispered accusations of favouritism. Actors have big egos, it's almost a requirement. And their egos are easily bruised. After all, you put yourself forward at auditions, and if you're rejected, it's hard not to take it personally. But it's a tight community. If an actor gets a reputation for being difficult, he'll find himself blacklisted. So everyone makes a real effort to co-operate."

"What kind of reputation does this theatre have?"

"Are you kidding? It's at the top of the heap. Having Jeremy here, it's amazing. He draws in the audiences, we have long runs, and that's what all actors crave. Look how much work has gone into this play! Think how discouraging it would be if it only ran for a week, to small numbers." She shrugs. "The advance sales have been fantastic. And they have more subscribers than most companies. It's quite a privilege to be a part of this production."

"Becky, I really admire your acting ability. I'm not as sure as you seem to be that you wouldn't have been a star wherever you landed."

"It's a long, hard struggle to be a professional actor. It means sacrificing a lot, and even then, success isn't always about talent. I had a child, and a deadbeat ex-husband. My daughter needed stability; that meant a nine-to-five job with benefits, and being home most nights. I've been fortunate, though, because both my parents and my in-laws have bent over backward to help give me some freedom to stay involved."

"Your in-laws help?"

"Oh yes. They're appalled by their son's behaviour, and they love Judith, their granddaughter. It's kept me from becoming bitter and angry like our friend here." She taps Norma's photo. "I'm one of those women who actually has it all." She pushes her chair back and stands. "Well, if that's all, I'll be heading off, but do let me know if there is anything else you need from me."

Left alone, I copy down names and phone numbers of those actors Becky didn't know well, and who didn't get the parts they wanted. I decide on a direct approach. I'll call them and see what they're up to, pretending we're interested in their future availability.

Hours later, no further ahead, I pack it in and head to the house.

In spite of their affection for one another, Jeremy and Charlene are ruthlessly competitive, even for an audience of one. They are as starved for attention and as relentless in searching out the spotlight as the neediest members of the drop-in. Some nights, when I'm over for dinner and the back garden lights cause the glass on the sliding doors to reflect mirror images of them, I see how they are both captivated by their own profiles, staring into their own eyes, enthralled as they talk, lifting their chins almost in unison, turning slightly to the left and right, judging the best pose. There is usually no room for my worries and concerns. I can lose myself completely in the ongoing clash of egos and the melodrama of the moment. It's the most relaxing environment I know, better than meditation.

But not tonight. Dinner is no fun. The food is as good as always, and the kitchen is as warm and cheerful as usual, but the conversation is stilted, very unusual for this table. Jeremy keeps casting sidelong looks at Charlene, and Charlene does the same to him. They're obviously worried about each other, but God forbid they should actually talk about what's going on.

Of course, I have my own secrets I'm keeping from them, believing they have enough to deal with. I'd love to tell them about Mallick, but instead I take another bite of chicken to keep my mouth occupied. I can hear myself chewing, and the scratch of my knife on the plate is as irritating as fingernails down a chalkboard in the frequent silences.

Jeremy clears his throat and puts down his fork. "Dana, I was wondering, the people you and Charlene work with at the drop-in, what do you think they'd make of this play we're putting on? Would they see any relevance to their lives?"

I feel like I'm back in the classroom, unfairly pinioned by a professor, and unprepared. I stall with a forkful of wild rice, a sip or two of wine, giving myself time to come up with an answer he'll respect and understand.

"I have thought about it; it's hard not to. Language would be a problem, but not insurmountable. I think if we talked about the play first, told them what was going on, they'd relate all right." More wine. "They know what it's like to be ostracized, whispered about and labelled. They've experienced it since grade school, a lot of them." I turn to Charlene for support. "And they know what it's like to be silenced. They've felt the way society protects itself from unpleasant truths, maintains its illusions by blaming the victim. Fathers don't molest their daughters. Mothers don't stand by and let it happen. They know the sting of being blamed for conditions they find themselves in, what it's like when other people decide who and what you are, decide why you're not working, or making the grade, or living in a house like everybody else. They also know, some of them, what it's like to lose a child, to have it taken away by Children's Aid. Most of all they know poverty, in all its aspects. Mrs. Erlynne would be a hero for them, for fighting back, for surviving, for winning. The fact that she resorted to blackmail to avoid sinking, that wouldn't be seen as such a bad thing. She's been victimized for years, shunned, and she got her own back. They'd probably cheer."

Jeremy nods. "Good. Maybe we can arrange a special showing, have a discussion after."

Charlene perks up. "Oh, what a good idea. Why didn't I think of that? Dana, it would be so much fun, and the drama group! I can just see how excited they'll be." She stands and kisses Jeremy on the top of his head, while he beams, then she leaves to visit the bathroom. He takes advantage of the moment.

"I called the lawyers. It took them no time at all to learn he's serving time in the States. Extortion."

He's clearly happy about that, and so am I. One less person to worry about. But that leaves the bigger mystery for him. I don't want to leave him hanging.

"Jeremy, Jason's a bastard, and I'm going to get him."

I see by the play of emotions over his handsome face that he's heard the poison Jason's been dripping in people's ears, that he's been paralyzed by not wanting to hurt Charlene. Flickers of hope dance in his eyes, and he leans toward me. "How?"

"Wait and see. A couple more days, that's all I'll need."

There is no doubt shading the relief I see. He squeezes my hand and smiles.

Charlene bustles back in, re-energized and almost manic with ideas, but it's time for me to take myself home. I refuse the offer of a lift; I want to walk and think. It's a lovely night, the heat of the day replaced by a cool, gentle breeze.

I haven't had this much going on in my life for a long time. I think back to my relatively sheltered existence before Maryanne's disappearance, before her murder. All that time to read, and think, and maybe heal. It all seems a bit idyllic now, and self-indulgent. I've re-engaged with the world big time, and I may well be out of my depth. There's Ed to think about, and the guys at the house, and now the theatre. Not to mention that tomorrow morning I'll dress in this hooker outfit I'm carrying, and Miss Semple and I will be knocking at Mallick's door. By the time I get home and drag my weary body up the stairs, I'm feeling very small. Sleep seems far away, but eventually it comes and before I know it, it's morning again.

We're stalled for a while at Ossington, as the perspiring, impatient driver argues with a woman who is trying to use a transfer that's a couple days old. She's carrying a number of plastic bags, stuffed with papers and scraps of clothing, and the lower half of a Barbie doll. For the passengers, it's a bit of a show; no one's in too much of a hurry, rush hour is behind us, and the sun is still high in the sky. The driver wins, and the lady exits with a string of impressive curses flung over her shoulder. He closes the door, muttering to himself, and keeps up his not-so-internal monologue through the next few stops.

I love the Queen streetcar. Even now, in its elongated, accordion-like form, it beats every other bus, every other route the TTC has to offer. I know people who spend all day riding back and forth, if they can cadge a ticket. When you don't have a life, it's a way of connecting, feeling a part of the world, and there's so much to see, briefly framed through the wide windows: bums panhandling, giggling children and their harried mothers, posturing teenagers, bemused tourists, all caught up in their own moments, their fleeting concerns.

And it's the same inside the car, where a variety of languages, colours and classes are thrown together, at least for the length of the ride, in wary, watchful tolerance. This time of day, it's comfortable, not crowded, everyone has a seat, with space for packages and baby carriages and invisible companions. Way in the back, a tall, wildly bearded man carries on an animated one-way conversation about the state of the world. A few seats ahead of him an Asian woman studiously ignores him, clutching her shopping bags, possibly fearing mayhem and murder. A gum-mangling teenage couple to the right of me, both wearing headphones from which rhythmic static can be heard, stare straight ahead; the young man frees up one ear long enough to hold a portable phone to it, creasing his forehead in an effort to hear. "Romance" in the modern world.

It's a little late to be second-guessing myself. Besides, it's not that unlikely a scenario. When I lived on my own, I was often bothered by canvassers, salespeople and the occasional Jehovah's Witnesses who'd gone floor to floor, door to door in the building, irritating everyone. I never looked too closely at them, or questioned their credentials.

Miss Semple, perched beside me, has been sorting through the papers pinned to her clipboard, checking for pencils, straightening her hair, rummaging in her purse, all unmistakable signs of nervousness. I'm not a paragon of calm either. In less than thirty minutes, we'll be at Mallick's door, and our ruse is starting to seem a little flimsy.

Gerry and Diamond had accompanied us to the bus stop, with last-minute advice and imprecations directed at Mallick if we didn't return safely. We had to appear confident for them, but now it's just us, and as we get closer the reality of what we're about to attempt looms large. Miss Semple seems so fragile, vulnerable. If anything happened to her, I would be responsible.

"I haven't told you how nice you look." Miss Semple is typically trying to calm me, distract me.

"Thank you. You're no slouch either. We'll dazzle him." She has carefully applied her makeup, shedding years in the process, and is wearing her best dress, one she used to wear to work. I'm in my seductress tight skirt and blouse, heels and nylons. My legs are feeling a bit raw and scraped. I had to borrow Diamond's razor, and it was very used.

She pats my hand. "We'll do fine. We've certainly practised enough. I think we could fool anyone at this point, especially an ignorant bully like Mallick. And I want you to know, whatever happens, how grateful I am that you're taking me along with you. The very worst thing is feeling useless. Some people believe older people can't do anything important. It can be very frustrating."

"You've done so much already," I say, gesturing toward the forms, some already filled out with fictitious answers we'd carefully crafted.

She is pleased. She's worked very hard, at the computer in the mission, and everything looks official and businesslike. I take a deep, slow, calming breath. We'll pull it off, and besides, what could Mallick do to us in broad daylight? Still, I find myself wishing the streetcar would go just a little slower.

"You've done stuff like this before," I said, curious now, "office stuff?"

"Oh my, yes, for years and years. It was part of my job at the firm, to sit in on meetings and take minutes."

"You miss it?"

"I suppose I do. I enjoyed working. We never had children, you see, though we did try. It was just the two of us, my husband and I. We had forty years together. He was a good provider, a decent man; he held a position at the same factory he'd started with as a teenager, right up to the time he got sick. He had cancer, the doctors said there was nothing they could do. I left work to take care of him. Neither of us wanted him to die in hospital."

"It must have been hard."

"Yes it was. Harder for him, of course. He hated being a burden, that's how he put it, though I told him every day that I loved our time together. After he died, three years after his diagnosis, I didn't know what to do with myself. There was the insurance, and our savings, I didn't have to worry about money, but the days were so long."

"Then how did you wind up here?" I wince at the insensitivity of my question.

"It's very embarrassing." To confirm that, little pink flushes appear on her cheeks. "My world had grown so small, in our old apartment, nothing was the same without him, it seemed more like a prison than a home. I think I was just waiting to join him. So it was exciting and very different to travel all that way with the girls, the buses were very comfortable, not like the TTC. I loved every minute of it. My friends, you see, encouraged me to join them on day trips, outings really, they said I needed to get out, see a bit of the world. There were free packages up to Niagara Falls, to the casinos there. It was fun at first, almost magical, all the lights and sounds, harmless, or so I thought. I felt a bit wicked, but I kept going back. In less than a year, I'd lost everything. If it hadn't been for the mission, for the forgiveness I found there, I really think I'd have died of shame."

I wince again, this time in sympathy. "It happens to a lot to people. Good people."

She went on as though I hadn't spoken. "He was such a decent man. We were both very careful, never extravagant. I just don't know how I'll face him when my time comes." Her voice breaks, I reach out for her hand, and we waited for her composure to return.

Hesitantly I offer, "I'm not well-versed on heaven, but from what I do know, I don't believe there's any shame or blame happening there. Too much of that down here."

She rummages around in her purse, pulls out a Kleenex, dries her eyes and blows her nose. "Thank you, dear, that's good of you to say. Maryanne told me much the same when we chatted together. She was so kind, so generous with me. I know she had problems, I know drink could turn her into a whole other person, but the woman we knew would always come back to us."

"Did she talk much about her life?"

"Just that between men and liquor, her life had been very difficult. I know her father had been a drinker; he would beat her mother, and Maryanne herself. She kept finding men like that, violent, abusive. She called herself an optimist, always hoping she could change people. But she felt she was too old to change herself. I tried to get her to come to the mission with me, but she just laughed, not in a mean way, she said they weren't ready to take on someone like her. That she'd drive them to drink."

"Tell me about the mission, is it new? Whereabouts is it?"

"Downtown. It's been around for years, apparently. We used to go there, the ladies from our church, on Christmas, Easter and Thanksgiving. We'd bring lots of food, and try to bring a little festivity to the place, a little cheer to the people there. They used to be mostly men, men who've lived on the streets for ages. But there's a separate group for women now, and that's where I help out. I fill in forms for pensions or home care, escort them to appointments, that kind of thing. It's brought meaning back to my life. The pastor is a good man; he doesn't preach at people, he listens, like he listened to me the day I broke down and confessed how much trouble I was in over the gambling. I'd thought he'd be appalled at what I had done, the money I'd thrown away, but he was angry at the government instead, for allowing such establishments in the province. Such a good man. You'd like him, Dana."

I wonder if she knows that compulsive gambling, like alcoholism, is supposed to be an illness, and whether that would make any difference. Probably not, I decide. She'd believe in personal responsibility, and wouldn't have much time for the addiction excuse.

We're at our stop, and we collect our things and disembark, standing for a moment in the bright sunlight. I peer up the street, and see Mallick's car parked a few doors away from his house. Show time.

I ring the first doorbell on a house a few down from Mallick's, pause, then ring it again. No one home. I turn to Miss Semple, grinning, about to say, well, that was easy, when the door opens a couple of inches, and an elderly female face peers out at us.

"Yes, can I help you?"

"Good morning. We're conducting a survey in the area, and I wonder if we could have a few moments of your time?"

"Oh, how nice. Do come in. I'm Ruth. Please watch the cat doesn't get out."

The cat is huge, a balloon monster of fur and fat and dandruff that can barely stand, never mind dart out the door. It collapses with a huff of expelled air as we carefully step over it, following the lady into a darkened, odoriferous hallway that ends at the kitchen. It's a nice kitchen, though quite tiny. If the cat grows any larger, they'll be no room for anything else. It's carefully kept, though there's a sharp smell here too, and Ruth seats us at a small table with plastic fruit as a centrepiece and creaky wooden chairs around it, while she puts on the kettle. She moves very slowly, though I suspect compared to her ordinary pace she's positively bustling.

"I can't remember the last time Matilda and I had callers. There were those Jehovah people, so neatly dressed and proper, remember, Matilda? But they stopped coming after a while. It's just us, Matilda and I, but we keep each other company."

Matilda has made it into the kitchen, her four legs straining under her weight; she mews plaintively and pees on the floor. We pretend not to notice. For the sake of apparent legitimacy, Miss Semple selects a blank form and a sharpened pencil from her stock, and begins with our first question, but it quickly becomes clear that we could have been axe murderers and Ruth would still have let us in, served us tea and talked our ears off.

"My husband and I bought this place over fifty years ago. I remember clear as day how excited we were to get out of his parents' basement, into our own home. It made our marriage more real, somehow, and then of course I was pregnant with Lilly. Just a moment, I'll show you."

She leaves us alone, splashing unaware through the puddle of urine on her way out, and we hear her searching for something, bringing back a small, framed picture.

"Here's my Lilly, my life, we took this in the back yard. Have you ever seen such a bright smile? It was a terrible tragedy, she was killed on the street, hit by a car, she was only nine and a half, always rushing, always eager to burst through the front door and wrap her arms around me. We knew everyone on the street back then, all the children and their parents, even their grandparents, the church was filled with mourners the day of her funeral. So many flowers, from people's own gardens, there were gardens everywhere then, people made an effort, not like now. And then my husband passed, about ten years ago, so it's just me and Matilda. There was no one left to call for his funeral. I don't know where everyone went, couldn't tell you who my neighbours are now, it's just noise and cars and shouting. I don't go out much anymore."

Miss Semple handles the picture like a holy relic, which I suppose it is. After making appreciative sounds she gamely moves on to the next question.

"Oh, I don't do much shopping. I used to know the Powells, they owned the local grocery store, and they had young boys, clean and polite, who'd load your bags on their bikes and deliver them right to your door. Now I feel like I live in China, or some other foreign place, no one seems to speak English anymore, or care who their customers are. I sometimes have to spend an hour searching for a decent piece of fruit or vegetable for my supper. And the children! They run around in packs; the girls dress, forgive me, like prostitutes, and the boys look like thugs. They frighten me. Matilda and I keep our own company, and we have our programs, our favourites, you know."

She brings out some stale biscuits from a battered tin and, placing them on a slightly chipped plate, sits down with a sigh of something approaching contentment, more than ready for the next inquiry.

Squishy with cups of Lipton's tea, it's forty-five minutes before we manage to extricate ourselves from the one-way conversation and make our escape.

Miss Semple's a bit wilted as we retrace our steps to the sidewalk. She dabs at her eyes with a tissue, sniffling a little. "That could have been me, all walled up inside my home, frightened and just waiting to die. How terribly sad that she's so alone. And Matilda will not last much longer, how ever will she cope with that? I think I'll talk to the pastor; perhaps he can arrange visitors for her."

"Good idea. Let's crisscross, in case anyone is watching, we'll be more visible."

We cross the street, get no response, and cross again, edging closer to our target. We smile at a young Asian mother with her arms full of a kicking, wailing toddler, she can't speak English, we gesture apologetically to each other and retreat. One man slams the door in our faces; we've woken him up and he's angry. Two more to go, and I'm starting to hope for another gabby resident—every time I look toward Mallick's my heart thumps in my chest. Which reminds me to undo the third button on my blouse; we need to get inside, and if a little cleavage will help, I'm game, nervous game. I almost trip up the stair as I try to look down my own blouse.

Chapter Eight

Here we are. After two more empty houses, this is the Mallick home. We don't dare pause, continuing without comment up the stairs and right to the front door. I look at Miss Semple, she nods encouragement, and I ring the bell. The door is flung open before the sound of the buzzer dies down, and there he is, in all his squat ugliness. I find my mouth drying up, leaving me without words.

Miss Semple comes to the rescue.

"Good afternoon, sir. We're with Advance Marketing, and we're canvassing a number of Riverdale streets. If you'll give us a few moments of your time, you'll be entered in a draw that has wonderful prizes: gift baskets, fun all-expense paid vacations and great discounts on groceries and clothing."

He glowers at us from underneath a low, protruding brow. He's in rumpled pants and a shirt that might have been white a few days ago, but now is covered with stains and sweat. The sleeves are rolled up, his arms are thick and covered with hair, and there's an aura of threat about him that's a bit chilling, even in this heat. He's shaking his head, about to close the door.

I step forward, leaning in confidentially. "If you don't mind, we've had so many cups of tea, this is such a friendly street, we'd really appreciate the use of your bathroom."

His head is even with my chest, and I'm offering him an unobstructed view. He seems a bit mesmerized. I actually reach out and touch one arm, keeping my fingers lightly on the curly black hair. "We're not supposed to ask to use the facilities, so don't tell our boss if he shows up, but we've been doing this for hours. I'm not sure what they expected us to do."

Miss Semple nods vigorously. Mallick laughs, a guttural explosion that sounds more like a fart, and waves us in.

"For ladies in distress, I will make time. Come into the kitchen, and I'll answer your questions."

He leads us down an ordinary hallway into his kitchen, which is bright with sun but could use a little darkness to disguise the mess. Dishes are piled in the sink, newspapers cover the table, and the garbage bin is overflowing. Ashtrays filled with butts are everywhere. This is a man's house, I doubt there's a Mrs. Mallick anywhere.

Miss Semple is pointed toward the bathroom, while he clears off a chair for me, and removes some of the clutter from the table.

"You will forgive the mess." He makes it sound more like an order than a request, and I nod quickly, and repeatedly, finally forcing myself to stop. He is hovering so close, he's taking all the oxygen. "A man without a woman is in a sad state, don't you agree?"

I hear with some relief the flush of the toilet, and Miss Semple appears in the entrance, smiling brightly.

"Your turn, Charlotte." It takes me a minute to remember who Charlotte is, then I'm back on script, trying to struggle out of the chair without knocking Mallick over. He barely gives me enough space, but I squeeze by, while Miss Semple settles herself and her files at the table.

The bathroom looks like the toilet in the drop-in after a busy night. Grime on all the surfaces, pubic hair clings to porcelain in the tub, towels and puddles on the floor that Matilda couldn't hope to compete with. I do have to pee, and I gingerly lower myself to the seat. Near my feet there's the body of a squashed cockroach, which is just the kind of accessory every bathroom needs. Afterward, standing at the sink, running the tap to mask the sound, I carefully open his medicine cabinet. There's a large collection of pill bottles, mostly sleeping pills and painkillers, and as I rummage through them, I have a eureka moment. None bear Mallick's name, though he may use them, either recreationally or to dull some ache of his. Why else would he have kept them? They're all for women, and all filled at a Parkdale pharmacy. I wish I had a pen with me; instead, I try to memorize some of the names on the labels.

Gingerly closing the cabinet door, I wash my hands and flush the toilet, taking a deep, calming breath, then go back to the kitchen where Miss Semple is dutifully proceeding with the questionnaire. Mallick's expression of bored impatience brightens at my reappearance. He evens stands, leads me back to my chair, one hand on my arm. I smile in a rigour of coquettish delight at his semblance of Old World manners.

"Now I will ask you a question. It's only fair, after all." He turns on me what he no doubt believes the full force of his charm, yellow teeth and all. "A beautiful young woman such as yourself, are you also alone?"

"At the moment, yes. My boyfriend was running around behind my back. I just found out a few days ago." I try for disillusioned and sad, and it seems to work.

"He's a fool. What you need is a real man who appreciates what he has. It's no good for us, in the prime of life, to have no one to turn to, no one to comfort us. Look at me, a man of property and substance, with so much to offer, and still I sleep alone."

His foul breath is overpowering, as is the thought of his hands on my body. I shiver, repulsed, and he thinks his charm and "substance" are getting to me.

"Next question," chirps Miss Semple.

"Allow me." He leans over, takes the questionnaire and her pencil, and begins to fill in his answers quickly. "It is easier this way. And then we can speak of other things."

It takes him less than two minutes, and he hands the form back to Miss Semple with a flourish. "How much does it pay, this job?"

"Minimum wage." It just popped into my brain.

"You are worth so much more than that. I have other properties, businesses, perhaps I could use an attractive young woman such as yourself."

"Oh," I say, batting my eyelashes at him, trying for coquettish but probably looking like I have something in my eye. "What kind of businesses?"

"Nursing homes, property management, investments. Since I emigrated from Serbia, I have worked very hard to establish myself in this city."

"It must be very lonely. Do you have any family here, or are they back in Serbia?"

"My sister and her husband live here. This is her house. I bought it for her. She is back home now, visiting family, but she wouldn't leave unless I agreed to stay with her husband. She said he would be too lonely, but I think she is a jealous woman who doesn't trust her man. Not that anyone else would have him, though I suppose he too is successful in a small way."

"It's good of you to relieve her mind. Are these homes you own in the downtown area? I don't drive, you see, don't own a car."

"You should have a car, and other fine things. Yes, my places are in the west end, easily reached. You live where?"

"Spadina and Queen."

"Perfect. Do you have a phone number?"

"Not yet. I moved recently, and the cost ..." I trail off, downcast.

"Here, this is my cell phone number; I can be reached anytime, day or night. We must speak more; there is much I can do for you."

The loud buzz isn't an alarm in my brain; it's the doorbell. He curses sharply, catches himself and shrugs apologetically. "One moment, please."

I look frantically around the kitchen, for anything that might be a clue. It's such chaos that it's impossible to find anything, not a scrap of mail, not a key to the Parkdale building. Men's voices speaking what I assume is Serbian are getting closer. Mallick is irritated, his seductive dance interrupted, and his face is angry and red as he stands at the entrance to the kitchen. Behind him is a man in a suit, carrying a fat briefcase. He's almost a clone of Mallick, only tidied up and taller, but that barely suppressed rage is there too. Mallick doesn't bother with introductions.

"Ladies, I fear I must attend to business." He walks over to me, takes my hand and plants a wet kiss on it. "Please call me. You will not regret it."

Miss Semple gathers up her files, as I try hard to memorize the face of the new villain. With the visitor glaring at us, we make it out the front door. I don't know about Miss Semple, but my legs are shaking, and I need to take in great gulps of fresh, clean air.

Once we hit the sidewalk, we abandon further pretense and quickly walk away. Only when we're at the bus stop does Miss Semple react. She starts to giggle helplessly, her whole body trembling, tears running down her cheeks. She holds on to me for support and I start laughing too, giddy and so relieved to be out of his reach. We're still in the throes of hysteria when the streetcar arrives, but we make it up the steps and collapse into our seats, abandoning any attempt at decorum.

"Oh my!" Miss Semple tries to leer at me, leaning close, mimicking Mallick. "You deserve the best, you deserve me! Come into my filthy home, ignore the unmade bed and roaches, I am a man of property!"

"Yuck! What a disgusting animal he is. What a pigsty of a place. Wait, let's see the form he grabbed. Thank God you had it laid out so professionally, can you imagine if we'd just faked it?"

We find his scribbled questionnaire, but his writing is hard to decipher, an obscure scrawl with lots of loops and flourishes.

"I can't try to read this now, but we have his cell phone number, and that's potentially useful. Your pencil?" She passes one to me, and I write down some of the names from the prescription bottles, asking Miss Semple if she'd also peered inside.

"I'm afraid I really did have to use the facilities," she says, a little embarrassed. "It never occurred to me."

"That's okay, I'm a natural snoop. Now, I need you to close your eyes and try to remember what his visitor looked like, what he was wearing, hair colour, anything you noticed."

We both close our eyes and think hard for a moment. I start a list. Between us we come up with a fairly accurate portrait, which I read back.

"Five nine, thick black hair, combed straight back, bushy eyebrows, bad complexion, stocky and muscular build, cheap suit, rumpled, black loafers with tassels, wrong colour socks, white or off-white, probably has to shave a couple of times a day, briefcase was faux leather, stuffed and well-used. Had a watch, and a wedding ring. Guttural voice. Bad temper. You know, this might be the guy who was with Mallick when he took Maryanne. Diamond and Gerry will be able to tell us. What a day we've had. What a woman you are!"

"What a team we make, you mean. I haven't felt so alive in years."

"A little terror goes a long way."

We're approaching our stop, and there are some very worried men waiting for our return. As soon as we hit the sidewalk, we hear cheering from the porch, and Diamond races across the street and grabs us both in a great embrace.

"You're back. You're safe!"

Gerry lumbers down the stairs, tears streaming down his cheeks, and I hold him while he convulses in body-wracking sobs.

"I was so scared. I thought he'd got you."

"We're all right, Gerry." I pat his back while he continues to cry. "Truly. We got inside, and made it out. C'mon into the house, we'll tell you all about it."

I hobble upstairs, desperate to get out of the shoes and hooker outfit. I have a new appreciation for my usual clothing, so loose and soft against my skin, and for my running shoes, which I tie while trying to ignore the rise of blisters on my poor feet. I'll have to scrounge up some Band-Aids if I'm to go for the walk I plan to take later this afternoon. Stress management, that's how I think of it. When I'm done, I go back downstairs, just in time to hear Gerry, who is anxious to get his room back, badgering Michael.

"I'm warning you, you lazy bastard, if you don't get out of my bed soon, I'm crawling right in on top of you! See what that does for your ribs! Flatten you like a bed bug, that'll get you moving!"

Michael makes wet kissing noises. "Come to me, big boy, I can handle you. 'Course, first you have to get off the floor. That should take a year or two."

"Talk about your floorplay." Diamond had gone for coffee, courtesy of Miss Semple, and returns just in time to add this nugget to the conversation. Balancing a full cardboard cup holder, he does the rounds, then finds his own spot on the floor. Gerry informs me that they have news of their own.

"Tommy's done a runner. The sorry junkie bastard's trying to hitchhike his way to B.C., like any sane person would pick him up."

"How come?"

"He was supposed to be in court today—possession, he would have done time. Anyway, he left us his cat. Name of Alex."

Michael lifts one edge of his blanket, just enough to show the mangy furball sound asleep next to him.

"We could manage, I suppose. We'd need a litter box, and a collar for him. He might help with the mice." Soft-hearted Miss Semple is hooked, especially when Alex, at the sound of her voice, lifts his little head and opens orange eyes, blinking at her. It's love. Alex stands, stretching each of his limbs, licking the odd bit of fur, then leaps down and does a slow, winding dance around her legs.

"I've given him a bath, so he shouldn't be carrying any nasties," says Diamond.

"Yeah, well, ya shoulda bathed Michael too, there's no telling what that poor cat picked up from him." Michael sends his pillow flying over to Gerry, who doesn't even have to duck; it lands on the floor a few feet from him.

The next few minutes are spent fussing over the cat, pouring out some of the creamers into a lid for him to lap up. When everyone is finally settled, Miss Semple holding the cat, she begins to recount our adventure, warned by Gerry not to leave anything out.

She's good at this; if most of her audience weren't on the floor they'd have been on the edge of their seats. When she reaches the point of my snooping into the medicine cabinet, I read out some of the names that were on the pill bottles, the few I'd been able to remember. No one recognizes any of them. Diamond and Gerry do recognize Mallick's angry visitor from our description.

"That's the evil bastard, all right," Gerry proclaims, while Diamond nods agreement.

Finally, Miss Semple pulls out the form, the one Mallick wrote his cell phone number on.

"Whoa," says Michael. "Let me see that."

"Me too, no hogging." Gerry has one arm out, but he's not getting up without assistance, so Michael wins. He whistles as he stares at the form.

"Will you look at that? Well, that's it then. We know what we have to do next."

"Oh yeah, Mr. Smart Guy, and what's that?" Gerry's impatient to see the paper; Miss Semple plucks it from Michael, and, gently unseating the cat, walks it over to him.

"We have to lure him into an ambush. He wants Dana for sure; he'll come if she calls. And we'll be waiting. All of us."

Everyone's thinking hard until Diamond interjects, "I'm sorry, Michael. You can't be part of this, not without damaging yourself again. But you're right; his interest in Dana is our hook. We just have to have a foolproof plan, one that won't get any of us hurt, especially Dana."

"The best thing would be to get him to agree to see me at Fortune Street." I'm thinking aloud now. "Find out when he's there, and I'll call him, tell him I need to see him right away, get him to invite me over."

"No bloody way. All that'll do is trap you too. We couldn't get through that door once it's locked again."

"Maybe I could unlock it, Gerry, while he's distracted. I told you Derek and his gang will help us, that'll give us more muscle."

Silence again, tinged with fear.

"I don't know, Dana. It seems like you'll be taking a big risk, being alone with him." Diamond is tense, his arms hugging his legs tightly.

"What if she slipped some of my pills into his drink, like a mickey? Knock him right out!"

Michael's suggestion isn't bad; we mull it over. The specifics elude us, though.

"Wouldn't he be able to taste it? The drugs, I mean?" asks a worried Miss Semple.

"Let's find out." Diamond's up, and dropping two pills into the remnants of his coffee. He swirls the still-hot liquid around till they melt, then takes a sip, instantly making a face. "Bitter," he pronounces. "Booze would hide it better, and I'm sure the bastard drinks."

"Or what if you have your friend Derek and his guys, have them hiding near the front porch, and if Mallick opens the door for you, they could rush him? At least then you'd have protection, and we'd be inside."

"That's not bad, Michael. But there'd be a terrible chance that we might get the door slammed in our faces. Game over."

He thinks about that. I'm feeling quite proud of him, he's using his brain to good effect.

"So we have to draw him out. We need a diversion. Something to bring him running outside." He lowers his head a moment, then says loudly, "His car! If something was happening to his car, he wouldn't stop to think, he'd come roaring out of that house."

I find myself nodding. "Yes, you've got something there. He's very proud of his car. If I was already inside, tracking down where he's keeping the ladies, and you and Derek's guys started trashing the car, being really, really noisy, he couldn't call the cops, could he? He wouldn't want them inside without time to hide whatever he's about. I don't think he'd even stop to lock the door, he'd be so furious."

"And once he's outside, the guys have to hold him so he can't get back in. So you'll be safe, and so will the women."

Diamond is nodding enthusiastically. "We have to be sure the other guy is gone first. There's usually a shift change when Mallick shows up at night, his confederate, he's a younger guy, just muscle I think, leaves a few minutes later."

"If he knows I'm coming over, he'll get rid of anyone else pretty quickly. He wouldn't want word getting back to his brother-in-law." It's breathtaking, absolutely breathtaking. We have a plan!

"Okay, that's it then. Diamond, can you take a message to Derek? I'll write it out, ask him to stand by tomorrow night, have his boys ready."

Miss Semple is worried. "Do you think this fellow Derek will be willing to break the law like this?"

I grin at her. "Oh yes. He has some experience. And don't worry about me, guys. I'm not anxious to take any unnecessary risks."

I urgently need to walk, I'm so filled with tension my brain has seized up. This is what it's like to have an addiction, I think to myself. This physical longing for movement, for a change of scene. "I've got to leave now, but we'll meet again in the morning, if that's all right with you, Miss Semple?"

She nods, willing to sacrifice another day at the mission to see this through.

"I can feel this coming to a resolution; we're very close to rescuing those women. By the way, who's got bandages for my poor, blistered feet?"

The best way I know to handle all this growing tension, and to open my mind to new ideas, is to walk, far and fast. I take the streetcar to the subway, and the subway to Broadview. From there I'll spend a good hour heading east along the Danforth, before hopping on the subway once again for High Park, as Charlene and Jeremy, anxious to show their appreciation for my efforts, have asked me to a back yard barbecue with just the three of us.

People have it easier in the east end, or perhaps they would say they've worked harder, made better choices, both of which are probably true. The tempo of the neighbourhood is more upbeat, laughter can be heard punctuating conversations between women who carry themselves with confidence. The houses that line the side streets are single-family dwellings, and sculpted gardens compete with each other. Even the stores are more welcoming, with none of the warning signs about shoplifters or credit notices that are ubiquitous in Parkdale. The fruit in the stalls looks healthier, plumper and free of bruises, and so do the children. Clothing stores rather than clothing outlets, coffee shops that don't carry doughnuts, two bookstores within blocks of each other, everything clean and dust-free. Here and there one does see the occasional panhandler, but even they look like they've made an effort to spruce up a bit, and never snarl invectives when you pass them by without yielding some change.

The familiar reasserts itself as prosperity peters out, walking farther east past Pape: shoppers thin out; the air seems to change, and not for the better. More men than women can be seen on the street, hands in their pockets, shoulders slumped, the burden of long hours with nothing to do lying heavily on them. And the prevalent skin colour changes abruptly from white to dark; English is heard less than other languages.

I wonder if they'll find the prosperity and acceptance evidenced by the Danforth Greeks, and whether it will come any time soon.

I can't help checking out Mallick's street, though I'm cautious enough not to approach the house itself. He's not there anyway, at least his car is not in evidence, so I keep walking, sparing a thought for the incontinent cat lady, wondering how she'll take to Miss Semple's pastor.

I like walking alone, perhaps because I live with so many people. It gives me time to think and, if necessary, time and space to change whatever mood I may find myself in. Not to mention it's the only exercise I can bear. The current fitness and health craze has led to so many establishments being created where people can lift weights or ride bikes that go nowhere. I use the city instead, seeking out different trails in various neighbourhoods, maintaining a fast pace, sometimes seeking out the hilly areas like Rosedale, sometimes just the flat concrete like the sidewalks here.

It's a few minutes to four as I enter the subway at Woodbine, anxious to beat the end-of-workday crowds. Though I prefer walking, or at least being above ground, Toronto's subway system is fast and efficient, as long as it's not either of the rush hours. *Rush hour* is a misnomer to start with, since it's at least two hours in the morning and another two in the early evening. During those times, breathing in the exhalations of so many strangers, a person could long for a thick shield of metal between him and the next person, even if it meant being stuck on the Gardiner. Currently, there's a contest on for TTC riders, looking for happy stories to bolster the pleasurable aspects of leaving the car at home.

Off-peak hours though, there are always seats, and the air is cool, especially if you stand strategically under the ceiling vents. For those without air-conditioning at home, it presents a lovely alternative to sweltering if tickets aren't a problem.

I'm happy with my exquisite timing: when the car doors open, there are only two other passengers aboard. One is a well-nourished, clean-cut suburban white kid in hip-hop gear, the other a young braided black man, scrawny and outfitted in combat pants and muscle shirt. He has a nice face, not much flesh on it, but pleasant enough. I take a seat equidistant between the two.

I close my eyes briefly, just enjoying the play of forced air on my head and body, and check in with myself to see if my subconscious has come up with any new ideas about Charlene's gremlin. Nothing yet, but I am much more relaxed now, if just a little tired.

When I open my eyes again, as we're pulling into the next gloriously empty station, I notice the white kid staring with a peculiarly longing expression down the rows to where the young black man is sprawled, feet on the bench in front of him. The black guy can't keep still, he is going through all his pockets, on the sides and in back, pulling out stuff and sorting everything into little piles.

It takes me a minute to realize he is sorting dime bags of pot. Living the suburban kid's wet dream. He must be quite stoned to be doing this so openly, and I feel an impulse, just before common sense kicks in, to caution him. There must be some event in the city tonight, some concert going on for him to be so busy and bursting with weed.

The expression on the white kid's face makes it clear that it's not easy for a white male who has to trek into the downtown area to radiate cool, no matter what FUBU gear he has on, no matter what Eminem has done to rehabilitate the image of white rappers, so damaged by Vanilla Ice. He doesn't know yet that the fix is in, that he just has to wait a few years to reassert his Darwinian destiny; it will all come together when he's settled into a career and bought his first home and sensible family car and he's shouting at his kids to turn off that godawful racket. The other will likely be doing time, another statistic of a devastated community.

I notice that a baggie full of smaller dime bags has dropped under the seat. Sometimes I think I'm a little too empathetic, and this is one of those times. I'm thinking he's probably been fronted the dope in advance of selling it, and that he'll be in big money trouble if he loses half his stock. And he's too high to notice.

I catch his eye, smile non-judgmentally, and point down near his feet. His initial alarm washes away in relief as he grabs the errant bag and settles it into his lap, smiling angelically at me. By the time we're at the major interchange station at Bloor, he's got everything together, and heads for the exit doors near me. He stops in front of me briefly, making a high-five, which I reciprocate, surprised that something is transferred during the salute. Two very big, very nice buds. I realize I'm staring at them as they nestle openly in my palm, even as people are starting to crowd in, so I quickly pocket them, as the suburban boy salivates.

I briefly play with the notion of submitting this episode to the TTC contest, laughing out loud at the probable reaction and disconcerting my new seatmates enough that they shuffle their bums a little away from me. This beats a bottle of wine or flowers, which I couldn't afford anyway; Charlene will be well pleased with my offering.

By the time we get to the Dundas West station, I'm so scrunched in that I can hardly extricate myself long enough to get out the doors. There's no way I'm going to crowd onto a bus after that, and it's early enough that I can walk the rest of the way.

High Park is not my favourite neighbourhood. While South Parkdale is ninety percent tenants, High Park is mostly made up of homeowners. The residents only associate themselves with Parkdale (adopting the geographic North Parkdale label) when they are trying to keep rooming houses and group homes out of their safe streets. For a time a number of homes on one of High Park's tree-lined streets had black and white lawn signs reading "One Is Too Many," protesting halfway houses and other down-market establishments encroaching on their area. Charlene and Jeremy contend that I shouldn't judge the whole community on the basis of a few "yahoos," and I grudgingly admit they're right.

I might have been travelling through Europe instead of barrelling through tunnels under the city: Greek storefronts and restaurants have been replaced by similar establishments bearing Polish signs; baklava and lamb supplanted by perogies and cabbage rolls. I look into shop windows along Roncesvalles as I pass by, many piled high with bakery items that remind me how ready I am for dinner.

A moment's inattention results in a pedestrian collision with two men exiting one of the smaller establishments.

"Charlotte!"

I'm in a bear hug, that is, I'm being hugged by a guy who smells much the same as a bear. I'm trying to extricate myself when the name seeps in, and as I step back with a heart that's stuttering wildly, I see that it's Mallick who has had his arms around me.

Standing beside him is his suspicious friend who'd demanded he get rid of us. He's no happier now, almost hissing at Mallick, rattling off commands to him. Mallick waves him off, and he spins on his heel and storms away.

"What a happy coincidence!" he burbles. I try to match his expression of pleased surprise, wondering if there's any colour left in my face. "I had hoped to hear from you today, I was desolated that you didn't call. Yet here you are."

Thinking fast, I lower my eyes and softly say, "My boyfriend came back."

"Oh, what a pity. You don't need him, you know, he's not worthy of a woman like you. You need a man who can appreciate you. A man like me."

"That's very kind of you."

"And what brings you to this neighbourhood?"

"I'm visiting my grandmother," I say, like Little Red Riding Hood to the wolf. "We always get together on Friday nights for dinner."

"Then allow me to drive you. No, I won't take no for an answer. It will give us time to talk!"

He has me securely by the arm, leading me across the street to his BMW, which is only marginally tidier than his house. He opens the passenger door with a flourish, and I get in, wondering if I'll ever get out again. I decide to give him Charlene's address, and hope for the best as he grunts his way into the driver's seat. He doesn't start the car right away, but turns to look at me, much as I was looking at those pastries. I take the initiative.

"Why is your friend always so angry?"

"Aach, he's no friend of mine, he's a fool. If he wasn't my sister's husband, I would not put up with him. He has no balls; he gave them to her on a plate when they got married. He thinks he is better than me, smarter, but he's just a glorified clerk. Do you know what he does? He hands money to drunks, so they can drink some more. What a strange country this is, paying people to be useless!"

"He's a welfare worker?"

"Something like that. For the province. And because of that, he thinks he's better than me." His face is red and angry, I've clearly pressed the right button. "Back home, he'd be nothing. Something under my shoe. Yet he talks to me like I am an idiot. Me!"

I must have learned something from Charlene and Jeremy after all these months of watching rehearsals and listening to the advice they give to their actors. I remember an exercise in which they take an established character like Ophelia and put her into situations that Shakespeare never imagined, asking the bright hopefuls to respond in character. So my character is a troubled young woman, overly dependent on the men in her life, who always let her down. Immature, resentful, she'd be impressed by a man with a fat wallet and an expensive car, who can take her places, buy her things. And she'd be more than ready to be rescued from the drudgery of minimum-wage jobs. And a brain wave hits!

"I hate drunks. My mother was a drunk, a nasty, falling-down drunk. And you're exactly right. As soon as she got her cheque, she'd drink it away. Didn't matter whether there were any groceries, or if I needed clothes. The only thing that mattered to her was the bottle." I swipe at my eyes angrily, and lower my head, seemingly on the verge of tears.

Mallick lays one meaty, sweaty hand, like a skinned animal carcass, over my own. I shudder at the contact, but don't pull away.

"You poor girl. You understand, then, what I'm telling you. People like my brother-in-law, they don't care where the money goes. Every month they send out the cheques, every month they're pissed away on cheap wine. It's insane. Meanwhile, deserving children like you, innocent, hard-working, pay the price. I'm sure the government doesn't offer to help you!"

"No. You should see how much tax they take off my paycheque

every week, and I hardly make anything. Yet my mother used to get money back! Every year! And she never paid any taxes to start with!"

Mallick tsks-tsks, squeezing my poor fingers painfully. He then sticks the key in the ignition, and starts the car.

"Perhaps you have a little time? I would love to show you one of my other properties, it's in the neighbourhood. Would you like to see?"

I shrug, still seemingly upset.

"We won't go in this time, so you won't be late for your grandmother. But you will see that I am a substantial businessman. Not some pimply, unfaithful boy. Charlotte, I like you very much, and I would like to take care of you. It is lonely for me, with only my sister and that arrogant bastard for company."

He pulls into traffic with his horn blaring, causing those behind him to stand on their brakes and honk back. That accomplished, we move half a block and we're at a standstill, the cars bumper-to-bumper in full rush-hour mode. He moves his hand from atop mine and places it on my knee. I'm thankful for the jeans I'm wearing, as he squeezes my thigh in a salacious parody of comfort.

"I'm so confused. I loved Gerald," I say, trying to recall if I've named the boyfriend yet. "And he's hurt me so badly. But I'm not sure I'm ready to jump into something else right away. You're a nice man, Mr. Mallick ..."

"Call me Stephan, please."

"Yes, Stephan." He squeezes so hard I almost yelp. "Gerald would never take me anywhere, buy me anything. He saved that for his other girlfriends."

We're moving again; I want to leap out of the car almost as

much as I want to get inside his house. There isn't enough water in Lake Ontario to shower off the slime of this guy, who belches contentedly by my side. What a Prince Charming!

"But I wouldn't want to come between you and your family."

"You don't worry about anything. Certainly not that bastard of a brother-in-law. Always at me to be careful, always double-checking everything I do. He sees spies everywhere, like an old woman looking under her bed at night. A man must be a man, he must risk to win. And I am such a man!" To emphasize this, he blares his horn again, this time at the ragged squeegee kid at the corner of Queen and Roncesvalles who dared to approach the car as it turned, but who now is startled into flipping Mallick the finger. I console myself that there's only a few more blocks to go till we arrive at his building.

"Garbage everywhere in this city. They should round them up, put them in jail. I don't believe in coddling people like that. Not those on drugs, not those on booze. Cut off their supply, cut off their money, make them work or starve. That's the only way. Teach them respect."

"I agree, I think. If my mother hadn't got those payments every month, if she'd had to work for a living, my life could have been better. There wouldn't have been all those terrible scenes, all that screaming at me."

He's touched. And to show it he squeezes my thigh again. I'm going to have bruises all over my leg.

"In my nursing homes, there is a regime of discipline. No drinking, no money to waste on liquor. Bad behaviour is punished. One day they will thank me for saving them, I am sure of that."

We are pulling into Fortune Street; I avert my head, not wanting to be recognized by Derek if he's out and about. Stephan parks by the house and points with pride to the building.

"This is mine."

"Oh, it's so big!"

"Yes. This property is very valuable. The whole area is going to be going up and up, very soon. Places like mine will double in price. When the time is right, I will sell, and pocket a fortune."

Sometimes I think every property owner in Parkdale is simply holding on, awaiting the boom—while every tenant and housing worker hopes it never happens.

"Can we go in?"

"Not yet. We must know each other better. Understand each other first."

I try pushing that red button. "'Cause your brother-in-law might not like it?"

He's very easy to get to. His face reddens angrily, but he shakes his head. "No, it has nothing to do with him, everything to do with us. Trust is important, critical here. There are some who might not understand the necessity of what I do." My heart sinks when he starts up the engine again; I was so close to getting inside. "When you and I, when we are together like a man and a woman should be, then I will show you everything."

I almost shout, "I'm ready now! Take me inside!" But I bite my bottom lip instead, understanding how reckless that would be. Mallick is a buffoon, but he's also dangerous, and no one knows I'm in his car. I don't want to disappear, or be beaten as badly as Michael. For the moment, I have to concentrate on getting to Charlene's, and away from him.

Chapter Nine

"Then what happened?" Charlene is leaning forward on the lawn chair, passing me the joint she rolled with alacrity a few minutes earlier.

"He drove me here, groped me a little more and planted a disgusting kiss right on my lips." I inhale deeply, holding the smoke for a long moment before breathing again.

We're sitting in the cool, shaded end of the garden, which is lush with ferns of all sizes and shapes, ranging from deep green to light. Classical Grecian busts of ethereal females peak up here and there through the fronds. Toward the front, nearer the house, the sun glares down on roses and flowering bushes, splashes of colour bathing in the light. Most people these days tear up their lawns and gardens in favour of a concrete parking space. Jeremy and Charlene did the opposite, as soon as Charlene had negotiated the rental of a garage down the street, parking being an ongoing problem in the area. They ripped up ragged chunks of cement, or the guys they hired did, imported what seemed like fifty tons of dark, rich earth, and started the wonder that was all around us.

We've finished the steaks Jeremy barbecued for us, along with ears of corn and a big salad, not to mention a bottle of wine. Charlene has cleared away all the plates, and we're settled back on the lawn chairs under the stars.

At some point in my narrative, Charlene excused herself, ran into the house for some paper and a pen, and started taking notes. Jeremy rolled his eyes and told me, in sonorous tones, "Grist for the mill." Now he plays with his wineglass (his drug of choice) while Charlene and I smoke.

"It seems to me you're playing a very dangerous game with this character. How far are you willing to take it?"

"I have to get inside. I have to see what's going on in there. Get evidence for the cops. Damn, I was so close!"

Charlene is rolling another; I like to watch her, having never mastered the art.

"Would you sleep with him?"

I respond like a teenage girl asked to shop at Kmart, but I know that's the question.

"I thought about it while we were parked there, thought hard, but I couldn't stand it. Not even to get the bastard locked up. He really is gross, his mind, his body; everything about him gives me the creeps."

Charlene is looking over the notes she's scrawled. "This is so good, so real. This is what I've been looking for. I feel rejuvenated; I have a million ideas all racing around my brain. How could you keep all this a secret?" she adds accusingly, as though I were personally responsible for extending her writing slump.

"What would you have done? Would you have slept with him?" I ask.

"Yes, just grabbed ahold of his prick, and led him to the door. I'm not squeamish about sex, God knows I've been with enough men to know how to fake it. But that's me. I'm an actress. It's what I do. I would be playing a role, it wouldn't be me touching him, it would be—what was the name you used?"

"Charlotte," I squeak out, trying to retain the smoke in my lungs.

"Yes, I would be Charlotte, totally."

"I tried to remember all the things I've learned from you about acting, but when his hand was on my thigh, when I saw his face coming at me, I almost puked. You can't totally divorce yourself from reality, can you?'

Jeremy says, "It's not so much divorcing yourself from reality as it is about entering another reality. Understanding your character as much as you understand yourself. What does Charlotte want, and why? What kind of life has she lived, what experiences have shaped her? What drives her?"

I think for a moment. "I've done some of that. Charlotte isn't as smart as she thinks she is. She's always been below average in school, partly because of what's happening at home, her mother being an abusive drunk. I'm sure she fantasized about being rescued from all that by some idealized father. And that's carried over to her adult life. She's lived with insecurity, she's known hunger and fear. It didn't make her a more empathetic person, it hardened her. Made her selfish and grasping. Boys made her feel better about herself, they didn't care what her marks were, they flattered her and hung around, competing for her attention. She felt her looks, and only her looks, made her special. She slept around, probably got a bit of a reputation in school. She'd have written that off as jealousy. I believe she doesn't like to be alone; her only sense of self-worth comes from having a boyfriend. So now she meets guys in bars, and it always starts out promisingly.

They win her over with compliments and small gifts, they move in and it all turns to crap. Sometimes they hit her. It's as bad as being with her mom. But she's stuck, so she tries again, and again, with the same sad results. She's getting older, too, maybe it's a little harder getting the attention she's used to. She has a deep sense of entitlement, that she's owed something better, and she's frustrated and a little panicky that it's not happening for her. Now this overweight, foul-breathed man, who owns his own car, and says he owns two houses, is gaga over her. Not exactly Prince Charming, but she's seen enough of what's out there to at least consider what he's offering."

"And why would it be important for her to see inside that house in Parkdale?" Jeremy has hit the nail on the head.

"Well, she's used to deceit. Tired of it. If she's going to sell herself, she wants the price to be high. And looking at him, thinking of his hands all over her, that just ups the ante. He may be her last chance. She's not worried about illegalities, and she's certainly not concerned about the welfare of others. Charlotte is out for herself. But she has to know. Has to see and touch."

Jeremy nods thoughtfully. "Yes, all that holds up. Still, I'm very concerned for you, for your safety. Are you sure there's no other way?"

"The cops aren't interested. No, there's no other way."

We sit silently, listening to the crickets serenade us. Jeremy stands, leans over and kisses the top of my head. "If there's any way we can help, let us know. I must go off to bed now. You two stay and talk."

As soon as he's out of range, Charlene leans close and says, "The gremlin's escalated his activities again. This morning—and thank God I'm always down first—I came to open up the theatre, and pasted on the door was this life-size blow-up from a tabloid, of Jeremy going into court, with all those lurid headlines scrawled across his body. Dana, I'm at my wit's end. Are you any closer to finding the bastard?"

I shake my head. "Now it's a process of elimination. Becky's asking around about the few actors she doesn't know, the ones who competed for the major roles. I think we'll find our gremlin is one of them. I know this is driving you crazy, but we'll find him. We just need more time."

"I can't believe this is happening. That someone would be so vicious. It's not like we've hurt anyone, or done anything to deserve this. And to go after Jeremy, to try to humiliate him this way! It's crazy, just crazy!"

I'm thinking about Jason, who's not crazy at all, just Machiavellian in his efforts to topple Jeremy. Charlene is going to be hurt, there's no way around that, when I manage to expose him. If I manage to expose him. Suddenly I'm struck by an idea, a plan, a hope; tonight might be the night.

I let Charlene think I was going home. I didn't want to get her hopes up in case nothing happened. I walked down the sidewalk and around the block a few times till the lights in their house went off, then I doubled back, creeping into the garden.

Now I'm waiting for the bogeyman. It's cold. And damp. There was a moon, but it's covered up by clouds. It's way after midnight, and I'm on my knees behind the bushes at the end of the garden. It was so hot today, who could have guessed the temperature would drop so precipitously? I'm trembling all over, all my muscles ache. And it's hard to see. My night vision has never been good, but tonight it's abandoned me altogether.

I want to catch the bastard. Never mind lists of suspects and spying on the actors, that's all taking too long and producing little of value except gossip and innuendo. I need to win one. And he needs to come back tonight, doesn't he? He must know that Charlene had ruined his effort to up the ante, destroying his handiwork before Jeremy could see it.

And we're coming close to the final confrontation with Mallick. I go over my part, to pass the time, thinking like Charlotte, being Charlotte, feeling her disappointment with life, the smallness of her soul. Imagining her growing up in a rundown apartment with her mother, coming home from school every day to find her passed out on the couch, no dinner on the stove, no groceries in the cupboard. Bills piled up like the butts in the ashtray, the phone cut off, the place still the way she left it this morning. Staring at her mother, school books still in hand, hoping she dies. Staying quiet, taking some comfort in remembering the admiring touch of the latest boyfriend, the marks of his mouth on her neck.

It's all a little too real, too depressing. Better to think about Ed, and the possibilities there. It's nice, and a little scary, to be wanted. He's decent, and funny, and caring. A take-charge kind of guy, and that has a lot of allure right now.

I give up trying to keep my jeans clean, setting my bum on the ground and bringing my knees up so that I can rest my head on my arms. It's funny how creepy this place gets in the dark, how many slithery, crawly things party under cover of blackness. It probably doesn't help that I'm still a little stoned on the pot and wine. I've been bitten too, increasing the depth of misery I'm feeling. And I have to pee. I close my eyes and pretend I'm back in my room, under my covers, warm and safe, out of the reach of mosquitoes, spiders and worms. Yowling, spitting cats are fighting in the neighbour's yard; I hear the drift of cars on the street and the occasional voices of passersby.

I remember when I was a child, playing in the small patch of land in front of our row house. Every inch of it was turned into a vegetable garden, where my father grew enough tomatoes, cucumbers, carrots and lettuce to feed us through the summer, and the tomatoes would be turned into sauces, delicious sauces, that would last most of the winter. I would help, or thought I was helping, with the weeding, and every now and then my father would pull out a cucumber, rub off the dirt, and cut me a section to eat. I used to love that. Of course, as I grew up, it became a source of embarrassment to me, this need to cultivate what other families called a front lawn. And I hated the worms that would hide in the lettuce leaves, hated washing them down the kitchen drain. I would have much preferred the store-bought, washed and wrapped and tasteless versions. I can almost see my father, on his knees in the dirt, a little trowel in his hand. And I can see my mother at the door, hair tied back in a scarf, bringing out cool drinks to us.

I must have drifted off. But I'm really awake now. There's someone coming. I hear the footsteps, stealthy, moving slowly. I'm not scared so much as relieved, I can catch him and go home. Go to the bathroom. I wonder if I can stand up, if my legs will work. I still can't see, but it's true what they say about blind people, about other senses taking over. I know where he is, just passing the barbecue, I can hear him breathing. I gather myself together, ready to spring.

Everything happens very fast. I aim myself at where I know he's standing, like an arrow from a crossbow. A crossbow held by a very inexperienced, incompetent archer, but I do connect. With two legs that collapse as I crash into him, bringing him down, we roll noisily into the foliage. We're both screaming, me to alert Charlene, him because of shock. Suddenly there's an explosion, not of sound, but of smell, and I have time to wonder if he's lost control of his bowels before the stench overwhelms me. The lights come on, Jeremy and Charlene rush out then rapidly retreat back into the house, driven in by the stench. I grab onto the man's pantlegs and stare into his face. It's not Jason, it's Jim Allan. He's starting to puke, and I don't blame him. I catch the striped tail of a skunk blundering off through a hole in the fence, followed by two smaller ones, before I'm also on my knees vomiting.

Charlene yells through a crack in the patio door, "Who's there? What's going on?"

In between bouts of retching, I yell back resentfully, "It's me. I've got the bastard." I grab the man's head by the hair and twist it around so they can see.

"Mr. Allan?" Charlene says, her voice filled with shock. "What are you doing here?"

"Later!" Where's her sense of priorities? "Please do something about the stink!!"

I hadn't expected a medal or a ticker-tape parade for catching the culprit, but they won't even open the door, other than to shout directions to the hose and to throw out a couple of cans of tomato juice and an opener.

"You've got to be kidding. You want me to hose myself down out here?"

"I'm really sorry, Dana, but there's no choice." The sliding door slams again, and I'm left with Mr. Allan. "Strip, you son of a bitch." There's no time for modesty, and he's practically ripping off all his clothes anyway. I drag him over to the hose and turn it on, with one hand spraying him, and with the other undoing my blouse. That's too awkward, so I hand him the hose, and he holds it over his head while I get out of my own clothes, puncture one can of juice and pour it over my own head. He puts down the hose to grab his own can while I massage tomato juice into my hair and over my body.

The door opens again, just wide enough for two plastic bottles to be tossed at my feet. I pick one up and yell, "What the hell am I supposed to do with this?" It's a douche contraption, but Charlene mimes pouring it over my head, so I do, and I take the other one too, screw Mr. Allan. Next comes a bottle of whisky. She sees me lift it compliantly over my head, but she bangs on the window and lifts her hand to her mouth, letting me know it's to drink. I take a healthy, warming swig, then pass it to Mr. Allan.

We both look like victims of the Texas Chainsaw Massacre, and we're shivering uncontrollably, partly from the shock and certainly from the chill of the water and the air. I hose him and he hoses me, over and over again, while the smell in the back yard recedes painfully slowly.

It seems like hours before we can close our mouths and breathe through our noses again. Charlene eases a couple of blankets out the door, along with two bath towels, and we towel off and wrap ourselves up gratefully. Jeremy eases his way out on the deck, sniffing carefully. "I'm so sorry, Dana, but that smell, we'd never get it out of the house. Please come in, both of you."

We're huddled in the kitchen drinking hot toddies. I'm wrapped in a scratchy woollen blanket, as is Mr. Allan, and I'm satisfied that he looks as miserable as me. His head is down, his thinning hair flopping in long strands over his eyes and face. He hasn't stopped shaking, and spills his drink every time he tries to bring the cup to his mouth. I'm mean-spirited enough to want to kick him under the table, several times, but I hold off. Charlene and Jeremy are still in shock. Mr. Allan owns the house next door. They've had no history of problems, they've always been cordial and polite with each other.

"Mr. Allan," Jeremy starts, "you're going to have to explain what the hell you were thinking. You've never said anything to indicate you had any bad feelings about us. And yet you resort to these guerrilla tactics?"

Mr. Allan shakes his head. Words spill out like the tea, hard to catch.

"Speak up, please, Mr. Allan."

With one trembling hand, he slicks back his hair and takes a few deep breaths, clearly penitent.

"Did you ever want to change your life? I mean, totally change directions? I'm fifty-four, I've been an accountant for thirty years, never missed a day at work, I raised my family, two boys at university now, my wife ..." He stops, gulps down some tea, and holds out the cup for a refill. "My wife left me last year. Said I was too boring, too predictable. She wanted some excitement, she said. Some newness. Routine was like a straitjacket to her, it was driving her crazy. I love my wife. I love my kids. I tried the best I knew to give them a good life. And it all came crashing down. So I thought, I really thought, that I should do something totally out of character."

"Sabotage?"

"No, no. I knew she was impressed with you two, she loved the productions you put on, loved to brag about her artistic neighbours. The more I thought about it, the more I was sure that if I could join you, get a part, she'd see that I wasn't just boring old Jim. That there more were layers to me than she gave me credit for. I was so sure, so ready. I bought a copy of the play, I walked around my empty house for weeks memorizing lines. I dyed my hair, grew a moustache, to look younger for the role. I was primed, you know, by the time the auditions started. And then, two days later, I get this call, and what it amounted to was that I wasn't good enough. Just like that. I couldn't stand it. I think I went a little crazy."

Jeremy, Charlene and I exchange looks, none of us remembering what must have been a highly forgettable performance.

"I wanted to get even. I started small, but it felt so good. I stole some scripts, broke a microphone, the coffee maker. Then I got more creative, undoing the stitching on some of the costumes. That got to you." He dared to look at Charlene, then Jeremy. "I was having an effect you couldn't ignore. Everyone was getting antsy, always looking over their shoulder. But it wasn't enough, so I ratcheted it up a notch. You hear things, hanging around, like about your court case, how it caused you to break down, fall apart." In a voice tinged with malice, he added, "I wanted you to feel some of that again."

Jeremy's eyes narrow, he speaks slowly. "You really are quite deplorable."

"Yeah, well, it seems I wasn't the only one who had it in for you. That guy Jason, he's been telling everyone how you were past it, how you were a glory hog, I almost felt like he was an ally ..."

Charlene's chair crashes back to the floor as she leaps up, furious and red-faced. "You lying bastard! You're still at it, aren't you? Trying to hurt us with lies!"

"No. I swear!"

"Swear all you want, you miserable worm, Jason's nothing like you!"

"He even told me directly, like I could help. I came really close to telling him what I was up to. I wanted to tell someone, it was too big a secret to keep."

Charlene is just standing there, staring at him in disbelief. Then she looks at me and Jeremy in turn. She reads the truth in our faces.

"You knew, both of you knew? Why didn't you tell me? Oh, that son of a bitch."

This is only the beginning of a spew of invective that includes every four-letter word ever invented, punctuated by flying dishes, pots and cutlery. Jeremy and I keep very still while Mr. Allan tries to make himself a smaller target, folding in on himself and covering his head. Charlene storms out of the kitchen, ranting her way up the stairs. Mr. Allan, open-mouthed, says, "Wow. I wish I could do that."

Jeremy clears his throat. "Yes, well, it certainly would be healthier for you. The question remains, Mr. Allan, what do we do with you?"

"Look," says Mr. Allan, peering nervously into the dark beyond the kitchen, afraid of the imminent return of the hurricane that's still raging upstairs, "I'll make good on everything. Return what I stole, pay for what I broke. It's out of my system, believe me. Tonight's been like shock therapy, it's woken me up. I'm not a bad man, sir, really, I just, well, I just lost it for a while. I'm really, really sorry."

Jeremy leans forward, and his voice thunders through the kitchen. "You lost it the moment you believed that a few weeks of reading from the pages of a play entitled you to a role in the production. Actors study for years, in school and out, to hone their craft, and it is a craft, not something one can pick up in a fit of pique. How singularly arrogant of you, to assume you deserved a part. How contemptuous you are of the theatre! Do you suppose that, if I found myself in your circumstances, I could pick up a few books on accounting and do your job? What were you thinking, man?"

The picture of misery, Mr. Allan hangs his head, shamed.

I have a suggestion.

"Jeremy, perhaps we can come to a resolution. If you have some paper and a pen, Mr. Allan"—I send him a fierce look—"will write out a confession as well as the steps he'll take to make restitution. And I suggest, Mr. Allan, that you see someone about your 'breakdown.' You need help."

"I'll do it," he says, eager to be out of the house. Jeremy sits for a moment, not quite ready to let the bastard go, but then he sighs and gets up to rummage around for paper and pen. Mr. Allan starts scribbling, and Jeremy and I stare across the table at each other, both of us shaking our heads.

It's grown very quiet in the house. Either Charlene has calmed down or she's broken everything that can be broken. Mr. Allan is taking a long time, itemizing everything he sabotaged or filched, including the phone calls to the cast and to Bell. He asks for more paper, and Jeremy glowers at him while I grab another sheet and lay it down in front of him.

He finally finishes his confession, signs it, and asks, "Please, can I go now?"

"By all means, get out of here."

He makes to hand us the blanket, but I've seen enough of his nakedness. "Keep it." He leaves through the back, and Jeremy and I sit alone.

"You've done us a great service tonight, Dana, and it's not the first time. You're a remarkable young woman." The glow I'm feeling has nothing to do with the whisky I've drunk. I'm so relieved to have pulled this off, so proud to hear his words. But there are footsteps coming down the stairs, and both of us straighten in our chairs, bracing for the onslaught. She's quite calm, though, as she enters the kitchen, carrying a change of clothes for me, which she lays on the counter. Her smile is tender as she faces us both.

"I've had a word with Jason. He denies everything, of course, quite passionately. Even accusing you, Dana, of poisoning our relationship. He really is quite transparent, isn't he? God, I'm an idiot." She picks up her overturned chair and sits down with us. "Jason won't be returning to the theatre. And you've dealt with our gremlin, have you?" Jeremy hands her the confession, she reads it quickly, nods, and puts it back on the table.

"I've been very foolish. And so have you. You should have told me. I should have seen through him. But he was very pretty, very eager, very energetic. It's been too long since a man has shown me such attention. I suppose I didn't want to examine his motives too closely. Oh, Jeremy, I'm so sorry." Tears now, as he stands and embraces her. She says into his shoulder, "You are the heart and soul of this company, and you are everything to me."

I take this moment to excuse myself to go into the second-floor bathroom to shower and change into the jeans and sweat-shirt and underwear she's found for me. It's bigger than my room at home, brighter too. I don't know how long I spend under the powerful spray, washing away tomato residue and the flowery douche smell. I soap every inch of my body, and a few crevices too.

After the woollen blanket, the towels are particularly plush and soft. I'm exhausted, and starting to get a headache, but the thrill of this first success feels great, and augurs well for the next confrontation. In a little while, Charlene will drive me home, and I'm so very ready for my own odd little bed, in my own odd little room. I have to remember to bum some Aspirin, otherwise I'm going to hurt tomorrow. Dressed, and somewhat revived, I go down and collect Charlene, who's glad to leave the business of cleaning up till tomorrow.

"You never liked him, did you? That's why we didn't see you for so long. You'd sussed him out totally," she says, opening my door, then walking around to her own.

"It's partly true." I wait till we both have our seatbelts on. "I didn't like him, but I knew you did." I sigh. "I had to ask myself why he got to me, if I just resented how close you guys seemed to be. I had no idea that he was bad-mouthing Jeremy till this week. I'm not much of a detective, Charlene. I was ninety percent sure it would be him tonight."

"No kidding? Wow. Still, look what the end result is, you got them both. I'd say you're on a roll, whereas I need to do some serious introspection. What was I thinking? Well, I wasn't thinking, was I? Here I am, a committed feminist, a smart, independent woman, falling for a piece of work like that. I'm ashamed of myself. God, poor Jeremy. And how will I show my face in the morning?"

"Triumphantly. There won't be any snide remarks coming your way. They love you, Charlene, that much I learned straight off. Now, where's the Aspirin?"

With a full bottle in hand, I trudge up the stairs of the silent house, open my new lock, think fleetingly of Ed, and fall into the deepest sleep I've experienced in weeks.

The first surprise of the day is that I slept so thoroughly; the second is that I don't have a hangover. I stay under the covers, preferring to relive last night's victory than to think of what lies ahead of me later today. It's very quiet in the house, as if everyone's holding their breath. Alarmed by this thought, I sniff at the air around me, but the skunk smell is gone, though I think I can still taste tomato juice in the back of my throat.

I play with the idea of telling the guys about the great adventure, but decide not to. They may feel (and I confess I'm a little worried about this too) that all our luck's been used up. I wish there was another way to do this, to get inside Mallick's lair, but we're as ready as we can be, and if Diamond has been able to confirm arrangements with Derek, we'll go ahead.

I wonder what I'll be feeling and thinking tomorrow morning, if I'll wake up in this same room, safe and sound. Or ... Can't go there, I tell myself, can't let myself think about "what ifs." Groaning a little, I throw off my covers and, still stiff from hours of crouching in the damp grass, limp over to my kettle and plug it in. Outside, it's just a regular summer morning; the sun is baking the streets, people are passing by the house, eyes front, as usual, intent on their business. "Easy for you," I mutter to myself. "You don't have to seduce a pig." There's a scratching at the door, and I undo Ed's lock (Ed: I wonder what he's doing right now, if he's wondering about me) and let in the cat.

Coffee in hand, I go back to bed and try to organize my thoughts, while Alex leaps up beside me and does his level best to knock the mug out of my hand. I don't want anyone getting hurt or arrested—except for Mallick, him I don't give a damn about. I close my eyes and say a prayer, for everyone's safety. It occurs to me I'm talking to God a lot more frequently these days, and I like to believe He's listening.

Two cups later, I've worked some of the kinks out of my limbs, showered and dressed for success. A padded bra, borrowed along with a cell phone from Charlene, a clingy blouse (I'll undo most of the buttons when the time is right), and my regular jeans and running shoes. I want to be able to move fast when necessary; Mallick will just have to forgo the visual stimulation of high heels.

Holding the cat at arm's length in front of my face, I practise my speech.

"Stephan, he tried to hit me." I work in a little hysteria, not so hard when I imagine his face on the poor beast. "I had to run out of the house. I've nothing with me, and I'm scared and alone. Please, I'm on Sorauren Avenue, at a pay phone, I need to see you."

Again. And again, increasing the intensity, the little sobs that break up my plea to him, till I can hear a semblance of veracity. The cat struggles and I let him down on the floor. Everyone's a critic. "But you're probably much smarter than him, even with your tiny little fur-covered brain. You'd never fall for that, would you?"

He flicks his tail, and meows loudly. I tidy up, trying not to trip over him, then make the bed and start to wonder what time it is. My stomach says it's late. As soon as I open my door, the cat scampers away, and I hear Gerry hollering, as if he's been standing at the bottom of the stairs just waiting for signs of life. "Jesus Christ, woman, we're all waiting on you! Hurry yourself up, will you?"

"Yeah, yeah, I'm coming down," I call back. Creaky knees and all, I get down to the first-floor landing.

Gerry has his arms folded across his chest. He's shaking his head at me. "I was about to kick the shit outta your door. This is the big day and you're wasting it in bed!"

He steps aside so I can go in, and yes, the gang's all here, big grins on their faces.

Diamond stands up and says, "We figured it would be nice to eat together before we start work. Gerry and I got our cheques, so as soon as we heard you moving around, we went down to McDonald's and picked up a few things." They certainly had: pop, hamburgers and fries, and those hot little pies that burn the roof of your mouth. Miss Semple is distributing napkins and goodies, and I take mine to my patch of floor, ravenous now.

"Thanks, guys, this is great."

"Okay, no business till everything's gone."

I'm wondering, as I bite into my Big Mac, if Jesus and his disciples felt this kind of camaraderie during their Last Supper. Not that this would be our last. I stifle an impulse to cross myself. Once every last scrap is down our throats, and the garbage collected by Diamond, it's time to talk. Diamond begins.

"I saw Derek. He's really nice, though his place is a real dump. He said to tell you to come around nine, it'll be dark enough by then. Oh yeah, and he wanted you to know that he's always dreamed about trashing a BMW. He's very enthusiastic. I stayed with him for a couple of hours, watched from his front window. Mallick arrived just like usual, his helper let him in. The two of them were still there at midnight when I came back home."

"So we're on, then. How are you guys feeling, are we all up to this?"

Gerry echoes my own thoughts. "I want this to be over. I want our regular lives back. And I want to punish this son of a bitch. Real bad."

He gets no disagreement. I tell them about the cell phone Charlene has donated to our cause, and how we're going to use it. "Miss Semple, it'll be up to you to watch the time really carefully. I've written down Ed's cell number, as soon as I'm inside you start counting minutes. I figure I can hold him off for half an hour. That should give me enough time to find out about the women. When Derek gets Mallick outside, that's when you make the calls: the first to 911, the second to Ed."

She nods carefully, but then adds, "Thirty minutes may feel like a lifetime, trapped in there with that monster."

"It won't be so bad, knowing you guys are out there. Knowing we've got him." I hope they can't tell this is just bravado on my part. Miss Semple is right, that will be the longest half-hour of my life. "We don't want him connecting the two events, me showing up and the attack on his car. I'm not sure thirty minutes is long enough, but it's all I'm willing to spend alone with him."

"Derek wanted me to remind you that his people need to be away from the scene as soon as the sirens get close. They apparently have some problems with cops."

"Yeah, that's okay, I expected they'd want to be out of the way. We won't need them after they draw Mallick out."

"I'll sit on the bastard if he tries to get back in," swore Gerry.

Michael has angry tears of frustration running down his face; he swipes at them and balls his fists. "I hate not being able to go with you. I just hate it. And it's my own stupid fault! I'm such a fuck-up!"

Diamond speaks calmly, soothingly, "It's your plan, Michael. You came up with it. You have to trust us to carry it out."

It's cold comfort to Michael, but he nods, keeping his head down.

"We have a long wait ahead of us till it gets dark, what do you want to do?"

Miss Semple reaches under her chair and pulls out the hardcover Evanovich, saying, "We should finish this. It will keep our minds nicely occupied. And when we're done, it might be good to try to sleep a little. I think it's going to be a long night."

For a moment I think that the very last thing I want to do is to read aloud, but then I realize it's actually quite a good idea. We already know the story will end with the mystery solved, and everyone we care about safe, and that's got to be a positive message for us. Maybe we should carry it with us. Like a talisman.

None of us managed to rest. Our little band dissected every part of the plan again and again in Michael's cramped room, looking for safer ways and finding none. The four of them were appalled by the risk that would be primarily mine, but Mallick wasn't going to invite any of them into his lair. I had the best chance, the only opportunity to breach that closed door. I talked up Derek and his crew, hedging a bit on their bad habits, extolling their experience breaking heads. I have no idea what Miss Semple's reaction is going to be to these ex-bikers, but she keeps surprising me, so it may be all right.

We decide to walk. We set a slow, solemn pace, partly because of Gerry's inability to move faster, but mostly because of our fear of reaching our destination, and our need to gather courage from one another. We use the less peopled, less distracting route along King Street, every step bringing us closer to the confrontation ahead. I'm remembering poor Michael's anguish, how he cried again and begged to go with us. It had been hard to leave him behind. So we were just four not-quite-intrepid detectives, heading for a showdown.

I'm still rehearsing my part in my head, the phone call I'll soon be making to Mallick. As we draw closer to his street, my heart starts missing beats, and my breath is too shallow to be calming. I start breathing slowly and deeply through my nose and mouth, filling my lungs and stilling my thoughts. Whatever happens tonight, I tell myself, we will have tried, we will have fought.

Diamond breaks through the silence enshrouding us. "We're almost there."

We stand in a small, ragged circle, which Diamond turns into a football-like huddle, our arms around each other, heads touching. We stay like this, reluctant to part, for a long moment, ignoring the rush of cars on the street, the curious looks of pedestrians. I'm sure Miss Semple is saying a prayer, at least I hope she is. I send one up myself, to Whoever might be watching over us, for protection, for victory.

"Okay, we're going to do this," I tell them, "and we're going to succeed."

I hope I'm projecting the confidence I wish I had. We break, and enter the side street leading to Mallick's hell house. I'm kept in the middle of Gerry and Diamond, just in case Mallick is looking out his window. It's time to forget I'm Dana, time to become Charlotte.

Chapter Ten

How could I have forgotten? This could mess up everything. Yesterday was cheque day and it's still party time. I look around Derek's living room, at the three men kicking back there with wide, sloppy grins, at the beer bottles, pizza and chicken boxes. I wave away the fume clouds of cigarettes, pot, alcohol and rumbling farts. Miss Semple, somewhere behind me, is going to walk right back out, if she doesn't have a heart attack first.

But I have to do it tonight. If I spend any more time thinking about it I'll be too afraid to try. It's now or never.

"Hiya," Derek says, coming into the room. "We're ready for you. On your feet, guys, our visitors are here."

He looks reassuringly steady on his feet, can't say the same for his crew, who struggle out of couches and chairs, all bellies and tattoos, torn and stained denim and leather.

"Come in, grab a chair." Reluctantly, I step inside, and hear the slightest gasp from Miss Semple as the scene is revealed. She moves with the caution of someone trapped in a nightmare, but the sight of her slight, aging figure galvanizes the boys into an attempt to hide the worst of the garbage. Bottles are kicked out of the way, boxes thrust under couches. The biggest of the three men steps forward, weaving only a little, and holds out his hand, the arm adorned with a large, open-mouthed serpent, to Miss Semple.

"Please to meetchu, ma'am. I'm Crusher."

We all hold our breath as she looks at the hand, the size of a Christmas turkey, and gingerly offers her own. Don't break it, I silently plead, watching her face for signs of pain.

"Nice to meet you, Mr. Crusher. It's good of you boys to offer to help us."

Crusher has a brilliant smile, even without his front teeth. With surprising delicacy, he leads her to the cleanest-looking armchair.

"It's our pleasure, ma'am, would you like something to drink?"

"Tea would be very nice, thank you."

As Crusher rumbles out, Derek makes the introductions. The two remaining behemoths are Harley and Rabbit. We all find seats, while crashing noises come from what must be the kitchen. Crusher is searching for a tea bag.

Diamond looks a little uneasy, but Gerry fits right in; he could go navel to navel, pound for pound, belch for belch with these guys.

"Don't worry, we're just fuelling up for the night," Derek says to me. "This is, like, breakfast, you know?"

I nod, but it's my life that's going to rest in their hands, and I wish they'd stuck to eggs and bacon. Our war council settles in, as pots clang in the kitchen, and a death-rattling sound shakes the house as the tap is turned on. Crusher sticks his head in the doorway.

"Would you like milk and sugar with your tea, ma'am?"

He's clearly in love, and that relaxes Miss Semple just a little. "Black will be fine, Mr. Crusher. You're very kind." He beams at her, and disappears again.

"You folks want a beer?" Derek asks.

Gerry and Diamond quickly nod, and I don't blame them; I'd

like a shot of something strong myself. I shake my head, though, knowing I need to keep clear-headed till it's done. Derek pops the caps and passes them each a Molson, as Crusher comes back with a steaming mug carefully balanced in both hands.

"Here you go, ma'am. Be careful, it's hot."

I don't want to think what that mug has held in its lifetime. Crusher stands over Miss Semple expectantly, like a child showing his first drawing to his mother, waiting for her to take a sip. I see her steel herself, and daintily blow on the brew before delicately putting it to her mouth.

"Lovely, thank you so much. That's just what I needed."

It's time. I survey my war council: four over-the-hill and inebriated bikers, one de-institutionalized mental patient, two runaways from the nuclear family and one senior citizen. How can we lose? I take a deep breath, and fish out the cell phone from my knapsack.

"Okay, here's the deal." I pause and take a deep breath. "Exactly thirty minutes from when I go through the door, Derek, you and the boys start trashing the car, breaking its windows, whatever it takes to get the asshole's attention. Miss Semple, you'll call 911. Remember to say shots fired, or they'll never show, too much happening out there around cheque day. Then call Ed."

Derek says, "You know, as soon as we hear the sirens closing, we'll have to melt away."

They all have long and questionable records; they can't be around when the cops come. Derek has underlined that point several times, but worries about me being left, even for a moment, unprotected. As for them "melting away," maybe in their youth that term could have been used, but there's a whole lot of Molson hanging over their belt buckles, and I can't see any of them actually sprinting out of sight. I wonder again if I'm quite mad, if we're all a little crazy. Too late for that.

"Okay, I'm heading out now." The house quakes with the force of motorcycle boots hitting the bare floor. The boys are up and ready. Baseball bats and crowbars appear like magic, Gerry grabs one, swinging it impressively, a broad grin on his face. I'm checking all my pockets for the quarter I'd saved for the call, relief flooding me when I find it. I have a heavy escort to the back door, everyone slapping my back and wishing me luck.

Outside in the dark, alone and scared, I snake my way through unfenced back yards up to the phone booth on Queen Street. I drop the quarter in the slot, and try to remember everything Charlene taught me as I slowly dial his number.

He answers on the second ring. A gruff, annoyed "Yah?"

"It's me. I need to see you. Need to come over. I had a fight, a terrible fight. He tried to hit me!" I'm pleased to hear the tremor in my voice. "We were visiting his friends, he thought I was flirting. When he came at me, I ran out without anything, no purse, nothing. Please, I'm at a pay phone at the doughnut shop at Queen and Lansdowne. Where are you?"

He is oozing concern. "The house on Fortune, the one I showed you. Can you get here? Or do you want me to come get you?" Aha, he's hooked.

"I can't wait here, Stephan, he may be looking for me. I'll come to you. Oh, Stephan, you did mean what you said to me? That there's a place for me? With you? I'm so tired of being lied to by men, promised everything, given nothing. If we're going to be together, then you have to be honest with me. Totally. I'm coming over. Okay?"

"Yah, sure." He's breathing heavily, I can almost see him touching himself. Gross. "How long will it take you?"

"Not long, maybe a few minutes. You won't let me down, Stephan?"

"Never."

I hang up the phone. Shake a bit. Rest my head against the door of the booth. I'm Charlotte now, I tell myself, gold-digging, desperate Charlotte, who's willing to trade her body for a life upgrade, and doesn't care who she steps on to get it.

People go to work eight hours a day, five days a week, at jobs they hate, trading in their freedom for a paycheque. Women stay with husbands they despise, to keep big houses and hefty bank balances. Sleeping with Mallick, keeping him happy and generous, it's not really any different. And I can control him. All I have are my looks, and they won't last long, living as I do. That last boyfriend hit me, right in the face, could have ruined my appearance, taken away any chance I have at something better. I just have to be sure Stephan has everything he says he does. That he can give me what I deserve. No more losers for me. No more lies.

The door opens before I realize I've rung the bell. Mallick wraps me in a bear hug, squeezing too hard. His shirt is sweaty, he hasn't shaved.

"I'm so glad you're here," he whispers into my ear, sausage and garlic breath wafting over me. "We will be partners, you and I, in life, in business. Come and see."

And I'm finally inside, the door closed and locked behind me.

There's a long hallway, and a living room (in much better shape than poor Derek's) with heavy drapes covering the windows, standard couch and stuffed chairs looking unused, a good rug on the floor.

"Oh, this is lovely," I gush, draping one arm around his large waist.

"This is just the beginning. Come see the kitchen." We bump thighs, he's that close, and like mismatched Siamese twins we trundle farther down the hall that lets out into a huge kitchen.

There's a mess, of course—supper things scattered about, a sink piled up with dishes—but the stove is new, so is the refrigerator and microwave. Here too the curtains on the window and on the back door are drawn. There's no sign of the women.

"It's so big," I gasp. What every man wants to hear. "Oh, Stephan, I could cook you great meals in here, there's so much space."

He opens the fridge, proudly displaying a large stockpile of goodies. The freezer section is crammed with cuts of meat. "Everything you could possibly want is here! Now, come, I'll show you upstairs."

That means bedrooms. I can't look at my watch, have no idea how much time has passed, but I know it's not nearly enough. He sends me ahead of him up a carpeted staircase, probably to watch my behind as I climb. In the three upstairs rooms he proudly displays, none shows any sign of being occupied.

His bedroom is the last door we come to. It's totally Mallick, the bed unmade, pictures of nude women cut from some porno magazine adorning the walls.

"This will be our room!" He stands very close, breathing heavily, then I'm on the bed, with his crushing weight on top of me. He's fumbling at my breasts, biting and pinching, almost tearing through my blouse, and I can feel his erection poking into my thigh. All the air is knocked out of me, but I try to grab at his hands, a move he interprets as passion. "Yes, pretend to fight me, I like that."

Then he seems to have some kind of seizure, his whole body going rigid for a long moment, and I realize he's already come. What a man. We lie there in silence for a few minutes, his breath coming in hot sobs against my neck. I fight my own revulsion and stroke his hair. "This is just the beginning, Stephan. We have all the time in the world, now that we're together."

He makes no apology for his premature ejaculation. "You make me so hot, I love your body. I dream about you. Now you are here." His voice is as spent as his seed, and I entertain a wild hope that he'll roll over and start snoring. Instead, he levers himself up, moving off me, and reaches for a pack of cigarettes on the night table. He lights one, hands it to me, and I take it. I like the idea of burning embers between us. We lie side by side, while I try to inhale without coughing, wondering how Charlotte would react. She'd probably be relieved.

"Stephan, I don't understand, where are the tenants?"

"In a moment. You have exhausted me." He grabs an ashtray and puts it on his chest. "You will stay with me? Tonight? And always?"

I could almost feel sorry for him, if my breasts weren't hurting so much.

"Once I know everything, once you show me you trust me. That I can trust you. I'm ready to trust you, Stephan."

He leans over, upsetting the ashtray on the cover, not the first time by the look of it, and plants his disgusting mouth on mine, shoving his repellent tongue in my mouth. I have to stifle a gag reflex, push him coyly away.

"Don't tell me you're ready to go again. You are an animal."

He likes that. "I want to see you naked."

"I want to eat first. All that food downstairs. Sex always makes me hungry, and I haven't had a proper meal for days. Can we eat, Stephan?"

He sighs, and with his grubby fingers collects some of the butts that have scattered over the blanket.

"You can do anything you want, as long as you keep me happy."

"I will." I manage to stand up, straighten my clothing, and smile down at him. "C'mon, I'm starving."

I get him on his feet, ignore his groping, and we go back down the stairs and into the kitchen. He opens the fridge and pulls out a bunch of leftovers, never pausing to wash his hands, and shoves dishes in the microwave. "Sit down at the table, I'll open some wine."

"But where are your tenants?" I ask, all innocent, almost batting my eyes.

"First we eat, then I'll show you." He rummages around, looking for clean plates and cutlery, while I pour us two tumblers of wine, immediately downing half of mine to kill whatever germs his tongue has left breeding in my mouth.

"They are pigs, they live in their own filth, it will ruin your appetite." He's positively bustling around the kitchen, re-energized and talkative. "I have to force them to shower, to wash their clothes. Still, without them, none of this would be possible."

He comes up behind me, standing too close, his hands once again torturing my breasts. "I will take you shopping for new clothes, whatever you like. Only the best for Mallick's woman. My sister, she is fat, she has a moustache. She could wear mink, and still she'd look like the peasant she is. But you, you are beautiful and young, thin but not too skinny." The timer dings, and he lets go of me long enough to dish out the food, some kind of chicken dish, into our plates. He watches as I try a forkful, as anxiously as a wife wanting to please her husband.

"It's very good." I have to eat it, subdue the gag reflex that again threatens to betray me. The wine he keeps refilling helps wash it down.

"You will stay here from now on, with me. We will be true partners. You have iron in your blood, same as me. You understand what must be done."

I have pretty much emptied my plate. He wolfed his down, and unless I want to be mauled again, I have to get him to take me to the tenants.

"Stephan, I'm ready now. Show me where you keep them."

"Okay. You must be strong, though. Remember your mother, everything she put you through, and you'll know that what I do is right."

There's another door I hadn't noticed, tucked into a corner of the kitchen, and he takes a key from a hook screwed into the wall nearby, and unlocks it. There's a stench that hits us the moment the door opens, a different kind of stench from the stale cooking odours. This is a stench of too many confined bodies in close spaces, of urine and feces and illness. He doesn't seem bothered by it. Flicking on a light switch, he heads down first. I'm trembling all over—now that I'm finally here I want to run away, while I still have my sanity—but I follow him, one shaky step at a time. We stand at the bottom of the stairs, in a weak pool of light from the bare bulb overhead, but still it's too bright, it still reveals too much.

The basement is not a finished basement, the walls are bare brick and the concrete floors are crowded with cots. I can't count them, they're too close to one another, there are too many of them. It's cold down here, an icy damp cold that the thin blankets covering the women will not ward off. The only sounds are of liquid, laboured breathing and soft whimpers, as though even the energy to scream is beyond them. In one corner, there is something moving in a bin of encrusted plates, something humpbacked and swift that flicks a tail and disappears. An open toilet is covered with filth and flies; the buzzing gets inside my head.

I step forward. Some of the faces I can see are merely jutting bone overlaid with slug-white, papery skin, mouths gaping open like hungry infants. They are barely alive. Others are too still, too quiet.

Mallick turns to me. I'm still shocked and horrified but manage a weak, malicious smile (I'm thinking of castrating him) as he says, "So here they are. My little money-makers."

He has no shame at all. I try to speak, it's difficult, impossible, but he's watching me closely—if I make the wrong move, say what I feel, he'll be the only one leaving the basement. The suffering, the degradation of the women presses in on me.

"Stephan, it's better than they deserve." God forgive me.

He grins broadly, and throws one arm around my shoulder. "I knew you were for me, the very first time I saw you, I knew. I'm never wrong."

I'm more frightened now than before. Standing so close to such soulless evil, being embraced, being claimed by it. "My good fortune, Stephan."

A figure lifts up from one of the cots, like Lazarus rising. A voice, thin and tremulous, calls, "Dana? Is that you, Dana?"

Oh shit. It's Janice, alive, thank God, but blowing my cover. Mallick, instead of confronting me, taps his left temple. "She's crazy. They're all crazy. Now you see. Let's go have a drink."

I can't move fast enough, stumbling up the stairs and into the kitchen, managing to call behind me, "Yes, I need a drink."

"Dana, don't leave us ..."

He shuts the door, cutting off the weak cry. He pockets the key without re-locking it, goes into one of the cupboards and produces a bottle of vodka. I sneak a look at my watch. Almost twenty minutes have passed. I ask for ice and a mixer, sitting down at the table before my legs collapse. This surpasses my worst nightmare.

"I know it's probably a shock at first." Mallick's being understanding as he puts a drink in front of me. I grab hold of the glass, knock back half of it, choke and try to get my breath back. He pats me on the back, then pulls his chair close to me so that we're knee to knee. "I warned you, they're little better than animals, never clean themselves. We feed them, they have everything they need. Still, they're ungrateful. Demanding. Whining all the time. You just have to be firm with them. Take no shit."

I finish the drink and hold out the glass for more. Maryanne's face rises before me, her mouth in a silent scream. Mallick laughs, looks almost tenderly at me, then gets up to make me another.

"How many are down there?" I keep my voice neutral, even.

"Fifteen. At $900 a head. Every month. My brother-in-law is their worker. I go with him to their houses. He tells them, 'you must move today, right now, this place is not recognized by us. We sent you three notices, you're out of time. If you refuse, you lose your benefits.' They remember nothing, of course, all the drink has made them stupid. But they want to keep their cheques coming. So they do what they're told. And we bring them here." He's becoming expansive, proud of the scheme, wants me to admire him. "At first they behave like your mother, screaming and crying, but we show them very fast what that brings. Make examples. They learn, like dogs learn."

I nod, slowly, remembering how calculating I'm supposed to be. "And what would I be expected to do? What would be my share?"

He laughs, like the devil would laugh when you sign over your soul, clapping his palms together. "I knew it, I knew it. You are perfect for me. What a team we'll make, Charlotte!"

Then all hell breaks loose. The front window shatters with a spectacular cracking, crashing sound; they're improvising, that wasn't supposed to happen. At the same time, there's the unmistakable tattooing and crunching of metal. Mallick goes white, then red within seconds; he curses and pushes back his chair, commanding me to stay in the kitchen. I stand and watch his back as he runs to the front door and flings it back, shouting more invective. I grab the iron frying pan from the top of the stove and dart to the basement door, open it, close it behind me and turn on the light, stumbling down the stairs, calling for Janice. As I do, I hear the front door slam, and Mallick's voice, tinged with hysteria, calling me. The coward, he's running from Derek and the guys, and he's looking for me.

Janice is up, she looks like a wraith, the others are starting to struggle out of their cots.

"Oh, Dana, I knew it was you. I knew you couldn't be part of this."

I shush her, put down the frying pan and hold her very thin body for a moment.

"It's not over yet. The cops are coming, but we have to ..."

"Charlotte! Where are you, Charlotte?" Mallick is in the kitchen, sounding frantic.

The door opens, he stands in the light like my worst nightmare. "Charlotte? What are you doing? Something's wrong, very wrong."

I decide to bluff, calling up to him. "There was screaming. I came to quiet them."

He's on his way down, slamming and locking the door behind him, taking two steps at a time. I gently push Janice to the side and look around for the frying pan, but it's too late. He has me by both arms, his face inches from mine.

"There are bad men outside. Some kind of gang. They are attacking my car, my house. I don't understand what's going on."

We can both hear loud footsteps from above, and men's voices calling out, "Dana, where are you?"

That tears it. I can see he remembers what Janice called me. He starts shaking me, violently, my head snapping back and forth.

"Who are you? Did you do this? Did you lie to me?"

He's so strong. I can barely get the words out. "No, Stephan, how can you think that?"

A moment's hesitation, he's unwilling to let go of his dream of us, of his perfect partner. Someone is pounding on the basement door. "Dana!"

I've totally lost contact with Charlotte, I'm Dana, and I'm terrified. From a dark corner, Janice calls out, her voice rising in triumph, "Now you're trapped in your own cellar, you bastard, see how you like it."

He abruptly releases me, and moves blindly toward the sound of her voice, enraged. I pull on his arm. "Stephan, no, we have to think, there's no time."

"Dana! Are you down there? Dana!"

Mallick needs to hurt someone, I see it in his eyes as he turns back to me. The confusion is gone. He knows.

"You will die now, you bitch, you lying bitch." He's choking me, both hands squeezing so hard I can't catch a breath, choking and shaking me, his face red with fury even in the weak light. There is an edge of blackness moving into my vision, his arms are like steel, I can't dislodge them. My knees are rubbery, I'm losing consciousness. Then the vise-like grip is gone, and I collapse.

Janice stands over Mallick, both hands still on the frying pan.

"Dana, are you all right?" I'm gasping for air, wanting to puke but needing to breathe. There are sirens cutting through the night out there. I can't get up. Mallick is lying very still. Janice drops the frying pan to the concrete floor, the sound echoes off the walls.

"God," she says, "I need a drink."

The kitchen is crowded with cops. Miss Semple, Gerry, Diamond and I are sitting around the table; I'm having more of the vodka, the rest are having tea. My throat still feels the pressure of Mallick's stranglehold. Ed's pulled up a stool he found, staying very close to me. He's trying to take notes, but he's obviously bewildered by events. There's a sudden commotion outside, voices raised in strenuous argument. We hear, "No one gets in, so move back now!"

"Oh, shit," Ed groans, "the media. That's all we need to make this night complete."

Derek and the boys did melt away, after trashing Mallick's car, and going one step further, smashing the bay window to gain entry. Miss Semple whispers to me that they'd decided on their own that that was the sensible thing to do, in case Mallick did exactly what he did, run back inside.

We're keeping them well out of it. Ed's beginning to suspect there are things we're not telling him, and I hope he's willing to let it go. The police, including Ed's partner, Price, as experienced as they are, were clearly as shocked as I was by what they'd found in the basement. Some of them, big and bad and powerful in their uniforms, had actual tears in their eyes, and at least one stepped outside and vomited on the grass. They'd called in a large ambulance bus, and one by one the women were taken out, some on stretchers, others cradled in the arms of weeping men, to local hospitals. Some of them had so little flesh on their bodies they could have been mistaken for cadavers. Others were confused and frightened; they didn't understand that their ordeal was over, they begged to be let go, and fought the attendants who were trying to help them up the stairs. Janice had bitched mightily, but I persuaded her to go along to be checked out rather than stay with us.

The basement is an empty crime scene now. Mallick, bleeding impressively from the head, was taken out, a little roughly, in handcuffs; he spat at me as he passed. One of the cops punched him in back of the head for that, and this is one time when I won't be complaining about police brutality.

As the four of us clink our cups and glass together, Miss Semple mouths, "We did it!"

"So let me understand this, you decided to trash his car, break the window, to draw him out?" Ed is still somewhat incredulous.

"Yep," says Gerry, all pride and innocence. "I liked swinging that bat. Always wanted to do that. And it worked. He came running out, cursing and screaming. Only problem was he was chicken shit. He saw us, got scared, and ran back inside. We got in through the front window, but by then he'd locked the bloody basement door on us. Shit, Dana, we thought you were dead. We pounded on that door, tried to break it down, we were so afraid for you."

"Thank God you came, Detective," says Diamond. "The other cops weren't listening to us, just shouting 'put your hands up,' 'drop your weapons,' like we were the bad guys."

"Can't see why they'd do that, with a smashed car and a broken window, you guys with bats in your hands." He leans forward, narrowing his eyes. "Is there something you're not telling me?"

The four of us shake our heads in unison. "No," says Miss Semple, staring forthrightly at him. "You've got everything there you need." She points to his notebook.

Diamond asks, "What about his partner? And the other guy, the younger one? Have you got them yet?"

"We will, don't worry. I still can't quite believe this. You guys took incredible risks."

"We didn't have any choice, Ed. We knew they were in here,

what else could we do? It wasn't your fault. You went as far as you could. You needed proof."

"You could have died!"

"But I didn't. Good old Janice. I think she thoroughly enjoyed bonking him."

He takes a deep breath, stares at his notepad as if waiting for the answers he's looking for to suddenly appear on the page. A very subdued Detective Price comes and stands by him. He looks younger, nicer, when he's not being all hard and judgmental.

Ed says, "Let's go through this again." We all sigh, realizing that we aren't getting out of here any time soon. "You followed him to his home in the east end?"

We all nod in unison.

"And you and Miss Semple got him to take ... a survey?"

"Well, Detective, that was mostly Dana. He took one look at her and opened his door to us."

"You shoulda seen the outfit she was wearing," bragged Gerry. "It woulda made your eyes pop out. He didn't stand a chance."

"And then," he said, turning his wonderful blue eyes back to me, "you ran into him on Roncesvalles?"

"Yes. He practically told me then what he was up to. I went along, pretending that I felt the same way he did about women who drank, but he wouldn't let me in the house yet. He said he had to be sure of me." I'm relieved when he turns back to the guys.

"And you boys had watched this place for days?"

"Yes, sir." Diamond, who had given his real name, Steven James, to the first officers at the scene, is all polite and middle class. "We kept track of his comings and goings, and we knew when he'd be on his own. Dana went in. We had decided to wait exactly thirty minutes, hoping she could find the women in that time, and then Miss Semple called you and 911, and we started to attack his car."

"You did this all on your own."

"Yes, sir. We're smarter than we look." We start to giggle helplessly, all of us, while Ed watches us, wonder in his eyes.

"Detective, I'm an old woman, and I'd like to go home now, if that's all right." Miss Semple is using the age card to draw the night to a close, probably the only way we're going to get out of here before dawn. Ed shakes off his doubts and stands up, looking quite handsome in his off-duty clothes of denim and a sports shirt. "Of course, I'll get you all rides. But this isn't over. You'll have to sign statements, under oath."

The four of us nod solemnly, unperturbed. Detective Price offers to drive us home himself.

The next morning, we're all a bit of a wreck. Some of us, like Gerry, got a few hours' sleep, but most of us just lay on our beds replaying the events of the night before, not quite believing what we'd done. By eight-thirty we're all in Michael's room, still in a state of shock.

Pete will be here soon, I called him around seven, knowing he'd be up and helping his kids with breakfast. It was a quick conversation; I didn't know how much juice was left in the cell phone.

"I heard," he told me. "It's all over the news. Is everyone okay? Are you okay?"

"We're fine, Pete. Listen, I left a backdated resignation letter on your desk, just in case it all went sour. I kept you out of it 'cause I didn't want the drop-in to be dragged into a mess if we screwed up. So if anyone asks, I don't work for you."

He brushed that off immediately. "I wish you'd have let me make that decision, but I appreciate the sentiment. What can I do to help?"

"Could you come by this morning? We're not sure what comes next, and we could use your advice."

And now here he was, walking through our front door, strong and calm, bigger than life. I'd forgotten about the livid bruising on my neck. He winces when he sees it, one hand reaching out almost wonderingly, then he hugs me, and for the first time in a while, I feel safe and secure, very willing to let someone else make the decisions. He looks at our ragtag assembly in some disbelief, and solemnly shakes hands with all the players, congratulating everyone.

"Who's going for coffee?" he asks, reaching for his wallet.

Diamond volunteers to make the run to McDonald's, and we wait till he gets back to tell our story, the whole story, including what we didn't tell the cops. Somewhere in the middle of our group recitation, Miss Semple, looking a little less put-together this morning, interrupts.

"I must say, I was just thinking, this is better than those stories we read."

We all fall silent for a long moment. Pete doesn't know what we're talking about, but he knows enough not to break the spell.

"Christ," breathes Gerry. "You're right. We made our own story. All of us, together."

We shake off the wonder of it, and continue to fill Pete in. Sometimes he laughs; sometimes he holds his breath like he doesn't already know how it turned out. Just as we're drawing to a close, we hear heavy footsteps coming toward the room. Ed, looking just a little weary, unshaven and still in the same clothes he wore last night, sticks his head in the room.

"Good morning, people." He crouches down on the other side

of me, reaching across to shake Pete's hand as I introduce him. He stares at Michael, who's still sporting bandages on his forehead. "I suppose you had nothing to do with all this. Just tripped over your shoelaces, did you?"

Michael pales, but rallies to say, "Never did learn how to tie them properly.'

Ed snorts in disbelief, but leaves it alone. "You've got a horde of reporters starting to gather outside. I showed them my badge, threatened them with trespassing, and made them get off the porch and onto the sidewalk, but they're not going to go away any time soon."

Gerry wasn't happy with that. "Bastards, bloody vultures, they almost put my eye out last night with their bloody cameras. Why don't you show them your gun, wave it around a little?"

"I'd love too, but they'd probably complain to my boss. You're going to have to face them sooner or later. Some better news for you. Mallick is squealing like the pig he is, blaming everything on his brother-in-law. This may not have to go to trial. We've interviewed some of the women who are able to talk to us, and they witnessed Mallick beating Maryanne. According to them, she fought like a tiger when he tried to force her into the basement, he got fed up and pushed her down the stairs. She must have hit her head pretty hard on the concrete floor, because she didn't get up again. He carried her out, that's all they saw. I'm sorry."

Michael is crying, so is Diamond. Gerry has his head down, but his shoulders are quaking. Miss Semple says softly, "There it is. Now we know everything. Now she can rest in peace."

We keep silent, all of us.

From outside, we hear loud voices calling to one another; they seem very close. Ed's right, we're surrounded. For the next half-hour we bang out a strategy for dealing with them. Ed suggests we simply say we can't talk about "aspects of the case that are still under investigation." We appoint Pete to be our official spokesman, and work on drafting a joint statement. In the midst of this, more footsteps, this time light and bouncy, head our way. Ed stands, ready to defend us against the invading press, but it's just Charlene, carrying bags of goodies, and just bubbling over with pride in us. We fall on the food, demolishing every bit, washing it down with cold juice. The room is getting really crowded, but none of us minds a bit.

"It's unreal out there. Reporters are pushing and shoving each other, pedestrians are getting into the act, cars are blocking traffic while they try to see what's going on. You guys are stars."

"We're working on a statement," says Pete.

"Keep it short, succinct. Don't give away too much. There are people who'd pay big money for your story. And it's not like you couldn't use the cash. Hell, it'd be a great Movie of the Week."

This is all getting to be a bit much. Miss Semple sums up our feelings. "I think that what we need is for Pete to go out there and talk to them, if you don't mind." She looks across at him from her perch on the one chair in the room. "None of us really wants to face what's out there. We haven't had time to think and we haven't really slept."

"It won't be enough," says Pete. "I'll do it, of course, but they won't leave without something from you guys. I agree with Charlene, you don't want to say too much, but how about one or two of you standing with me?"

Diamond looks across at me. "If you and Miss Semple could do it, that would be great. Then maybe we could all go to bed."

Miss Semple closes her eyes, and I wonder if she's praying. "All right, if it's okay with Dana. Goodness me, I thought last night was bad."

Pete reads through our press release, we change a word here and there, but we're happy with it. It talks about the need to pay more attention to those who are on the margins, especially the elderly and the vulnerable; the consequences of abandoning them are too clear. How it's our hope that this terrible incident will trigger an investigation into the matter. It explains that our group simply wanted to know the truth of what had happened to our friend Maryanne, and when the police could go no further, we'd decided to find out on our own. That we've been requested to make no further comment about what happened till the case is resolved in the courts. It concludes with a polite request that the reporters utilize their time better by surrounding city and provincial officials rather than our house. As Miss Semple and I stand nervously, along with Pete and Ed, Gerry groans loudly.

"We can't do this to them, Diamond. Send them out by themselves. We're a group, we're together."

Diamond nods slowly, and gets to his feet. "Miss Semple, you're right. This is going to be a lot harder than last night."

We all stop by Michael's bed, and I hear Gerry mutter to him, "You lucky bastard. It's almost worth getting the shit beat out of you."

And out we go, into the babble and the harsh artificial lights, together.

Epilogue

You'd think from the noise that someone was trying to drown a cat. I don't go looking, though, I know it's just Gerry, splashing and bitching, cackling and splashing, and soaking both Michael and the floor. It's a bit of a miracle that Michael got him into the tub, and, for my part, I've donated my shampoo and left them to it. I'm upstairs, getting dressed in another borrowed outfit, but this one is sombre and more in tune with who I am and where I'll be going later today.

Charlene will be here soon to trim Gerry's hair and beard, and to drive us to the drop-in. Jeremy will come a little later. He's taken his Cadillac out of storage for the occasion, and Miss Semple, Diamond and Michael will ride with him. Miss Semple (and her iron) has kept busy, trying to turn Gerry's freshly laundered T-shirts and jeans into something approximating clean and respectable. Not even the redoubtable wardrobe lady, Eloise, could find a suit jacket to fit him, though she did locate suits, white shirts and shoes for Diamond and Michael. I was glad to leave that to Charlene, who dropped off the outfits last night; so much of her stock moving out the door must have rattled Eloise badly.

There's a rare air of excitement permeating the building, a sense that we're approaching the final pages of the story we've written together. All the publicity that followed our home invasion means that we've become minor celebrities in the neighbourhood, even in the city. Our pictures, except for Michael and the ex-bikers, captured as we left the infamous building with the cops, have been splashed across the front pages of all four dailies. Karen from the bar across the street saved them all and brought them over; she assures us we looked great on the television news shows. That isn't the reason for the excitement though. We're about to celebrate the life of our friend Maryanne. She's no longer an anonymous victim of the system and of Mallick. Her murder, and how it spurred us to act, has elevated her into a public figure who won't soon be forgotten.

Pete has arranged for the drop-in to host the memorial; Maryanne would have liked that, maybe even been a little proud, seeing us all brought together, like a real family, to say our final goodbyes.

I worry that the bruises on my neck are still lurid and impressive, so I've opted for a black turtleneck, like a teenager hiding hickeys from her parents. I hope the lump on Mallick's head is still causing him grief, as he sits in his cell and awaits trial. The cops busted his brother-in-law at his home off the Danforth: Mallick had been eager to hand them the address, and he was taken out in handcuffs like the felon he is in the middle of the night. They also picked up the young thug, who's also talking. Numerous investigations are under way, both the province and the city launching their own, and seniors' groups and their advocates are demanding answers.

I hear Charlene call from the bottom of the stairs, so with one quick check of myself in the mirror, I head down. She's grown very fond of Gerry since she first laid eyes on him a couple of days ago, and he is absolutely smitten with her.

"Hurry up, Gerry, the scissors await!" yells Charlene, as I join her.

"Just hold your horses, woman—I'm getting outta the tub! Jeez!" I hear the pleasure behind his words, and so does Charlene as she grins at me.

"Well, you look great, Dana. I went by the drop-in first and everything's ready. Pete's done a magnificent job on the place. There were already people, and media, lining up to get in."

I wince at the addition of the media, but both Charlene and Pete have said that if we want changes to the system, keeping pressure on the two levels of government is critical. Gerry has had to jam the front door closed to keep out the "snoops" who, in spite of our efforts, have camped out on the porch for hours at a time. Gerry trundles down the stairs in his newly laundered jeans and T-shirt, bitching at every step, with Michael herding him from behind.

"One torture after another, that's what this is. Some way to treat a hero."

Charlene clicks the large pair of scissors she's pulled out of her bag. "We're ready for you, Gerry. Your public awaits."

He snorts and tries to turn back upstairs, but is effectively blocked by a grinning Michael. "Get down there and take your medicine, big guy!"

Using one of the straight-back chairs in the common room, we get the barber shop set up for Gerry, and Michael, who also wants a trim. Diamond makes his way in, looking tall and confident in his suit. His parents had shown up shortly after we hit the news. I'd been across the street at the time, eating breakfast and relaxing. He told me later how it went.

"When Gerry called up to me that my parents were at the door, it was like none of this had happened. All I could think about was how I'd failed them, disappointed them. I stayed in my room at first, pretty much wringing my hands and pacing. I could hardly face them. But when I came down, they both held on to me, wrapped their arms around me. I can't ever remember them doing that before. Of course, they wanted me to go back home with them, right that minute. But I told them, and my heart was in my mouth, we have some things to work out, and for now, this was my home. My father was crying, it was so strange, he kept saying, we love you, we love you, over and over. It was like they'd changed even more than me. I don't know what I'll be doing with my life now, but I'm very glad to have them back, Dana."

I couldn't help thinking about my own parents at the time, still trapped in their ghetto of fear and intolerance. I couldn't imagine such a familial scene being played out with them—not that it was likely, since they didn't read the papers, didn't watch much of the news. I hugged him, genuinely pleased that he had stood up for himself. There was no trace of the halting, inarticulate young man he'd been, and whatever he decided to do, I knew he'd do it well.

"Hey, how much are you cutting off? I don't want to be a bloody skinhead."

"Keep still, or you'll lose one of your ears."

Hair is flying everywhere, but when Charlene stands back, the final result is impressive. I'm so used to his hair being matted and sticking up every which way that it's going to take some time to get used to his new 'do.

Michael's next, and Gerry stays in the room to harass him. "Cut it all off. Make it smooth as a baby's bum, that's the best look for him." Michael looks good too, freshly shaved and showered, wearing (a little uncomfortably) the suit Charlene brought for him.

"I hope Maryanne appreciates all this," Gerry grouses. "I'm raw from him scraping me in the bath."

"There were so many layers of dirt, I didn't have a choice. Now you're all pink and shiny. She'd say, what have you done with Gerry?"

This is the first time they've been able to say Maryanne's name lightly, and it feels good.

No cigarette butts around the entrance. That's the first thing I notice. Someone has swept up all the detritus, the discarded Styrofoam coffee cups and chip bags and fag ends, and laid down a lovely, colourful, indoor (but what the hell) knotted rug over the much abused pavement. The glass door and window are gleaming, sparkling even, in the strong sunlight. There's a notice taped to the door, black felt pen on white typing paper: "Memorial Service Today, 2 p.m. to 4 p.m. All Welcome."

We hang around out front till Jeremy drives up with the others, so that we can enter together, as seems right. As I hold the door for Jerry, Diamond and a slightly dazed Miss Semple to walk through, I hear Michael ask Jeremy, "C'mon, that's not how you talk when you're home by yourself, is it?" followed by a loud guffaw from Jeremy.

Just inside the door, Miss Semple uncharacteristically grabs my arm, whispering excitedly. "He kissed my hand! Jeremy! I've seen him on the stage at Stratford. I almost swooned like a schoolgirl. He's so ... so debonair!"

Pete has piled up the tables behind a few baffles and created rows of chairs, many of which are already occupied with members of the drop-in centre, everyone looking as though they've made a real effort to spruce up. The chairs are facing a makeshift stage, and there are flowers too, lovely arrangements of roses and carnations, lilies and peonies. Pete's wearing a suit, the first time I've seen him in one, and he smiles, shaking hands and congratulating all of us, one by one.

"The front section is reserved for you folks, whenever you're ready."

"Pete, thanks, it all looks lovely." We hang back, taking it all in.

Miss Semple had asked us if her pastor could lead the service today, and we all agreed, with Gerry's proviso that he "keep God out of it." And here he is, a slender, red-haired man, with watery eyes behind his metal spectacles, nothing unctuous about him that I can detect as he briefly and gently hugs Miss Semple. He tells us that whenever we're ready, he'll begin. I have no idea how this is going to go, what to expect, but Miss Semple has spent a lot of time talking with the pastor, so I'm not too worried.

There's a rush at the door as CityTV and the CBC jostle to get in, joining a group of reporters at the back. And wonder of wonders, there's the sombre police chief in full regalia, accompanied by his deputies and a dark-suited, grinning Ed, who formally introduces all of us—except for Michael, who's left quickly to take a seat in the second row. Ed had put in writing his request to keep Maryanne's case open, citing our concerns. That has served him well, though not his immediate supervisor.

I notice that Derek and his cheerful gang of felons are here, for the moment keeping their heads down. And some of the liberated women who've been released from hospital, including Janice, who looks a little tipsy or perhaps it's just the rakish tilt of the wig she's borrowed from Vera, who's holding on to her like life itself. Pete whispers to me that the MPP from the area is also here, along with the mayor and a handful of city councillors. "Never saw any of them in here before. Probably never will again." It's time, the place is packed, camera lights are adding to the heat. We take our seats, and suddenly all the coughing and murmuring cease.

Pete goes to the microphone (rented for the occasion) and welcomes everyone to the service and to the drop-in. Then he calls up, and I almost swallow my tongue, the wardrobe lady, who appears carrying a violin. She's in a severe black dress, and I have a moment of panic as I recall how much of her stock is clothing us, but she does an odd little bow to the audience, and begins to play. The first strains of "Amazing Gracc" fill the place, their beauty and clarity calling forth our grief and hope. We are all crying as the last notes fall on us, Maryanne almost a visible presence.

The Pastor takes the stage. His voice, coming out of that slender body, is deep and resonant.

"We are here today to bid goodbye to Maryanne. She left us no photographs, there's no estate to apportion out, no relatives to bury her. There are no visible traces of the life she lived, and that might be a very sad thing. Yet, if we look around us, we can see that Maryanne, in her living and her dying, has profoundly affected her friends, her community, even the system that failed her.

"Maryanne was loved. So much so, that when she was taken from us, in such a brutal and senseless manner, a small bereft group of friends stood up for her, demanding justice for the woman they had come to know. Maryanne had a difficult life, it was easy to dismiss her living and dying with labels that society frequently uses to categorize those we've pushed to the margins. Official records would describe her simply as an alcoholic. But the official records would be wrong. Maryanne cared about people, she reached out to those around her, building a community out of the isolated and the lost. And it was that very community that found its courage and strength to fight for the truth, when others wished simply to close the books.

"Look around you today. Here we are, the powerful and the powerless, the wealthy and the poor, in communion together. A miracle in itself, many might think. This, our dawning awareness of our common humanity, our individual responsibility for those in need, is Maryanne's legacy. She lives today in our hearts and minds, a symbol for us all of what we've lost, and what we've gained.

"May she now rest in peace."

There is more music wrung from the violin, a sad lament that morphs into "Ode to Joy," and then Jeremy is called up. He looks so handsome, so dignified, as he takes the mike to murmurs of recognition. He stares out at the audience, waits for the hush to deepen, and begins to perform—there's no other word for it—a very fitting poem, the last verse of which captures Maryanne's fight perfectly. "Do not go gentle into that good night/ Rage, rage, against the dying of the light." Then the ceremony is over.

Gerry wants to go home, his eyes are red and teary, his nose is running, but we persuade him to stay a while, finding him his own box of Kleenex. Charlene takes a seat beside him, and they murmur quietly together.

I see Pete having a very serious conversation with Michael, and wander over.

"Two breaking and entering, and theft unders," Michael is confessing, his eyes down.

"And those are the only charges outstanding?"

"The only ones they caught me for. Since I was in juvie."

"Okay, I think I can arrange a way out for you. It would mean doing community service hours here, real work for no pay. What do you say?"

"Hell, yeah. Do you mean it?"

"Leave it with me. We'll work it out."

They shake hands, Michael turns to me, relief clear in his eyes. "Did you hear that? I could do my time here, with you!"

"Cool. Of course, that means staying legal. Are you ready for that?"

"So ready, you have no idea."

The police chief and the mayor are standing together in a scrum of reporters, and I see the indomitable Miss Semple chatting away with Mr. Crusher. Ed comes up behind me, whispering, "After the boss leaves, would you like to take a ride with me?"

"Love to."

And I would. I realized some time last week that things are never going back to normal, that that time has passed. It was Charlene and Jeremy who underlined this for me, back at the boarding house. In a little ceremony of our own, held in the common room before we left today, they'd presented me with a copper plaque bearing my name: "Dana Leoni, Private Detective." The plaque came with pamphlets advertising P.I. courses, and I have to admit, I'm seriously thinking about it.

I don't think I'll mention all this to Ed just yet.

Author's Note

This is a work of fiction, anchored in the very real community of Parkdale, located in the west end of the city of Toronto. There have been changes, some good, some bad, since I lived and worked there in the eighties. The poor are still poor; if anything, their lives have become even more difficult, with severe cutbacks to social programs and benefits.

Homelessness is rampant, and has spread throughout the downtown area and, for that matter, the country. The introduction of crack cocaine has brought its own evils to the troubled neighbourhood, and shows no signs of leaving.

Still, artists and actors and writers have discovered how vibrant and affordable Parkdale is, and the long-awaited real estate boom seems to have begun. Due in part to this influx of new blood, and to efforts made by both sides, relationships between the marginalized and the ratepayer and business associations have improved immeasurably, leading me to hope that a Parkdale address may once again become something to brag about.

Acknowledgments

For their unwavering support, I wish to thank the following individuals: Paul Quinn; Reva Gerstein; June Callwood; Elizabeth Gray; Diana and Julia Capponi; Becky McFarlane; Nora McCabe and Joey Slinger; my agent, Bev Slopen; Pamela Rodgerson; Michelle Grinstein; and Dushan Jojkic.

To Erica Kopyto, and to the folks at the Bloor West Village Players, thank you for the world you opened up for me.

To my editor and best friend, Cynthia Good, I couldn't have done it without you. And to Iris Tupholme, publisher and editor, thanks for taking a chance on a fiction novice.

And very special thanks to Lynne Ford, who came up with the idea for this book and pushed to make it a reality.